BOOK ONE

Moon Child

United with the Stone

By Simon L. Swink

First paperback edition 2024

Cover illustration created by Kenshjn Park
Book design created by Swink Designs
Map created by Swink Designs
Character illustrations (Nars, Reiji-Arashi, Kio, Mel) created by Kenshjn Park
Other illustration, unless noted otherwise, created by Swink Designs
Logo & Book Graphics created by Swink Designs

www.facebook.com/Simonlswink

979-8-9909677-1-7

*Let the moon be your light
in the darkest
of nights.*

Contents

Prologue

The young sorceress ran through the cursed forest, tenderly holding a bundle in her arms. Rain fell from the blackened sky and the wind howled overhead. The ground quaked beneath, and every leap she landed lasted less than a second as she dodged the branches of the whippet willows. Their roots pulled up from the wet soil and lashed out with attempts to grab her. Every moment was vital.

The forest opened to a small clearing. Smooth, petrified roots formed a crest of a crescent moon and seven stars on the ground. She ran to the center, barely catching her breath. The roar behind stopped her heart as she turned to gaze up upon the monstrous, horned beast that traumatized her world.

"GIVE HER TO ME NOW!" The behemoth demanded—his eyes flamed with fire. His roar boomed like thunder. A brisk wind of damp rain hit her skin like icy shards.

"She is not yours to have." The sorceress's words were silenced by the wind, and she started with a whisper, "*Tr'u me Ah,*" The beast's growl vibrated her bones as he charged. Unmoved, she held the bundle of blankets high above her head—"*tare-os ess!*"

The beast clawed forward, but both the moonstone and small baby she held vanished with a blinding flash of the teleshifting spell. The sorceress smiled to herself. *She's safe now... transported to a safer place.* Blood dripped from her wounded arm onto the smooth stone beneath. It streamed through the lines of the petrified roots—illuminating the stars within the seal—as she began the incantations of her next spell.

"I WILL FIND HER!" The behemoth's words rumbled the earth as the petrified seal unraveled the gate to his prison. The ground opened to consume him—trapping him beneath the surface for another thousand years. His rage thundered against the storm, "AND THE WORLD WILL BE MINE!"

The beast reached out and his claws smacked the sorceress back into the forest before bursting into embers. She hit hard against the weeping tree with red vines.

The woman laid her head back on the tree. *It's done now...*

The whipplet willow encased her, wrapping its red vines—prickled with long, dark thorns—around her limbs to absorb the life from her body.

Years from now... It'll be someone else's destiny... She felt the tree's hunger as she drifted off into darkness...

Whipplet
Willow

CHAPTER 1

The Moonstone

The city was sound asleep as the hooded figure crept through the back allies, dodging the night guards who surveillance the grounds for anything suspicious that could harm the citizens of Adrienan. The king made sure his people were safe and secure from the outside threats beyond the castle walls.

Knowing exactly which way to turn, the hooded figure walked lightly through the paths of the tall buildings. Left, right, straight, around the corner, and towards the brick wall that surrounded the kingdom. After making sure the path was clear, the figure sprinted towards the wall, and jumped up—catching on the bricks that stood out. Hastily, it climbed up the wall and down the other side.

Landing lightly, the girl threw off her hood and smiled, *hee-hee, I've made it!* She thought to herself while dancing around excitedly to celebrate. Her heart nearly stopped when she heard a voice from behind—

"Sneaking out again, Princess Taemi!"

"Holy geez! Susia, you scared the hell out of me!"

The princess' guardian was a sturdy, plump woman with a bun of silver hair atop of a hard face. She was an old woman as she had also taken care of the king when he was a child, but her voice still cracked like a whip and demanded obedience.

Vexed, Taemi's nana frowned as she pointed a bony finger to the gate of the inner wall. "Now, march your royal arse back to the castle." She clapped her palms together, "Come, come."

The princess lowered her head sulking as she walked, "Yes, Susia...."

"Don't give me that attitude; you'd have your bottom whipped if your father had known you're out of your room at such an hour—much less outside the castle walls."

The princess clenched her cloak and mumbled under her breath, "Stay in the castle, must always stay in the castle. A princess may never leave the kingdom—nope! Must always be safe and bored and locked up in her room!"

The girl had never been outside the walls, yet the stories she read in the library talked of such wonderful adventures. She just wanted to live and fall in love with a true love—instead of some suited, cocky prince she was *destined* to marry just so her kingdom could be expanded. She grimaced, *why is my life so BORING?!*

Susia never missed a beat in her constant lectures, and the princess was certain she had every word from her nana memorized, but the last bit caught her attention. "You know very well you have a banquet ceremony tomorrow; you should be getting your night's rest."

The ceremony had completely escaped the princess' mind, even though it was all the talk from her servants and father. *That's right. Since my eighteenth birthday, I'm now eligible to take part in the council and speak for the good of my people.* It wasn't something exciting, but important, nonetheless.

Princess Taemi loved her people and believed that they were her responsibility, but sometimes she wished she could be a regular girl with no strings attached to her royal responsibilities and go off adventuring. She sighed.

Susia led her to her bedchambers and ordered the maidens to prepare the nightly rituals. They filled the washstand, put paste on her mouth-brush, and laid out her nightgown. Tired and annoyed, the princess obeyed and rested in her soft bed.

The servants came into her room early the next morning, pulling open the drapes that blocked the bright, warm sun. The blinding rays hit Taemi's eyes and the girl threw her thick covers over her head.

"Come on, your Highness—you must get up and get ready for the banquet." She could hear the servants—some pouring steamed cider into a glass, some fumbling through her closet for the clothes, and others turning on the faucet to fill up a hot bath.

Taemi laid in bed wishing they'd all leave her be to sleep. *The banquet didn't even start until a few hours after midday. Why do I have to get ready so early?* She thought, letting out an exasperated groan.

The girl flinched at the sudden breeze of cold air as the covers were pulled off. "Here you go, Princess. Hurry up and eat your breakfast." A small tray with toast, fried eggs, and sausage was placed on her lap, accompanied by the smell of the hot cider on the small table. Led by the authority of her handmaid Susia, the servants did everything for her. She was relieved that they didn't hand-feed her as well. She hated the idea that she wasn't able to do anything herself or her own way.

After the princess ate her breakfast, she was taken to the hot bath. The all-female servants went on to washing and rinsing. The water was still hot by the time they ushered Taemi out and toweled her dry.

The servants began their work on polishing the princess—from plucking her eyebrows to cutting her nails.

While her nails were being trimmed, filed, shined, and polished, the rest worked on her hair. They pinned it up in multiple curls, weaving decorated jewels and white pearls to contrast her dark hair.

When her nails were done, the servants moved on to her make-up, adding powders of foundation and blush to her face. They painted on eyeliner, lip liner, and touched up her eyebrows with a dark liner. They added shimmery shadow to the girl's eyes and drew on the thick, tasteless lipstick—topped with a glitter gloss scented with vanilla and berries—to her thin lips. The servants added additional glitter around her eyes and glued on small white diamonds by the corner of her right eye in a shape of the crescent moon.

As some still tugged and twirled with her hair, the other servants moved on to dressing the princess. Already wearing the satin undergarments, the servants pushed her into nylon stockings, and a tight corset around her thin figure in an attempt to lift what she had into a boisterous bosom. Then they added on the wire hoop skirt and layered on white satin petticoats with sparkly lace. Over the top, she wore a navy dress with the skirt crinkled in waved layers that glittered pink, purple, and blue—depending on how the light hit it. The top was designed to fit her curves smoothly as it strapped up by her neck—exposing a little cleavage—and then white, satin gloves stretched up her arms. Small gems outlined the straps of her halter and down across her bosom to the back where the servants laced her up.

Taemi caught a glimpse of her reflection and was struck by her own appearance. *So elegant and mesmerizing!* Her painted face accented her high cheekbones and the lipstick complimented her deep, emerald-green eyes. Her long, dark, straight hair was stacked high on her head with curls and buns, and a dozen gems twinkled like stars as the light flickered off them. Her dress fit her form perfectly, despite that she felt like a late bloomer, lacking the feminine curves of her upper chest. It was a sight that pleased her to be a princess for once. The final touch-ups to her outfit were earrings that hung like chandeliers, a heavy necklace made out of gemstones, and a crown that sat perfectly on her head.

"Oh, my—Darling you look beautiful." Taemi turned to see Susia who had just entered the room. "The banquet is about to begin."

Taemi looked out the window to see the sun across the midday sky. *It took four hours to get ready?!*

The plump woman crossed her arms, "Now you remember, dear, we announce your new upcoming position, and then we eat and celebrate. Today, from now on, you'll take part in the council for the responsibility of the kingdom."

Taemi let out a sigh as she continued to gaze beyond the gates where she longed to venture, "I know Susia."

"Quit dreaming, girl." Taemi jumped at the snap of her nana's hard voice. "You'll never know how easy you has it until you lived in another's shoes—but let me tell you, be grateful with anything you can have—or maybe one time you won't have it. Now, come away from that window, it's about time you learn where you're meant to be."

Taemi bowed her head, "Yes, Susia..."

Susia continued on as they walked down the corridors of the castle. Tapestries of flowers decorated the walls with hints of gold on the columns every few paces, and the white and blue tiles were brightly polished for the evening. "From here on, we'll have you be meeting tons of nobles and princes for your hand in marriage, and you'll be Queen of Adrienan. Not everyone gets to live a life of comfort. You keep that in mind now, when it comes to thinking how miserable being a princess is."

"Well, maybe I don't want an easy life." Taemi mumbled to keep her voice from drifting too far down the corridor as she crossed her arms. She avoided looking at her reflection in every mirror she passed. Life was perfect, but something was missing and she knew she wasn't going to find it being cooped up in a castle.

Susia pivoted around and put her hard fist on her round hip and glared down at the princess, "You're a stubborn child. You best be careful to watch what you wish for—especially in that manner. Now, get a move on child! We've squandered too much time arguing about you're childish fantasies."

They continued down the hall, taking multiple turns until the corridor opened to the large dome ballroom where the banquet was held. They walked onto the balcony where two curved staircases led down to the ballroom floor.

The room roared loudly of chatter from all of the high authorities and superior minorities who ruled around her kingdom. Taemi gasped at the sight of the large crowd below her. Everyone was dressed in elegant clothing—clattered with gold, silver and jewels. The lords and ladies paid no mind to the servants who walked around with trays of goblets—grabbing at the drinks as if they were floating right into their hands, and refilled by magic. The sound of harps and strings echoed softly through the hall.

The girl never thought that her position in the council would be so important to other kingdoms around her, but it was one of the next steps to becoming queen. But such an audience felt overwhelming; she could almost faint.

Adrienian soldiers were posted near all the exits for the safety of her guests. They were all dressed in their red and gold uniforms with the embroidered symbol of Adrienan's crest on the upper-right of their chest.

Entering into the ballroom, her eye caught a handsome soldier. He watched—alerted, saw her, and cast his eyes down towards the floor—avoiding direct eye contact with her until she passed. He was young and attractive with strands of his brown hair falling in front of his dark eyes. She figured he was new to the guarding position. The other soldiers didn't mind her presence like the common peasants. They were there to protect her.

Her father sat in his gilded throne on the balcony. As soon as Taemi joined him, the king stood up, and everyone within the ballroom became quiet. "Welcome all my fair comrades and my fellow Adrienians." His voice carried loudly in the ballroom, "Tonight, my dear beloved daughter, Princess Taemi Lor Equillis of Adrienan, becomes part of our council. She will join the politics and become responsible for the well-being of the Adrienian people." Her father glanced back at her and gestured that she should come forth and stand next to him.

"She will make good choices, for we know she has a good heart. I proclaim you the title that has been passed down for generations, *The Crescent of Adrienan.*" The entire crowd cheered and applauded. "Let us feast!"

Music played cheerfully while the food was being served, and a few lords and ladies even started to dance as they drank down wine with joy. Taemi watched, wondering if she should even go down and talk amongst the others. She swayed to the music with a glass of spiced wine that she had no intention of drinking in her hand.

"Taemi," Her father's voice broke through her thoughts as he stood up from his throne. "There's something I need to give to you, privately." The princess nodded and followed the king out of the ballroom, and up to her parent's chamber room. Taemi waited patiently as her father rummaged through the closet—moving items out and away—and finally pulled out a small, black, wooden box with a small lock.

"Taemi, my dear daughter, you are... special, as we all say. For the Faiths have blessed us with the Daughter of the Moon." The girl watched her father retrieve a key from his pocket to open the box. Once opened, he lifted out a pendant on a silver chain. "You are now old enough to be the guardian of the moonstone and use its power as your own. Keep it safe—don't let anyone know of its power, for many will attempt to use you."

He handed her the necklace. The teardrop-shaped moonstone shimmered in every color—from purple to blue, to red and green, shifting in the light. As soon as Taemi held the pendant in her hand, the stone glowed, and she felt a warm source flow through her.

The princess looked up at her father who only smiled brightly. "With this stone, you have the ability to possess magic like the elves and mages."

"...But father, but how? I thought you had to be born with the power."

Amused, her father laughed. "Yes—but this stone also allows the same gift to the female descendants of the moon, so in a way, you are. This moonstone has been in our family for seven generations—when an Adrienian prince fell in love with a loving and selfless woman. She was a descendant of the moon and used the power to protect the kingdom. Unfortunately, she only gave birth to sons, and they, too, had only sons. The elves said to keep this stone within our family until finally, it could be bestowed onto a daughter. They said, '*She'll come when she is needed once more.*' Her father took the chain and clasped it around Taemi's already-decorated neck. It hung down by her heart. "I'll send for Madeem from the Laquar Forest so that he can teach you how to use your power."

Taemi stared down at the pendant in disbelief, "My power..." She could hear Susia's voice in the dim of her mind, "*You best be careful for what you wish for.*" This wasn't anything nearly as close to what she could possibly ask for, but... it was enough for her to stay in the castle. She tucked the moonstone under her dress to keep it hidden.

As she and her father walked back to the ballroom, they heard loud screams of terror. Her father hastily ran ahead to the ballroom, accompanied by standing guards "— Come, Taemi!"

The princess attempted to keep up in her heavy dress, but from the midst of the shadows beneath the curtains, a dark, undefined figure appeared before her. Taemi halted, gasping in fear. The shadow formed into a ghostly appearance of a large wolf with maroon eyes. It bared its long, sharp teeth with a low growl.

Taemi stepped back slowly, but slipped on her dress and fell back onto her hands. The shadow wolf lunged towards her.

"PRINCESS!"

The girl stared in horror at the beast as a sword sliced through its smoky body before her eyes. The shadow evaporated away.

"Princess, are you alright? Princess?"

It took the girl a moment to realize what was happening. She looked up at the young soldier boy who wouldn't glance at her earlier. Now, he studied her condition as he helped her up on her feet. "You alright, Princess?"

She nodded, "Yea... I'm fine." Her voice was shaky as she glanced around looking for more of the shadow wolves.

"It's alright, I'm here, Princess." The boy took her by the hand, "Follow me." He led her down the corridor, passing injured servants holding their bloody wounds from spilling across the floor. Taemi couldn't pull her gaze away from the frightful horror. She saw their insides spilled across the freshly polished tile as they lay in red pools, reaching out for help. The walls and tapestries dripped blood.

The soldier came to a quick stop and Taemi slid from the slick floor into his hard figure. She looked up, and covered her mouth—her eyes wide from fright. Ahead, one of the high noble women who ran from the ballroom was pinned by two wolves tugging at her flesh. The poor woman screamed in agony, pleading for help, but she was too far-gone as her limbs were torn away one-by-one. Her screech echoed down the hall until she was completely torn in half.

"This way." The boy whispered softly and slipped behind the tapestry—keeping Taemi close by. He took her down a short, narrow passage that the girl never even knew existed, and came out into the ballroom behind another tapestry.

It was a battlefield of soldiers and lords, fighting against the large shadow wolves.

"Taemi!" The girl glanced over to see her father slice through a shadow wolf with a large axe and ran towards her. "Taemi, you must leave from this place—nothing can happen to you. Quick! Go to Laquar and find Madeem!" Her father's arm was drenched in dark blood that dripped off his fingertips. "You boy, take her—and get out of here—"

A shadow shifted from the wall and formed into another wolf. It gouged its teeth into the king's shoulder and threw him across the room.

"FATHER!" The princess lunged forward in a pitched scream—but was pulled back and hoisted over the boy's shoulder.

At a run, the soldier carried the princess in and out through the tapestries and down long narrow paths until they arrived at the stables where the horses slept calmly. The footman jumped to his feet at their presence and awaited orders.

"Tack up the princess' horse and your fastest one—quick!" The stables man rushed off to obey.

The boy set the girl on her feet as he fetched her a cloak and packed up a bundle of items. Within ten minutes, the horses were ready to go and they ran out of the kingdom in a canter. The princess glanced back at her castle, dimly lit by the moonlight.

The gusty night wind blew harshly, forcing Princess Taemi to tug her cloak closer around her neck. They ran straight to the nearest forest after passing the outer gates, for it was the best shelter in the dark night. The wind still managed to cut through her cloak like a knife and her feet were practically numb in her damp slippers. She wanted to take a hot bath and sleep away the nightmare that she had just endured.

After running for an hour, the horses walked at a slow pace; Taemi herself was exhausted from the rough ride. Kio—the soldier boy ordered to protect her—traveled ahead, but glanced back continuously, watching Taemi, as well as the woods.

She packed away her crown and necklace into a bag, but the jewels in her hair still weighed down her head, as well as the thick layers of her dress. She felt guilty that she may have to trade in her prized dress for something more comfortable to travel in. Removing the satin gloves she brushed her face. She could feel the powders of make-up clumping up and running down her face.

"How long until we reach an inn? I need to change, and take this stuff out of my hair, and wash my face, and eat some food..."

"I don't think we'd reach an inn until another two hours or so."

Taemi gave a start, "Two hours!" She didn't remember the towns being so far when she studied the maps. The princess sighed and slouched in the saddle. Exhaustion was quickly consuming her.

Kio glanced back with a concerned look, "We'll stop for a rest here, then." He pulled his horse off the narrow path and into the forest to a grassy spot. Taking the reins, he tied the horse to a branch with a quick-release knot. Then he came over to help Taemi off her black gelding. "You can rest over here and try to take down your hair. I'll tend to the horses and build a fire."

He took the saddle and pack off his horse, and dug for the canteen and food. "Here's some dried meat that'll hold you over for the night. Tomorrow we'll stop and gather enough supplies for the journey to Laquar."

Taking in the food, she watched Kio un-tack the horses and tie them up. "Do you even know where Laquar is?"

"I've only ever heard of it. I'll purchase a map as soon as we can. I'm sure it's east from here, but I don't want to travel in the wrong direction for a long time." The horses grazed on the soft grass when he finished.

Kio disappeared into the woods to gather dry wood for a possible fire and Taemi began to undress from the heavy layers. She took off her dress first and packed it away with her crown and gemmed necklace. She wanted to keep it as clean as possible, just because of its elegance. Afterward, she took off the wire hoop and threw it aside. *Perhaps that could be sold... as well as this corset.* Taemi tugged at the corset strings, but she couldn't reach the high knot to untie and loosen it. She heard Kio walking back and quickly dodged behind the tree.

"Princess? Are you alright?"

"Oh.. Um....yea—I'm good...." She tugged at the strings, but cried out in exasperation, "Ugh... why do they have to make these things tie up in the back!" She gave a sigh and quit her struggle. "Kio...?"

"Yes, Princess?"

"...Could you... maybe help me with something?"

He hesitated for a moment, "...Sure?"

Taemi debated on him seeing her in the undergarments, but she also wanted to breathe. She stepped out from behind the tree, and Kio immediately glanced down at the ground. Even in the darkness, she could see his face color.

"P-princess, y-your..."

"It's okay, I need your help getting this corset off."

"Uh...Um, y-yea—As you w-wish, P-Princess."

The poor, nervous soldier fumbled with the knot, Taemi couldn't help, but to be amused at how shy he was. After two minutes, though, she came to think that it was ridiculous that he still couldn't get the knot out. "You having trouble back there?" Her statement was mostly for teasing, but she couldn't hide the hint of irritation in it.

"...The strings... they can be replaced, right?"

"Yea—I don't care, just get the thing off." Before the girl knew what he was doing, she felt a stiff object up her back that sliced the strings.

"There you go." The corset fell to the ground as Kio put his dagger away. His eyes were still on the ground when Taemi turned around to pick up the corset and put it away. "Princess, can you please put your cloak back on?" He handed her the cloak.

"Oh, thank you—I'm freezing!"

"I know..."

The princess looked back at him confused for a moment, but simply shrugged her shoulders and ignored it. "Did you find any dry wood?"

"Yea, I got some." He bent over the pile and took out two stones and flicked them together until the sparks ignited a flame and the wood started to burn. "Get some, rest Princess, I'll keep watch."

Taemi eased back, trying to find a comfortable groove in the tree to sleep against. *That's silly, he couldn't possibly stay up the* whole *night—he must be tired too.* But before she could argue, her mind drifted off to sleep.

"Seems like your shadow mongrels have failed you, Lord Reiji-Arashi."

Arashi, dressed in black with sun-kissed skin from the southern kingdom of Narpal, stood poised as he watched the princess gallop off into the woods on her black gelding through a crystal disc. The crystal disc showed visions of whatever the sorcerer wished to see outside of his fortress. The platinum-haired man only glanced back and gave a mischievous grin. "On the contraire, Nars—I have her right where I want her."

Nars sat on her cushion throne like a seductive feline, petting a large white tiger that lay by the side of the chair. The sorceress stretched, peeled herself off the throne with a graceful twist, and prowled towards Arashi, "I don't understand." Her reflection on the marble pillars caught her attention. She brushed her blonde bangs out of her eyes. The rest was pulled back with spikes coiled in her hair, twisting it up into a bun. She smiled at her attractive appearance—a pretty face, fair skin, and well-formed curves expressed through her silky, sleeveless magenta top hanging by thin straps. It swooped low, exposing generous cleavage, and stopped short revealing her toned mid-rift.

She wore the arm clasps of the Eithsa's fashion. The ones she wore today were simply a silver clasp that encased her whole forearm—below her wrist to her elbows—and another clasp encased her upper arm. Light silk swooped down to the ground from the clasps, like unnecessary drapes, but she was fond of them, nevertheless. Her outfit was complete with a loose matching tulle skirt that hung from her hips and knee-high, high-heeled boots that clipped the floor's surface when she wanted to be noticed.

"I thought you wanted the stone, not the girl. You could have killed her—like her father—and we could waltz in picking up the gems." She trailed her hand across the back of Arashi's shoulder and down the back of his black leather

NARS

top. She pushed herself against him and looked up with her persuasive blue eyes, "And you could have all the magic to rule over the kingdoms, one by one." Her voice chimed pleasantly as it echoed through the empty tower.

"You speak so rash, my dear. The point of attacking the castle was merely to scare the princess off to where she is now—alone without the protection of her father, nor the knowledge of the moonstone."

Nars pulled back coolly and crossed her arms, "So?"

"Well, why put all the work and fight for the kingdom—it's so tiring—when all it takes is a little patience, and I can have the world within the palm of my hand by doing little-to-no work at all."

"...So you mean to keep the girl ...alive." Nars flattened her voice and her charming eyes switched to an icy glare.

Arashi looked down at his loyal servant and smiled—likely amused by her jealousy. He turned to cup her chin in his black leather gloves, making Nars' glare soften in his grip. "It's the perfect plan. You'll see, and I'll promise you all the wealth you deserve." He walked around her, grazing the gloves against her soft warm skin—it prickled at his cool touch—and he leaned in to whisper in her ear. "Now sit, watch, and wait." She melted under his warm breath. "Keep watch while I rest for the night."

He walked out of the room, leaving Nars with chills running down her body, and blood rushing to her face, but she was quick to ignore the infatuation. Her lips formed into a pout, and sulkily turned to the crystal. She had helped him with his plans for nearly ten years—fetching rare crystals and using her contortion spell at his command—but her reward wasn't even mild affection. His touch was only to ease her temper, and it did so hypnotically. She accepted that the man refused to mix pleasure with his work, *but suddenly today, he's interested in this girl?*

Nars summoned her goblet, generously filled with a dry, smoky, red wine with hints of deep cherry. She attempted not to glare at the crystal and simmered in her drink until she felt nothing.

CHAPTER 2

The Country Rose

The shadow wolves were catching up as Taemi ran down the dark tunnels. She tried her hardest not to slip on the damp floor where the puddles splashed up at her. The wolves' deep growls were getting louder. Suddenly, the girl's leg gave out and she slid down on the hard, wet stone. She could feel the pain of a bruise developing on her leg. The dampness made her shiver. She was alone in the dark as the wolves were closing in.

"Let the moon be your light in the darkest of the night."

Taemi woke up shivering. She was lying against the tree drenched in the morning dew. The air smelled crisp as the orange glow of the sun shined over the trees and lit the sky pink. Small golden rays seeped through the trees. The faint coos of the morning dove drifted overhead.

"Oh, you're up." The princess glanced over at Kio who was already tacking up the horses. "I thought we head out early and try to get to an inn. And from then on—only rest at inns. You shouldn't be freezing in the cold like this." He came over and helped the princess to her feet, but stalled for a moment before helping her on the horse. "You need a little more coverage than just that cloak—especially if we're going into the village."

"But that dress is far too inappropriate if I'm to pass as a normal commoner."

The boy nodded. He untied the strings to the armor that covered his shoulders, took off his red coat from underneath, and wrapped it over the princess. It was very heavy, but warmer than what she was wearing. It bore the crest of Adrienan on the back; two gold intersecting crescent moons—wax and wane—circled by four stars, and a fifth one in the middle of the two moons.

"That should keep you warm until we get a different outfit for you. Maybe it'd be best to get a warmer cloak as well."

Taemi studied his exposed arms. Even though he seemed to have the appearance of a boy, his arms were trimmed and muscular. She looked away quickly to control the flushing of her face.

Kio helped her up on her horse, and they headed through the forest.

Taemi shivered as the morning wind brushed against her. It didn't help that she was only wearing her undergarments and slip beneath the cloak and wool coat. The sun was rising, but not quick enough to dry the dampness that covered the earth. Her clothes were wet, her legs were sore, and she had a cramp in her back from sleeping on the ground. The girl's stomach rumbled for hot food. Yet, half-dazed and miserable, she rode on.

After an hour and forty minutes, they arrived on a dirt path that led to a small town. Chickens roamed freely as they passed the tiny, wooden houses. The country folk were already up and working on their morning chores. Women and children formed a line at the well to fill their pails with water. The men groomed the horses and packed their saddles for the day's hunt.

At the edge of town was a large building—two levels high—with tan brick siding. "The Country Rose?" Taemi questioned as she stared up at the wooden sign with a rose sigil and read the name written in black paint, "Sounds pleasant. Do they get a lot of business?" The inns within the city walls were acceptable for traveling lords and ladies, but she'd never seen those outside of the walls. It appeared well-kept as Taemi inspected the siding for flaws.

"I imagine enough. It's the only place to stop between the castle and the next town. Unless someone doesn't have time to rest from riding for sixteen hours."

"...That's a lot of riding." Taemi halted her gelding as Kio got down from his horse and headed towards the barn. He came back briefly followed by a stable boy. He aided the princess down, but the girl fell into his arms from exhaustion.

"Are you all right, Princess?"

Still processing the words, she answered after a long pause, "Oh...wha? I'm alright."

"Can you stand?"

"Yea... of course."

Kio let her go, but alerted to catch her if she fainted again. He handed the reigns off to the stable boy on their way to the inn. "Be sure to feed and groom them right away; we won't be staying for more than an hour or so."

The stable boy nodded.

As Kio and the princess came through the door, the innkeeper put down her mug and stared at the two of them, shocked, "Oh, my dear, you look dreadful!" She was a middle-aged woman with burgundy hair, streaked with stands of gray, and pulled back into a bun. "Come in and take a hot bath—I'll have the hot water ready as soon as possible." She gave a clap of her hands, and two young girls in matching maid gowns ran off to ready the bath. "You two must be hungry—come sit—and I'll bring you some fresh toast and tea."

"Oh, miss, I don't like tea."

She paused at Taemi's words and turned around with slight sympathy on her face, "Well, I would offer wine, but we ran out after toasting the princess' new title last night."

Taemi almost forgot about the banquet as if it was just a nightmare she had as a child long ago. "Oh... Have you heard any news as to ...what happened?"

The woman shook her head, "You're the first guests to come by since. Are you two coming or going from Adrienan?"

"Um..." Taemi paused, uncertain of what to say.

"We're leaving." The princess gave a sigh as Kio answered, assured that he would know what to say. But he said nothing more.

The innkeeper nodded and continued to prepare their meal and tea. She came back with the bread stacked on a plate and every slice already buttered. Behind her were the same girls who got the bath ready, carrying in jam, honey, and cinnamon. "The bath is all set, but you should eat first anyway. Would you like some coffee instead of the tea? I have a fresh brew already made."

Taemi wasn't a fan of coffee either. In the castle, she was offered juice from exotic fruits, and the occasional hot cocoa when they had it. She completely forgot that common folk didn't have such luxury. She forgot it *was* a luxury.

"Um, no, it's okay. I'll try some of the tea."

The innkeeper nodded with a hint of annoyance. Perhaps she was wondering if Taemi was one of the high ladies, yet—her wardrobe showed different. The girl blushed. She wondered if the innkeeper had any idea what she was wearing under Kio's coat. *...Or what she thought about me* wearing *Kio's coat!*

Taemi finished her first piece of toast when the

innkeeper came back with the hot tea, already poured into cups. The teacup was hot against Taemi's hands, and she welcomed it as much as the buttery toast with the sweet berry jam. She took a small sip. *Light, this is hot!* She cursed, but it definitely made her insides melt pleasantly. The tea had a strong root flavor with a hint of raspberry that made her lips puckered in distaste.

She heard Kio snicker from across the table and shot him a flat look. "Here." He pushed a ceramic jar towards her with a smile, "You can sweeten it with honey."

She poured in the thick, golden syrup and stirred. She sipped the cup slowly. It added a strange taste—nothing at all like the sugar in the castle—but it subdued the bitterness enough to her satisfaction.

After the meal, Kio left to gather supplies and the princess was escorted to the back bathing room. She entered a personal chamber with a bubbling in-ground tub that misted the room with hot steam. "That's incredible..." Taemi has never seen the like! Even her private tub at the castle was small with a burner underneath—but this tub was big enough for two—*no, four people*—to sit and bathe, and it looked like it kept warm for hours.

The maid girl carrying the towels giggled at her reaction, "It's our new installment—invented personally by the innkeeper's husband. There's a boiler underneath that heats up the tub and a hose that blows in the hot air to make the bubbles." She smiled proudly, "I personally take my baths in here, as well, so it's a hundred percent safe."

The maidens left Taemi to her privacy. She wondered how long she'd be able to soak before Kio's return. She undressed and hung her clothes on the hangers. There was a small shelf stacked with the towels, so the girls wouldn't have to come in again when she was finished. *Clever,* Taemi thought.

She paused briefly about what to do with her

pendant. She heard her father's warning to keep it safe repeat in her mind. It wasn't something she should just leave somewhere and forget—but she'd hate to maybe distort it in the bathtub—just in case.

She took a towel, placed it on the floor next to the tub, and put the pendant on top. *Now it'll be close by, and safe.*

The princess stepped cautiously into the tub. The water's heat went up her leg, welcoming her in. She eagerly immersed her body in the hot tub. The warmth softened her frozen toes and fingers, and soothed every ache throbbing throughout her body. *Oh, how I could simply daze off to sleep!*

She closed her eyes—*just for a second*—she thought. But once she relaxed, her eyelids felt far too heavy to lift again. The princess drifted off joyously in the spa, letting her worries melt away, and her frustration fade.

She fantasized about how her adventure outside was supposed to be like: observing exotic creatures, discovering secluded places, and witnessing mages using their magical powers. She imagined meeting travelers who told exciting stories, and those that played talented notes on strange beautiful instruments. To befriend acquaintances from different cultures, adapting to their fashions and ideas, *and maybe...* She hoped, *maybe I'd meet someone who wasn't just a prince—but a man—a traveler of great experience who will protect me from dangers and treat me with respect and devotion.*

Her worst fears of traveling would simply be being robbed, or attacked by an animal—something alike a wolf. She never imagined the creature to be a giant, shadow monster where its transparent appearance shifted like smoke, but able to rip a human's body into pieces at the same time...

Taemi felt a prickle of terror and suddenly wished for Kio to be there with her. It was an odd feeling—something that developed in the pit of her stomach. She wanted to reach out for him and drag him back to her side. *Was it loneliness?*

Despite the heat of the tub, she could feel her skin perk as a cold shiver ran through her body. She became aware that her left arm tingled and slowly going numb.

The princess glanced over and opened her eyes to a black mist with two large maroon pools for eyes. The shadow wolf exhaled.

Quickly, Taemi pulled herself away, but noticed a swirl of black smoke wrapped around her arm—nearly up to her shoulder. Her nerves were numbed by the touch. Taemi reached out with her other arm in an attempt to pull herself out of the tub. She kicked at the walls while trying to get out. But the shadow had her arm bound in the dark smoke coils, creating the unnatural, yet tangible shape of the wolf.

Taemi thrashed to get away and remembered the pendant. She had no clue how it would help—but she had to get to it. She turned and reached out with her right hand—tugging away from the invisible pull that encased her numb arm. The chain of her pendant was just inches away. She felt a strain from her neck. She'd have to rip her arm off in order to get free, but she was getting closer...

A stabbing pain ran down her back like a hundred pins. She took a deep breath and reached again—flicking the chain closer with her fingertips—until finally pulling the chain into her hand.

She cupped the pendant in her palm, but she hadn't the slightest clue what to do. The wolf merely stood there in a trance and the smoke tricked off like shadow snakes swimming in the water towards her legs. Her toes became numb as the shadows began to wrap around her legs.

She held the pendant close and tried to think, but her only thoughts were of the creature's tainted darkness, and how she wished for it to let go—for it to shrivel away by... light!

A flash of light blinded her and there was a hiss of something burning near. Opening her eyes, she watched the howling wolf flinch back from a vibrant, bright glow that shined off of the stone. The smoke released Taemi. The girl looked at the creature in bewilderment. The wolf shook his head—a swirl of clouded darkness—and gave a deep growl, peering at Taemi.

The girl jumped out of the tub quickly, and backed away from the beast as far as the room would let her.

There was a loud thud on the door that averted the wolf's attention for a moment, but it focused back to Taemi, ready to spring.

The door broke open—splinters of wood crashing to the floor—as Kio charged in with his sword unsheathed, and attacked at the shadow wolf with an upward slash. The beast turned into a smoke cloud to avoid the hit and reformed again behind the soldier.

"KIO!"

The shadow wolf chomped the boy's arm and threw him across the room. Kio's sword slid away as he hit the ground with a roll, and landed face down.

Taemi watched—holding the pendant in her hand, but uncertain of what she could do. *I can do something; I have to do something. It worked before... somehow.* She couldn't recall what she did that activated the light before. She was thrashing from fear and pain... but that's it.

The wolf growled at the soldier who slowly lifted himself up, gaining his senses. The wolf lunged in the air and Taemi's mind raced for a conclusion. She wished she could have more time to control herself, and actually *think* about what she could do to help. The pendant grew unusually warm in her hands like a burning coal.

The creature's movement slowed and floated in the

air. Everything was slowing down. Her mind must be racing faster than she thought; she had to take this chance to really think.

Kio swiftly grabbed his sword and held it up at the shadow wolf. Taemi blinked. That wolf moved at such an unusual pace... but as quick as she realized it, the wolf crashed down on Kio's sword and vanished with a yelp. The boy sighed and tossed his sword aside.

The princess scurried to his side to inspect his injuries, "Kio, Kio, are you hurt? How did you know the shadow wolf was here? I thought you went to get supplies? ...Was I really in the bath that long?"

The soldier shut his eyes tightly and turned away—avoiding to look at Taemi. *What's with him now?* She noticed his flushed, red face, "Kio, I need to know you're okay. I'm not going to have you ignore me like this."

"P-princess, c-co-could you p-please put on... a towel."

Towel? The girl tilted her head briefly confused, then blushed, "Oh!" She grabbed the towel near the tub with a giggle and covered herself.

"There—Decent!"

"DAMN IT!"

Arashi threw his goblet across the black marble floor—the red wine splattered out like blood as the cup shattered into shards. The sorcerer boiled in rage.

Nars t'sk behind him and mouthed, "Such temper..." Her voice dazed as if to imply a feeling Arashi could not identify. He didn't care—he was so close to just taking the girl, but the little brat already started to use the pendant. *How had she known?* "That little scoundrel of a child! The girl—she's already found some hold on how to use the pendant for magic—how can this be?" *And the boy he is a complete nuisance. It's best to have him killed and quick!*

Nars approached for a closer glimpse at the crystal disc, "Hmm...There was something strange about that boy's presence. Didn't we just watch him walk across town to the merchant shop?"

Arashi shrugged her comment off and glared, *I have to come up with a way to get rid of that boy somehow.*

"My *Lord*," Nars continued, "don't you think it's *odd* that he got there so *quick*?"

Reiji-Arashi finally glanced down at his servant. Nars' eyes narrowed to study the crystal disc. Arashi was intrigued—as well as amused—with how she sometimes demeans herself by calling him *my lord*. Most of the time she considered herself as an equal—calling him directly by his name and ignoring orders—while other times, at surprise, she would acknowledge him as her master and surrender beneath him. It would be easier to know when she would switch back and forth, but she did it... randomly as if she was toying with him. However, when she did address him seriously, Arashi always found himself yielding to her statements.

But he was still irritated, "What is it that you're inferring?"

She watched, her eyes flickering to the images displayed on the crystal, "...I'm ...not sure." She stated while lost in a trance.

Arashi growled at her empty answer, *Useless!* He immediately regretted the wasted time, listening to her nonsense. He stormed out of the crystal room towards his chamber to think, "Bring me something to eat!"

Reiji-
Arashi

CHAPTER 3

A Veil

The sun was close to mid-sky when Taemi and Kio set off again. The temperature was much warmer compared to the morning chill, but Taemi was glad she was wearing a new outfit. She was satisfied with the plain, wool, gray dress that covered down to her ankles and a slit on the side for riding. She also wore a thick, white cloak with red trim, wool socks up to her knees and sturdy boots with a slight heel, but comfortable enough for walking. They were warm.

Kio had taken her into town to shop for supplies and clothes. He rarely left her alone after the incident in the inn. He did all the bargaining—though he was certainly well-paid for a solider—but Taemi let him do his job.

They left the town with a large bundle of bread, smoked meat, and cheese, and a few water bags. A lack of a map, however, frustrated Taemi most. There was a small one in the common room, but it only showed as far east as the Mythic Sea. The Laquar Forest wasn't even on there.

"We will just have to go to Sandar and look at their map. You will be welcomed there, Princess, since they're an ally. They will most likely grant you a better escort—not that I intend to leave you, Princess—but danger seems to be everywhere. You shouldn't expect to travel a far journey on your own. It's so dangerous for a..."

The girl drifted off in thought as Kio continued. She remembered visiting Sandar. *Yes, I should be highly welcomed.* She used to travel there for studies during the summer until her father found a new teacher. She knew King Nigan came to her banquet—he was a dear friend of her father's—but that would leave his son, Prince Willis, left in charge. A very quiet and passive boy, Willis was. But, if King Nigan did not return, Willis would be the next king... *Who would have attacked so many high lords and ladies... and killing them with shadow wolves?*

"Kio?"

Even though Taemi spoke softly, the boy stopped his chatter with a startled look. When she looked up at him, he turned away with a flushed face, "Oh, I'm sorry Princess, I should be keeping watch."

"Kio, what are these *shadow wolves*? Who do you think is after me? And *why* me?"

The boy stood silent for a while. Taemi thought he intentionally ignored her to keep watch. *Boys are always so one-track minded when it comes to duty!* She was just about to give him her opinion on the nonsense until he cleared his throat and spoke with tightness in his voice.

"There was only ...one recollection of a sorcerer who could control wolves—shadow wolves are just one form—he can control more. I don't know what he's after, but I bet it's the same guy."

"How do you know it's a sorcerer? Have you met him?"

"No." Kio cleared his throat again and shifted in his saddle, to sit up taller. "It used to be an old fairy tale my parents used to tell me."

He turned to her and smiled as bright as the sun, "But don't you worry, Princess. I'll make sure you reach Laquar safe and unharmed. I know the way to Sandar from here; it'll be a stroll in the garden after that."

The dirt road became busier since the morning as oxen and mules pulled carts for farmers and merchants. A few carriages sped by at a brisk pace that nearly pushed Taemi and Kio off the road. For a moment, the girl wondered if it was a lesser lord leaving her city. She wondered if anyone else made it out alive and if her father was doing well. *He'll take care of the people,* she nodded to herself. *I have my own duties to fulfill.*

The sun passed its peak and the cold wind started to pick up once again. Taemi pulled her cloak closer. They ate lunch, which was bread and slices of cheese, in the saddle to keep moving. In a few hours, the sun would set and the road would fade into darkness. Kio had already prepared lamps for lighting, but Taemi was more concerned as to what creatures came out at night.

Susia used to tell her bedtime stories of trolls, gremlins, hydras, kelpies, dar'rakars—beasts that were part animal-part human, created from the rotting soil of the bogs—and bloodhounds as big as horses. The stories were to keep her from venturing out late at night. She was mostly over her childish fears. Mostly. The one thing that terrified her now were the shadow wolves—she knew *those* existed.

"Kio?"

"Yes, Princess?"

"You really should stop calling me Princess." There wasn't anyone on the road at this time anymore. Most of the travelers have reached their destination or have already set up camp off the road, *but he shouldn't be calling me Princess all the time. It was silly.*

"As you wish, Princess—" Kio winced as soon as the last word habitually slipped off his tongue. Taemi glanced at him sternly. "As you wish... Taemi." Kio almost choked.

The princess held back a giggle from his struggle

and smiled, "How long have you been a soldier in the castle?"

"Almost two years now."

"You're quite younger than what my father normally hires for guards."

Kio smiled to himself. "Young. But far from inexperienced." His face glowed with pride. He had such a gorgeous smile when it was there.

"You're not even from my kingdom, are you?" She guessed, based on his light brown hair and dark brown eyes.

"No, Prince—" He cleared his throat, "No. I was born near Nishe, to the south. I traveled a lot. I know roads, dangers, and how to avoid them. I ran into a brawl while passing through your kingdom. It happened to be a fight against your sword master. I lost the fight, but he was impressed with my skill. The king thought I would become a good captain with a few years of training."

"A brawl? With Master Gallanver?!" He was one of the best sword masters of all seven kingdoms, but Taemi knew him to be a modest man with the tolerance of a mountain. He taught that rash moves and raw emotions lost battles. "What in the creator of heavens did you *do*?!"

Amused by Taemi's shocked eyes, the boy laughed, "He decided to teach me a lesson of manners. Nothing more."

A bird caught his attention and he glanced towards the sun sitting on top of the tree line. Vibrant colors of deep red, pink and purple painted the sky. The boyish smile slipped from his face and appeared stone. "We should search for a place to stay. The night will be upon us in a half hour or so. The road won't be so safe then."

The princess nodded.

"There looks to be a farm up ahead." He gestured slightly towards a transparent stream of smoke from the treetops. "We'll merely ask for a place to stay; your kingdom is certainly known for warm hospitality. We could always stow away in the barn though."

A gust of wind blew through the trees. Along with it came an eerie howl, and Taemi's breath caught. The blood in her veins froze to ice.

Kio's expression never altered.

It must have been the wind. I'm letting my imagination get the best of me.

"You heard it, too."

It wasn't a question, and Taemi found herself struggling for breath. There was another howl, a little louder... *a little closer.*

"What do we do?"

Kio looked at the sun, and then scanned the hills, twisting in his saddle. Suddenly, he sat upright. "You see the smoke from the chimney up ahead, right? The one I pointed to?"

"Yes."

"Run." He kicked hard and his horse cantered down the road.

Taemi kicked Zipper, her gelding, and followed after. Refusing to look back, she heard the howls getting closer. The jolts of the canter heaved her stomach, which was already sickened with fear.

She stayed a heartbeat behind Kio; the smoke of the chimney was already covered by the treeline as they raced deeper into the wooded countryside. The echoes of howls grew into growls behind her. *So close!* She refused to look back.

"This way!" Kio led his horse abruptly off the road and down a cleared narrow path. Taemi gave a hard kick to turn, as the shadows manifested, taking the form of a large dog in front of her.

Zipper reared up and took off into the woods at a fast pace Taemi couldn't control. She clutched the mane as every tree branch tugged and scraped her. The horse's unpredictable steps lurched her up and down hard on the saddle. She could still hear the wolves' snarls practically next to her.

Another sudden jolt threw her up into the air. Her grip on the mane seemed to vanish—leaving only stands of black hair in her hands. The air was harshly knocked out of her, leaving her lungs to burn from the lack of oxygen as her back hit the rough ground.

I'm on the ground... Her horse cantered away. The wolves were in the darkness nearby. Without another thought, she pushed herself up and ran. Suddenly, she slipped and her body tumbled down, landing lightly on a soft pillow of grass.

She opened her eyes to the full orb of the moon glowing through a pinhole view of the sky. Knowing she fell in a hole, she glanced around the dark edges. Dirt and the musky smell of tree roots surrounded her.

Panic overwhelmed her at the thought of being trapped. She watched shadows pass over the narrow opening above her, but none stopped to look down

She lay there, waiting.

The howls soon faded, and the night was silent once again.

Taemi shifted upwards—her head ached and she felt nauseous, but she was able to sit upright within the cavern. The hole she fell through was high above her head, nearly impossible for her to reach even if she stood up on her toes. The cavern was a large dome with the slightest opening at the top. She sighed, knowing she couldn't climb out on her own.

Beneath her, was the softest patch of grass she ever felt; her fall would have been worse if it wasn't for that. Before her was a luminous, blue glow. She moved slowly towards it—mainly because of her head—and saw that it was an underground spring. The teal water shimmered like crystals; *perhaps there are crystals forming below it?*

As she stared at it, tiny, lights flew up towards her like specks of glowing dust. But instead of floating, they moved like insects. *Flies?*

They embraced her face with a warm flutter instead of the buzz she was expecting.

"What poor child."

The whispers were so soft; she thought it was her imagination. There was no one in the cavern, but herself.

"Moon Child, you are far from your home."

"—You are of great importance."

"Rest."

"Drink from the well—it will heal your aches, your sorrow..."

There were so many different whispers talking over each other. The tiny lights fluttered across Taemi's face, as they spoke.

"Drink child."

"Drink from the well."

"Rest."

"There are dangers along your path."

Rest? Here, in this cave? Taemi shook her head, "I... I can't. I need to get out." She looked around unsure which of the lights to direct her request to, "Will you help me get out? I need to find Kio. I need to get out."

"Rest."

"You're safe for the night."

"The moon protects the pure."

"Light hails over darkness."

"Evil will fester."

"Protect."

"Protect, Moon Child."

"Rest, child."

"The world depends solely on you."

Taemi sighed. *They speak in riddles and they're not very helpful.* "I know of the dangers. I will go to Laquar, defeat the shadow wolves and save my people, but…"

"*Shadow wolves?*" The lights giggled with amusement.

"*Silly child.*"

"*She is young.*"

"*Yes, so young.*"

Why are they laughing at me? Taemi glared at the lights. *Wait, did they say the world solely depends on me?* She looked at the lights with confusion. "Why does the world depend on me? I know nothing other than my kingdom."

"*Evil hasn't touched yet.*"

"*But it will come.*"

"*Yes, it will come.*"

"*You must rest, Moon Child.*"

"*Drink from the well.*"

"*Rest…*"

Taemi looked down at the spring again. The water didn't reflect her image, or anything else. She scooped her hands in—a chill ran through her whole body—not a numbing cold, but an unexpected splash of a refreshing coolness that tingled every nerve down her spine. She brought the water to her lips and drank. She could feel it spreading throughout her body—to her lungs, to her head, to her toes. Suddenly, the briskness warmed her body and dispersed. The aches and nausea instantly vanished, but Taemi was still shocked by the water from the crystal spring.

The whispers and lights vanished. Taemi pushed herself up to stand, but her body collapsed and she drifted off to sleep under the light of the moon.

"Wake up, Princess!"

Taemi opened her eyes to the slight shake. The sun had already started to rise and the forest chirped melodiously to the sound of the birds.

"Are you hurt, Princess? Are you okay?"

"Kio?" The name was a mumble on her mouth and her eyes winced at the light. Kio stood over her with a relief on his face. He had both of their horses tied to a tree branch. The forest surrounded her. She vaguely remembered being down in a hole—*but maybe it was a dream?*

A strange dream...

"Are you hurt anywhere? You fell off your horse in the night... and when I finally found you, I was worried you wouldn't wake up."

Taemi took a moment and realized her head didn't hurt. Nothing was sore. She might have had the best sleep since leaving the castle. She smiled, "I'm fine. Not hurt. Thank you for...watching over me."

"I didn't find you until midnight. I almost thought I failed. The wolves seemed to have vanished shortly after dusk."

"You think they can't stay out that long?"

"That, or..." Kio grew pensive, "Whoever was looking for you gave up shortly..."

Taemi watched him as his dark eyes drifted into thought and strands of his brown hair fell over his face. His appearance looked slightly fatigued, but no less than Taemi would have expected from someone who stood watch every hour of the day.

The boy shook his head, "We better start heading out. Sandar is still a good day away."

Taemi nodded. *What was that boy thinking of?*

CHAPTER 4

Dragon Cavern

Arashi's dark minions chased after the girl as she was bucked from her horse. The sorcerer smiled over his goblet of spiced wine while he watched the images on the crystal disc. *So close now—we just need to grab hold...*

The princess suddenly vanished from sight. His wolves continued to chase at nothing through the forest. The wolves dispersed as Arashi's shock released the spell that created them from the black obsidian crystal. *She's gone?!* "How? How could she simply disappear?"

Nars was at his side watching, amused at another one of his failed attempts. "What a tricky little brat, isn't she?" She giggled, "Something must have masked her presence from you. I doubt she is capable of creating that spell herself for the lack of magic knowledge."

Arashi's fist clenched tighter around his goblet.

"Hmm..." Nars smiled brightly up at him, "Perhaps the elves of Laquar have sensed what you're doing and decided to help?"

The elves helping? Not the sort of news he'd like to hear. They mostly kept to themselves unless the outside world affected them. *What's one little girl to them?* "Let us hope they remain to be hermits and mind their trees." He returned Nars' smile with a stern gaze. He swirled his wine,

"In the meantime…" He paused to take a sip, "I'll have you scout and keep watch for me."

He knew that Nars wouldn't like the sound of that. Her toothy smile was wiped clean off, leaving him a flat glare. Her dark icy eyes could pierce a man's soul—if he had one—but to Arashi, it was the look he found quite entertaining; the woman was hard to read otherwise—hiding behind hollow smiles and fluttering eyes.

She said nothing. She wouldn't. Arguing against a command was above her place, and as much as she stretched the lines, she never overstepped. But Arashi could see the tightness of her lips compressed in distaste, reducing her to a lap dog. She always thought of herself better than that.

Arashi went on, hiding his grin, "Don't do anything rash. Be invisible and watch. Let her think that she has surpassed the dangers. Report back to me."

He expected her eyes to be aflame by his request, but the woman was perfectly composed and gave a small bow of her head and responded in a cool voice, "As you wish, my lord."

"She would be near the Dragon Cavern, continuing her way to Sandar."

"Dragon Cavern? I had no idea you had dragons this far west."

"We don't."

She shrugged, "Pity, *your* side of the world. I enjoyed dragons' company as they told the best of stories. Though, some emperors would have rather eat them." She placed her index finger on her lips, "I'd imagine their meat to be tough and tasteless. Who named it the Dragon Cavern if there are no dragons?"

"Questions are for philosophers." Arashi stated sharply, sipping his goblet, "Now get going."

"So why is it called the Dragon Cavern? We don't have any dragons," the princess asked as they continued on their journey together. Kio explained earlier that traveling through the cavern would be the fastest route to Sandar— her sister kingdom. As they came to a clearing at the bottom of the hill, Taemi gasped at the dark opening—big enough to take a large wagon through.

Kio laughed, "Can't you tell? It's like walking right into a dragon's mouth!"

"Oh, stop it, Kio— you don't even know what a dragon's mouth looks like."

He smiled, "Okay, Princess. It's called Dragon Cavern based off of a long-ago folk tale. You know, those things made up to explain how rock formations are made. For a princess, I'm surprised you don't know about the geography of this country. You said you've been to Sandar before, haven't you?"

Taemi's face flushed. "Well, it was a long time ago and usually princesses travel in carriages ...and long travels make me sleepy." She kicked her horse and trotted to the cavern entrance with the echo of Kio's laughter following close behind her.

As they approached the darkness, Kio slowed his horse to light the oil lamps and handed one to the princess. They both had one lamp tied to a post stretched out in front of their hoses, and another to hold in their hands. The darkness of the cavern almost engulfed the light. A large draft made the flames flicker, but after a few more paces, it died down. The cave was cool, stuffy and moist.

Taemi held her lamp up to study the spectrum of colors—dark reds, oranges, yellows, glittering blues and purples—that covered the cavern's walls. They were layered in rows like a cake, but in some areas, they twirled and swirled like the whirlpool illustrations she had seen on tapestries.

The ground sloped deeper and the path became narrow. The colorful walls became waterfalls of melted rock—the wetness glistened in the candlelight. In some areas, the wall disappeared into darker passages, framed by shapeless columns. She wondered if they led to multiple tunnels.

"Nine hundred years ago," Kio began as they walked—his voice echoing softly off the walls—"there used to be a giant dragon that tormented the kingdoms. Its fire breath would level villages in one blow! So the Elves of Laquar came together and cast the dragon asleep for eternity. It fell from the sky and crashed here. The ground took him and petrified his body into rock, but his teeth," Kio pointed up at the stalactites forming from the ceiling, "still grow."

Taemi giggled, "Oh Kio, you should be a gleeman for how well you tell stories."

"You've really never heard that tale before?"

"Of course not! That's peasant folk talk. My teachings are about true history and politics."

"A princess' head shouldn't be filled with fantasy tales." She remembered her father saying whenever he caught her reading books about love stories instead of her studies.

Kio laughed at the girl's stubbornness, "That might be so. I'd like to venture for it, but with your luck, Princess, it might just come awake and eat us."

The princess scowled at the boy, "I am *not* bad luck!"

"Well, traveling with you has been interesting."

"Hmph!" She sniffed and sharply turned her head from him. They walked through the cavern in silence from there. The rock formations changed the further down they went, and never the same. Pillars that formed from the ground looked spongy, and the dragon teeth from the ceiling dripped down, forming complicated arrangements. The princess reached out to touch them. They were slick, smooth, and left her hand feeling damp and grimy. Grimacing at the feel, she pulled out a handkerchief to wipe the silt off.

"How much longer is this cavern?"

"I'd say we still have an hour yet." Kio looked back at the girl, "Are you hungry? Tired?"

"No, just—" There was a low, raspy hiss that cut the girl off. It was the first thing she heard aside from the echoing hoof prints and water droplets.

Kio glanced at Taemi quizzical. His unchanged face says he heard nothing out of the ordinary.

"Kio, are there… are there snakes in these caverns?"

"Snakes, Princess?"

"Yes. The slithering, hissing kind." She remarked, looking at the walls now with caution.

The boy laughed, "Haha, I suppose there could be. It is a cave after all. There are tons of little tunnels and paths through here; a person could get lost for days." *That explained those dark passages…* "But creatures usually aren't visible on the main path because of so many travelers."

"If it's so often used, how come we haven't *seen* other travelers?"

The boy's face went blank upon realizing Taemi's concern. They saw dozens of other wagons on the road in the morning, but no one since entering the cavern.

The rasping hiss echoed again. This time, it made Zipper rear up and prance around. It was hard to tell where the noise was—in front of them, behind them, or … *above them?* Holding tight onto Zipper's reigns to control the animal, Taemi glanced around in every direction, but couldn't see anything past what her lamps would illuminate.

Kio jumped down from his horse and handed Taemi the reigns, so he could unsheathe his sword. "That did not sound like just an ordinary snake, Princess…"

The hissing came again with a clatter of falling rocks. Taemi looked ahead and gasped as the red layer of the cavern wall shifted.

"Princess…" Kio whispered, "Get ready to run." The soldier held up his lantern towards the moving wall ahead. The light reflected off the thick, scaly body as Kio traced the wall, and ended at a barbed tail.

Suddenly, Kio whipped around and dropped his lantern, "Run!"

Taemi looked behind and saw the head of the beast with long white fangs, as big as her forearms, slithering out from the shadows. It flashed towards her, but Kio blocked the snake's mouth from eating her whole with a heavy strike of his sword.

Zipper sprinted without a kick and Kio's horse was close behind. Taemi held tight onto the horse's mane as both Kio and the snake were engulfed by the darkness behind. Taemi could only hear his attacks and the snake's hiss echoing down the cavern.

The lamps were rattling so much that it was hard to see what was ahead. Zipper lunged and leaped blindly and Taemi could only hold on, crashing into the hollow pillars. *At this rate, the horse was bound to break his own neck!*

Suddenly, the horse came to a dead halt, skidding across the stone floor. "Whoa!" Taemi pulled in the reigns to regain control. The horse snorted and pranced a few steps, but did not take off. Taemi raised her lamp up and saw that the path narrowed so small, it was no longer big enough for Zipper to fit through. It might as well be a dead end.

Taemi looked around with her lamp, "We must have took a wrong turn somewhere." Many of the stalactites in this part of the cavern grew so far down, creating columns. It was hard to see how Zipper even ran through without hitting most of them.

Kio's horse was nowhere to be seen.

The girl dismounted. Her body trembled from fright. *If something spooked Zipper again, we might veer even further into the tunnels and be lost for days.* "Alright, Zipper, we have to find the main path. That's our way out of here."

Taemi tried to walk back the way she thought Zipper came from, but the horse barely nudged. It was hard to tell what direction they came from in the dark. She found a path to lead the horse, but Zipper now resisted going under the low stalactites after already breaking some when cantering through. Taemi only hoped their spikes didn't puncture Zipper too badly. She would have to check him when they got out.

"Ugh, come on, Zip. I don't see how you couldn't just stay on the main path like the other horse." *Kio's horse was probably already roaming the hills of Sandar, and she was stuck in here with a stubborn mule-brained animal!* It was a struggle to get a good footing to pull the gelding. The main path was solid rock ground, but here the ground was uneven with large, thick stalagmites that Taemi had to ease Zipper around.

The horse stamped and snorted, but Taemi couldn't get the animal to budge further. "I will go without you!" the girl snarled, but it did nothing to persuade Zipper. The girl finally sighed and released the horse. "I'm serious, you can stay here all you want, but I'm leaving."

Zipper stamped and pulled back two steps. Taemi watched as the horse's ears perked up, flicked back and forth, and a second later it dashed off down the tunnel again.

"Wait, Zipper! Blast that horse!" Taemi ran after him until she heard the raspy hiss echo from the tunnel. *With all of Zipper's commotion before, I must have missed it...*

The girl could feel her heart pounding against her chest. The hissing grew louder. Without wasting a moment to look behind, Taemi rushed to the narrow path ahead—the sound of scraping rocks growing louder behind her. *It's right behind me!*

She lowered her head and turned sideways to squeeze through the narrow crack as fast as she could. She barely fit, but she continued to push herself through until she fell out onto the other side, snagging the bottom of her dress.

The flame went out as her lamp hit the ground with her. The girl heard it roll and tumble over a ledge. It filled the cave with a rhythm of echoes as it fell further and further. She was left alone in the dark. The hissing noise was coming through the crack. The thing could eat her whole and she wouldn't see it coming.

Wait. I made light before! The princess held her pendant and hoped for light! The snake snarled as Taemi's pendant illuminated brighter than the flame in the lantern. The creature flinched away from the light and she was able to see the beast completely. The gigantic snake had yellow and black scales. Red, spiked fins sprang out from the side of its head like a pair of wings as it hissed, and larger spikes down its scaly body.

Taemi's light only staggered the beast for a moment. The girl scooted back but stopped once her fingers felt the edge of the ledge. *A drop.* She was trapped between the snake and a cliff.

The snake took only seconds to recoil itself and then it striked forward at the girl. Taemi blocked her face with a scream, "KIO—"

A loud slash jolted Taemi's eyes open. The snake slithered back with a hiss and blood dripping from its face. A figure dropped in front of the girl so lightly, it barely made a sound. "Kio?" Taemi glanced up and in the light of her pendant; she saw that the person wasn't at all Kio. Dressed in satin and armor, the figure was a woman wielding two long swords—one in each hand.

The woman glared down at Taemi, and when their eyes met, she snarled, whipped her head away, and back-kicked Taemi off the edge—hard in the chest. All the air was kicked out of her, as the princess fell into the darkness.

In the midst of tumbling down the steep slide of gravel, Taemi struggled for breath. Her whole chest burned. *That lady had high heels?!* The rocks scraped her arms, and her pendant no longer bared light.

As if she wasn't dizzy enough, the ground disappeared from under her and she landed even harder on a large, smooth boulder. Its smoothness did not ease the pain. Taemi lay there for a moment to catch her breath. Her whole body ached, her chest felt bruised, her arms throbbed, her head spun, and her lungs burned.

Taemi rubbed her bruised chest with a moan and lay still until the aches faded away. *She didn't have to kick me... Although, she didn't have to save me either... Who was that woman? Why would someone save me and then kick me down a cliff?* "And she glared at me!" *Whomever it was, guess she didn't want me lurking around the cave?*

Taemi didn't spend the time to ponder; she'll tell Kio about it later—perhaps he'll understand. Peasants are his territory of knowledge. *But she was wearing satin and armor? Peasants don't wield two swords... No.* The girl shook her head. *It must have been my imagination. But she did* kick *me.*

Finally, the girl pushed herself up to her feet. Slightly dazed, as if the ground was still moving, Taemi cast light from her pendant again, and looked up from where she had fallen. She could see the slide of gravel, but only the end of it. The ceiling and walls were lost in the dark. Taemi thought a slight disturbance of the smallest stone would echo throughout the whole cavern, but it was quiet.

The girl stood on a large, but oddly smooth boulder with stalagmites forming up in a uniformed row. Or, like

stalagmites, but the formation was more defined and smoother as it reflected the light from the pendant.

Is the ground moving? Maybe she just hit her head a little harder than she thought. *The boulder couldn't be moving.* But it felt like it. The girl tried to peer over the round edge, carefully, looking for a path. But the boulder shifted again and her footing slipped over the small pebbles.

With a yell, the girl slid off the boulder down another slide, much smoother though, hitting few bumps, and landed in a pool of silt at the bottom—the least painful of her falls so far.

The pool was shallow enough, but completely soaked the girl's knee-high boots, elbows, and the back half of her dress. Her stomach sank in distaste feeling the soft slime under her fingers. She got on her feet again and frowned at her dress covered in the murky clay water.

The pendant still glowed like a lamp around Taemi. She could only see a few paces ahead of herself. She lifted herself up and chose a direction, hoping to find something to pull herself out of the water.

There was a ledge that looked like claws. As she got

closer, they were as big as her, white, and uniquely smooth. They felt like marble. *If only they didn't look like a creatures teeth!*

The princess grimaced and looked for an easier climb. Following the wall that the white stones reached out of, she turned and gasped.

It was a gigantic creature with scales like a snake, but with large horns that sprouted from its head. It was carved so realistically into the wall that it gave her a start, but soon realized that the creature didn't move.

Much like the snake—this one had large white fangs—probably made with the same marble as the claws— its jaw was wide open with a roar of agony. The wide, violent eyes shimmered like gold even with the small cast of light of the pendant. The carving gave a feeling of distress, anger and rage. The rest of the creature was consumed by the darkness.

Whomever had the time to create this had such skill and an eye for detail! Shaping every form and scale by removing the rock. Who would spend so much time in a cavern creating something that no one would ever see?

She had to ask Kio about it. He might know. *If I find him... and a way out.*

Taemi continued on through the water, staying near the wall. The ground eventually sloped upward out from the water like a steep ramp. The path took her up and out of the dome. She passed through a narrow tunnel that could only fit a single person. It was more of a climb than a walk, and she pulled herself up into a bright clearing that was somehow exposed to the sunlight. The princess' heart was at ease, assuming she was close to the exit of the cave. She could see the structures without the light of her pendant now.

Before her was a solid, level path much like the main road. She looked back and studied the small hole she crawled out of. It was big enough for a body, but not more noticeable than any other part of the cavern. If she didn't know where it would have led, she would have dismissed it as any other tight, dead-end passage. *Maybe all the tunnels lead into that giant dome?* Maybe. She hoped she might find it one day. *Art like that should be seen, but maybe the mystery was part of the beauty.* She would definitely show it to Kio someday.

Kio... The princess panicked. *What if...* She couldn't bear the thought, "Kio! Kio!" Taemi ran down the path and called out for him. "Kio!"

She didn't want to go back further into the cavern, so she followed the light, running and calling for him. Maybe if she found the exit, she could convince Sandar to create a search party and help her find him.

"Kio!"

The girl rounded the corner and came face-to-face with the wide mouth of the giant cobra. She let out a horrid scream and flailed her arms to shield herself, falling to her back.

"Princess!"

As she heard steps close by, she opened her eyes up towards the reptilian beast that was about to prey upon her, but it was still. Its broken jaw hung open, and its long thick, spiky body coiled tightly around the stalagmite it was staked on. Blood oozed out from where the spire pierced through the limp body, and pooled at the base.

"Princess, are you okay?" Kio was down on his knees holding Taemi in his arms as she stared at the monument before her.

"I... I thought it was alive..." She breathed.

"Well..." He glanced up at the creature, "it's very much dead now."

"Kio, did you..."

The boy chuckled as he helped the princess to her

feet, her eyes still fixated on the creature. "No, I can't take credit for this. That thing weighs a ton."

"Who do you think could have done it?" Even though it tried to attack them first, there was something *off* about it being mounted on a stake and left to suffer. It was merciless.

"No idea, Princess. But light, I hope I never face them in combat." He tried to guide Taemi's eyes away and towards the main path, "C'mon. The horses are up ahead. They seemed to have known their way through."

"Those wool-headed animals would, wouldn't they?" The princess mumbled. *Zipper almost broke his own neck, with* me *right on him!*

Kio looked quizzically at the girl's sour comment, but continued leading the way to the horses. They walked up a ramp that led to the main path in the cavern. The light showed through like a giant, welcoming sun from the other side. The horses' silhouettes danced restlessly on the grassy hill.

"Something's not right. Quickly Princess." Kio ran ahead and unsheathed his sword. Taemi hoisted her wet garments and tried to keep up with his pace.

As they got closer, there were other figures up ahead. Taemi hoped they weren't creatures. *Bandits maybe?*

"Hey! Get away from those horses!" Kio yelled out, but the thieves held their stance.

Once out of the cave's entrance, Kio halted to a complete stop, but kept his sword out in defense. "Princess—stay back!"

Eight spears were pointed at them from every direction. They were soldiers dressed in forest green uniforms with gold-plated armor. A sigil of three spears pointed upward was embossed on the upper-right corner of their breastplates.

...Sandar soldiers. Taemi wondered if they were expecting her.

"Passing through this cave is strictly forbidden by the orders of both rulers of Sandar and Adrienan." The one who spoke was the only one who wore a pendant with a ribbon. He had a stern face and a dark mustache. "How you got past the soldiers of Adrienan guarding the other side is enough to hold you two captive to be taken to the Prince of Sandar."

...There wasn't anyone guarding the other side... soldiers of Adrienan?

Taemi looked at Kio who resisted putting his sword down. In fact, his stance became more tense.

"Kio..."

"Put your spears down, Sandar! I *am* a soldier of Adrienan!"

"Kio Stop! Put *your* sword down!"

"You look like a child to *us*, much less a soldier." The officer kept his face expressionless, yet there was a hint of amusement in his voice. "You likely stole that coat."

"Kio please drop your sword—they'll take us to Sandar!"

"They're going to lock us up like prisoners! We've done nothing wrong! No one was guarding the other side. We didn't sneak in!"

The Sandar soldiers watched him with calm calculating eyes. Soldiers were able to control their emotions, but Kio was still much of a boy. There wasn't anything Taemi could say that wouldn't hurt his pride as her protector.

She turned to the officer, "Please forgive us." She bowed her head in modesty, "We were ignorant and my brother is quite fond of me." Kio looked at her in confusion. "We will go in peace to Sandar to meet with the Prince." After Kio's reactions, now wasn't the time to reveal her identity—not that she looked like the princess in simpleton garb, and Kio wouldn't be taken seriously as an Adrienian soldier.

"Sheath your sword, and we will take you to the Prince."

Kio hesitated, glancing at Taemi, but finally he obeyed. Two of the Sandar soldiers stayed to guard the cave while the others and the officer escorted them to the castle. Zipper and Kio's horse's reins were each tied to one of the soldier's horses.

Most of the attention was kept on Kio in case he decided to do anything irrational. Taemi hoped he wouldn't after the humiliation of her apology. He should have known better than to stand up against eight trained soldiers. The travel to the castle was silent, but she intended to speak with Kio in private about his actions.

CHAPTER 5

Sandar

Sandar, the kingdom built on the coast of the Mythic Sea, was just as big as Adrienan. Six, giant, brick bridges arched over the river that streamed around the kingdom. The shores of the Mythic Sea could be seen from any one of the bridges, and each bridge had a large gate controlling passage into the city. Ships traveling from the north to trade docked at the harbor. Smaller boats were used to sail on the river for a faster passage to their destination.

Upon passing through the front gate, Taemi's nostalgic memories came rushing back. The gate used to tower over her like a giant as she rode with her father. The bridge led to the market area of tall buildings—each filled with multiple stores. She remembered having to walk through a flower shop and fabric factory to get to the seamstress on the top floor.

She saw now, that there were signs for each level, indicating the stores. Due to the river that restricted the kingdom's growth, the citizens utilized the vertical space. Passage through Sandar was slow-paced, as the roads were narrow. The buildings were built right up against the next, where only small animals were able to use the alleys in between.

The castle was in the center of the city and stood on a hill higher than the market grounds. Seven towers with green and gold flags stretched out high from the castle. Six of the towers aligned with the six large bridges. The seventh tower stood the tallest in the middle. The outer towers were all connected at the bottom, while smaller bridges connected them to the middle, for easier transportation from one to the next.

Taemi only recalled ever being inside the Fifth Tower—the tallest tower in the middle. How they named their towers was beyond her logic of understanding. The middle tower was to only be used by royalty. The other six were meeting rooms, servant chambers, armories, and enforced protection for the castle. No one could get to the middle tower without entering the outside towers first.

Before entering through one of the towers of the castle, the officer dismounted his horse and exchanged information with one of the castle guards. Their uniforms were similar, except the guards were bulkier and heavily armored with long spears and thick helms. The captives were kept back from hearing what was said. The guard called over a pageboy, spoke to him briefly, and sent him off running.

The officer turned back to Kio and Taemi. "Dismount the horses and come with me to the Third Tower."

Servants came for their horses and took them away. Taemi thought it odd that they let Kio keep his sword, but she was glad they did. He certainly would not give it up without a fight.

The officer and two castle guards led them towards the tower. Maids and servants populated the grounds, running errands and goods for the lords. Wealthy merchants were also granted passage to the towers for business and shipping contracts.

The inside of the Third Tower's lower level looked

similar to all the other towers. There were two hallways, with the left leading towards the second & first, and the right went towards the fourth and sixth. A large, spiral staircase before them would take them to the top with rooms and corridors along the way. At some point near the middle of each tower would be another hallway to enter the Fifth Tower.

There were no decorations on the lower level, but as they went up to the staircase, the walls became more furnished with tapestries and paintings. There were few windows along the way, but the gold markings on the doorways indicated each level. By the time they passed four rooms and three windows, they reached a doorway marked with a large gold 'V'. The level had castle guards here at all times because it was the first marked corridor that would lead to the Fifth Tower.

They passed this level quickly and continued up. After passing a doorway with a 'XIII', the officer slowed his pace, and Taemi had the opportunity to glance out one of the windows.

She gasped at the sight and stopped. At this level, she could see the entire kingdom and more. The rooftops of market buildings had flat, narrow roads for guards to patrol the city. She could see one of the bridges directly in line with the tower she stood in. Out in the distance, she saw the white sails gliding on the sea that glistened under the sunlight. She has been in the tallest room of her castle and never once had seen so much!

Kio touched her arm and she remembered this was no time for sightseeing. She was to meet with Prince Willis. Her soldier hadn't said a word to her since they left the Dragon Cavern. Even though he was next to her the whole time, it felt oddly lonely.

They left the staircase and went through a doorway marked with "XVII" and entered a meeting room. It was very plain with lit oil lamps, a wooden desk with ink and parchment scattered about, two chairs, a small bookcase in the corner, and a map on the wall.

A map!

"Taemi Lor Equillis of Adrienan."

The princess turned around at the pronunciation of her title. The gentleman was already mid-bow at the entrance of the room, addressing her, but she knew his face as soon as he straightened. Prince Willis used to be a shy, timid boy with short blonde hair and grey eyes. Now, he was a tall, toned, handsome prince, dressed in a fine green, high-neck coat with gold embroidery. His long, golden hair was held back at the nape of his neck by a leather band, but his long bangs still fell into his eyes. He walked towards Taemi, brushing his hair out of his face with black gauntlets. Her breath caught at the sight of his smooth, flawless face with high cheekbones and stormy blue eyes.

He knelt before her, took her hand into his and gave her a kiss, "Thank the Heavens you are safe and well."

Taemi's heart was racing and she forgot her formal manners of receiving his presence. "Prince... Prince Willis of Sandar." *...what was his last name?*

He rose to his feet and grinned, "You don't have to be formal with me. 'Willis' will do just fine, just as you used to call me when we were kids." He brushed a strand of her hair from her face, and her skin pricked at his touch. "You have grown so beautiful... I regret not being at your coronation ceremony."

The castle guards left the room, but the officer stayed to guard the door. Prince Willis backed away from the princess and continued, "Which brings up the remarkable question as to why you are here... and in such a tragic state." An obvious remark on her peasant clothing, no doubt, but the princess imagined she looked worse than that from her fall in the cave. Already, she'll have to get a new dress and boots.

Kio spoke up first, "How did you know she was the Princess?"

Willis gestured to the office, "Sir Reverance informed me."

The officer nodded. "Your majesty, from my long years of service, I'd recognize the face of your father and mother on you any given day."

"And you dared to threaten us..." Kio's grumble was bitter as he crossed his arms and slouched up against the wall.

The officer kept his attention focused on Taemi and bowed, "Forgive me, my lady, but I didn't think it was wise to expose your identity."

"Yes, that *was* probably wise, wouldn't you agree, *Kio*?" Taemi didn't look in his direction as she asked him flatly.

"Yes... your majesty."

The princess turned her attention back to the prince, "Something terrible has happened in my kingdom, Prince Willis. During the ceremony, we were attacked... by sorcery. Creatures that look like wolves, but lay in the shadows and can disassemble bodies like parchment." She studied his face, but the prince showed no expression. The hardest part was what she had to say next, "I have no information if King Nigan is well. I escaped with the escort of my guard in the night during the attack."

"Well," Willis pursed his lips and took a moment to process the information. He sighed and gave a small smile back at Taemi. "My father would not have gone down so easily in an attack. I can assure your concern that he's either well or did not perish in vain.

"I will send out troops to hunt down this sorcerer. Princess Taemi, you are welcome to stay here as long as you need; you will be safe here. As allies, we fought alongside

Adrienan—any threat against you is a threat against us."

"Thank you... Willis," Taemi bowed her head at his generous offer, "However, I feel that whatever attacked my kingdom is solely after me. I'd like to request assistance to Laquar."

"Oh..." Willis stroked his chin, "That's quite the travel. Even by carriage, it would take more than fourteen days, not to mention the trouble on the way." He shook his head softly. "It would be best if I send for someone from Laquar for you."

"Willis..." Taemi reached for his cuff, "... my father wishes that I go there. I can not disobey him."

"Very well." The prince sighed again. "How soon do you intend to leave?"

"As soon as necessary to arrange an escort for me and the fastest ship to sail on the Mythic Sea."

The prince smiled, a gorgeous one at that, "I can have an escort ready by tomorrow morning after the sun rises. Princess Taemi," Willis held out his hand to her, "Will you do me the honor of joining me for dinner? I have a small banquet for the lords and ladies visiting from our western manors—business matters, really—but I'd feel better if you were with me than being left alone."

The princess bowed, "Of course, Prince Willis."

His smile became even more gorgeous, "Pleased to hear. I had your things moved into a room at the Fifth Tower. Sir Reverance will take you there to get cleaned up for the evening." He took her hand, kissed it, and left the room.

Sir Reverance bowed, "If you will please follow me, Princess."

"Actually, if you could leave me with my guard in private for just a moment."

"As you wish. I'll be waiting just outside the door."

As soon as the door closed behind Sir Reverence, Taemi spun to face Kio with one hand on her hip, and a finger in the air—the same way Susia posed when she was getting scolded—but to her surprise, the boy was already down on one knee, hand over his heart and face down towards the floor.

"Princess…" His voice was soft and choked, "I am no longer worthy of serving you. My actions were of a child rather than of your protector and I disobeyed you." He unlaced the sheath around his belt and held out his sword. "The most acceptable punishment would be to relieve me of your service."

All the anger she felt towards him vanished. Even if he reacted in a blind rage, he was only trying to protect her. He would take on all of Sandar's trained soldiers if he had to.

She sighed and shook her head, "Kio, get up and put your sword back on." He did so, but kept his eyes towards the floor. "My father appointed *you* to get me to Laquar. You will carry out his orders whether or not they be his last."

He looked at her and nodded. "Yes, your majesty."

Taemi couldn't help smiling at his modesty. "Besides, I couldn't waste effort learning the name of a new bodyguard." She was most amused by his blank stare and half-opened mouth as she turned and left the room.

Chimes of strings and flutes hummed through the dining hall, vibrating over the low buzz of chatter from Willis' enthusiastic dinner party. The princess stopped counting the guests after fifty couples, and they were still flooding the hall with laughter and hefty garments. For a small gathering of friends, Willis sure knew a lot of lords in the area.

"Your majesty, I'm very concerned about the mydrallchobria looming in the Dragon Cavern. It's really delaying our trade from—"

Willis cut him off with a simple hand gesture, "No

worries, Sir Mornay. I'll have my finest men sent into the cavern tomorrow to slay the mydrallchobria."

Taemi frowned, *He promised* me *his finest men as my escort nearly five hours ago...* But I suppose a king has to comfort their lords with something. *Perhaps he has an army of the* finest *men of all Sandar.* She thought mockingly with a smirk.

"Well, I hope they do away with it quickly," The lady that accompanied Sir Mornay was quite in her years. Rare diamonds lavished her garments generously and sparkled blindingly in the light. It was too much for even the Princess of Adrienan. "Ever since that slithery monster burrowed in the cavern, I had to wait six weeks for the cheese of Norwin."

Bored with petty talk of men's trade and women's secret shop findings, Taemi couldn't help missing the engaging conversations with her comrade, standing guard in the shadows, ten paces away with the other Sandarians. It was the distance between royalty and paid help that really made her feel lonely. *Black, vicious wolves are chasing me, and these lords are* literally *complaining about the mold in their cheese!*

Taemi took another sip of her wine, only to realize her drink cup was long dry. She never even noticed when it was half full. *Who's not filling my drink cup—are they blind?* She glanced around for someone with a pitcher while raising her cup in the air. She received eye contact from someone across the room, and smiled as they ascended towards her... and then they vanished immediately into the crowd.

She sniffed and slumped further in her chair. Willis laughed among the lords and ladies, and her bodyguard stood just out of sight behind a pillar nearby. Servers ignored her empty wine glass and her body still hurt from her adventure through the cavern.

Taemi glared at the woman a few tables away, laughing over her scarlet wine while taking bites from a steak that was so rare—it likely never had been near a flame before appearing on her plate. The woman's complexion was fair, and her sun-blonde hair was contoured within a nest of thin sticks that crowned her head when you looked at her straight on. She was elegantly graceful, yet—other than the silver lining of her magenta arm-cuffs and star-shaped earrings that glistened in the light with a necklace to match—her attire was free of gems and jewels, unlike the other ladies. *Her attire was rather strange entirely...*

Why does she look so familiar...?

"My Lady, do you care for a dance?" Prince Willis held out his hand and patiently waited for Taemi to realize he was addressing her.

"Oh..." Taemi blinked and looked up at Willis and then back at the table to point in the direction of the lady in satin, but she was gone. Her seat replaced by a gruff, fat man covered in gold embroidery.

Willis smiled amusingly at Taemi's confused stare off into the crowd, took her hand and carefully led her to the dance floor.

"Is the wine a little too strong for you, Miss Equillis?" Willis asked as he led the dance of Three Bliss Queens.

Right palm to his right palm, Taemi surveyed the dance floor as they moved circularly. "I thought I saw someone odd... and I wanted to ask you about them."

"Odd...?"

They changed hands—her left palm to his left. "Perhaps maybe I did have a lot." *Maybe Willis told the servants to cut me off...?*

Willis smiled with a small laugh, "Everyone in this kingdom is odd—they come all over the country land to trade." Willis brushed a black, stray hair from Taemi's face. "You have a very protective guardian. His eyes alone seem to threaten anyone with a pitcher near you."

"*Kio* cut me off?!"

Willis laughed more openly as he pulled the girl into his arms near his chest in a surprising spin, yet fully supportive. "He started to get restless after your third glass, and then stopped the servers on your fifth."

Five glasses... The room circled around them as they danced.

He whispered in her ear, "He may be a boy, but he doesn't overlook a single detail."

In a daze, Taemi saw the crowned blonde in satin over Willis' shoulder dancing among the couples. Her mouth curved in a smile and then a scowl as soon as their eyes met. *Just like right before she kicked me...*

The spinning stopped abruptly and support of Willis was gone as a large drunk pushed through and tumbled into another couple. Taemi's footing was hindered and she fell back grabbing at air.

Until she saw Kio's kind, brown eyes.

"Kio..." the fall into his strong arms left Taemi breathless. Blood pounded in her ears so loud, she could only hear fragments of the current commotion:

"My Lord!

"...He's a bloody fast one."

"—Badgering right into me!"

"...My Apologies, Prince Willis..."

Kio looked down at the princess with a smirk, "I think it's long past time for bed, Princess."

It was well into the late hours and Kio could still hear the merriment of the party echo through the halls while he settled outside against the door of the guest chambers where the princess slumbered the wine off. After taking her upstairs, she spilled up cups worth, but still. *Five glasses is far too much for even* his *age.* He frowned. He didn't like that Prince Willis either—*completely*

preoccupied in the princess' presence and then asking her to dance while she could barely hold a conversation. ...Far too casual towards her too!

Torches dimly lit the corridor where the soldier rested his head back against the door and stared off into the dancing shadows. Every moment he thought it secure to rest for a while, there was a flicker of movement in the corner of his eyes that made him jump in panic. There haven't been any shadow wolves since the chase before the cave, and it doesn't seem like the mydrallchobria from the Dragon Cavern was connected to the same dark magic.

...Or maybe that's just what they want *me to think?*

Kio shook his head, *No, you'll never sleep if you keep over-thinking everything.*

Yet, he couldn't help but wonder who killed the mydrallchobria. It slithered into one of the narrow passages as soon as he countered its attack. He grabbed onto its tail to keep it from following Taemi and the horses, but the beast flung him off like a fly. It was long gone by the time he recovered and he found his horse not too far down the main path. He didn't hear a sound from the princess until he reached the exit. When he saw the mydrallchobria staked, he knew it was the same one as it bore the small scratch where Kio slashed its head.

No normal human would be able to pierce that thing like a trophy, but would it be the same monster after the princess...?

Perhaps he should have had a glass or two of wine.

He heard a cheer echo from the halls. As it grew louder, he peered over to watch four figures develop into focus. For a moment, he could only make out well-dressed lords, grinning and cheering to each other while a woman's laughter filled the hall. As they passed by, he then saw that the four lords carried a young blonde among themselves— the front two lords supported her back with their shoulders as she drank her wine and giggled, and the other two held up her legs. The lady was dressed in high-end fabric of the north and knee-high boots, all in the same color. A noble sort, for sure.

These people are so weird... was his first thought as he watched them pass, *but what if—*

"Stop."

They were only a few paces from where Kio rested up against the door when the woman raised her slim arm—draped in satin—palm faced open. With a quick whisk of her wrist, the men halted on command.

They eased her down onto her feet like a queen. Gently enough—not even a drop of the full glass of red wine that she held dripped to the floor. The men smiled at her like drunken fools, but behaved like trained soldiers. Once she was fully supported on her own feet, they simply stood upright waiting for her next command.

"Ah. Thank you, Vlad," and she took down a few gulps of her drink.

Obviously, they're not any danger... Kio sat and eyed them all up, uncertain of what to expect *...am I in danger?*

"Aw, it looks like you've been up for days—why don't you ever just take a nap?" The woman smiled as she walked towards him, the click of her heels echoed down the hall. She brushed up against the door to the princess' chamber and slid down onto the floor to sit next to him. "Trust me, no one is coming after you tonight." She spoke softly with squinted eyes and patted him limply on the cheek with the back of her icy hand, "So relax, have a drink." Her words faded into a whisper.

He raised his hand to block her less-than-gentle pats, but she stopped promptly and giggled. *...What is this? She's harmless, right?* She was just confusing and annoying like a typical drunk, but she did everything in a manner of a lady. The boy glanced back at the men who chuckled

Kio

as she laughed, but said nothing and stood where she left them.

"Ah-ha—I have something that will help you sleep," She lifted his chin and poured a strong liquid into his mouth faster than he could react. It smelled of alcohol as it burned down his throat and pushed her off while gagging at the taste.

"Ahk! What. What *is* that?!"

Giggling, she slipped down to rest her head in Kio's lap, peering up at him amusingly with vivid eyes—bluer than the cloudless, midday sky. Her curved lips, stained from the dark, red wine, smile innocently up at him, "*That,* they call Dragon's Breath."

"...A poison?" he began to recover from the taste, but everything started to feel dreamier by the second. Giggling, she slowly gestured her head from side to side while still lying in his lap. The statues mimicking her emotions became blurrier as their laughter faded into murmurs. His eyes became heavy, but he could hear her voice as clearly as before.

"It's because it does this—"

A blast of fire roared up from her mouth.

Kio blocked himself from the flare and shuffled to his feet, unsheathing his sword in seconds, "What—what the bloody hell—was *that*!?"

The woman lay on the floor where she was tossed and looked up at him repulsively, "It was just a trick..." Her voice quieted and the lords behind scowled at him.

Heat flowed through his body from his own sudden movement. His vision was normal for a brief moment, but the dizzy haze swiftly returned.

"You're so uptight," she muttered, but as she lifted herself up, so did her spirit, "but you're probably grumpy because of the lack of sleep. Alright, Vlad let's go."

Kio kept his blade raised, but his eyes became

too heavy to keep open. The four lords carried the woman further down the hall, and before he could force his eyes to open again, he felt the cold concrete floor on his face and everything faded out of touch.

CHAPTER 6

The Last Rest

Rays of light beamed through the small office window where Taemi reviewed the old parchments of Sandar's landscape for the quickest path to Laquar. She came to Sandar from the west through the Dragon Cavern, the Mythic Sea surrounded the kingdom at the North and East where Sandar's wealthy trades sailed. The Mydral Marshes were south—a path most choose not to take—because just beyond the marches laid an evil-infested forest.

None of the kingdoms declared ownership of the forest; therefore, it stayed unlabeled on all the maps. Commoners referred to it as the 'Forest of the Damned', 'The Devils Tomb' or simply, 'Death'. Royals stayed clear of mentioning its existence at all—assuming that it would cease to exist.

Rumors of the forest spoke of trees that devoured the flesh of anything that entered. Their red-thorn branches latch onto their prey and then feed off their victim until the body is infused within the trunk. If anyone survived those, then it was the monstrous beast with large fangs and multiple heads—roaring and screeching—that would kill them off within the night. Though, some have said that the forest is so thick, it was always night.

She shuddered at the thought of encountering one of those creatures and reverted her attention back towards the map. *The best path would be to take a ship across the Mythic Sea.*

"It'll be about a week's trip of sailing, Lady Equillis." Master Mavean mentioned quietly on the other side of the table. He was the kingdom's cartographer—weathered by age; his thin skin clung to his boney hands. He mapped all of the areas surrounding Sandar and even some of the largest cities across the sea in his younger days. Now, he advises the king, pointing out safe roads and dangerous paths noted on his maps in small, intricate detail.

"You'll have to stay south and sail inland because there's a large whirlpool here," His boney finger grazed the map across the Mythic Sea, and between the two continents, he motioned a spiral. "The current makes an easy travel from the north coming to Sandar, and riding it back up, but it's quite large during this season and will pull your ship north instead of straight to Laquar."

"Princess Taemi, won't you reconsider staying here for a while?" Willis frowned down at the map. He was quiet for most of the morning, drinking hot herbal tea for his headache. "A week's travel near the south inland is just as dangerous as traveling through... the forest." He forced a swallow. "Those creatures are less contained by the elves' spell each day, according to my field patrol. Wait another month, and traveling to Laquar would only be four days at sea."

Taemi hesitated about her answer as she studied the map. *It'll just keep getting more dangerous.* She wondered if these were the small choices that determined one's fate of life or death. Her stories never gave the heroes options; they were weaved into their journeys as if they knew what they had to do. *A month?* Hiding away for a month could be just as dangerous as sailing. *Whoever is*

To the Land of
Krah-Haareen
N
Mythic Sea
Sandar
Adrienan
Dragon
Cavern
SANDAR
ADRIENAN
Mydral Marshes
NISHE
Forest of
the Damned

The North Islands
To Eithsa
Whirlpool
LAQUAR
Laquar Forest
TERRALIN
Cloymein Plains
To Narpal

after me will only attack Sandar just as they did in Adrienan.

"I would like to leave as soon as a ship can take us."

Willis exhaled loudly, but nodded. "Not many will travel *that* route even with a large fare. I'll send men to the harbor and prepare one of our naval teams."

"Thank you, Willis."

"You should be able to leave tomorrow morning. Your soldier should be well-rested by then."

Kio was given a bed after the princess found him lying asleep outside her door. She admired his persistence of staying awake so long, but days without sleep were bound to catch up with him. This was perhaps the best place for him to finally give in for one night. She assumed that he'd sleep most of the day.

"Lady Equillis, while I arrange your team for Laquar, how about spending some tea time in the gardens?" Prince Willis reached out and cupped Taemi's chin, directing her attention to his stormy eyes. "Lady Iriene and Lady Teirine would be ecstatic to have you accompany them."

"Oh... um no." Taemi shifted out of his hand and back to reviewing the map. *The last thing I want is to talk to anyone from last night.* "I think it's safer that fewer people knew I was still here, and I should really probably check up on my guardsman—to see how he's feeling, and brief him of our travel plans."

Willis nodded. "Just... one more thing then." He reached down and unclipped a knife from his belt. "I want you to take this with you." He held out a dagger with an emerald gem on the hilt. "Even with an escort and trained soldiers, a lady should never travel without a weapon."

She hesitated. *I have my pendant.*

"I won't let you leave my kingdom without it." He insisted with a smile. Taemi nodded and took the dagger before leaving the study to Kio's room.

The sun was low in the autumn sky and the brisk wind grew colder as Kio walked home with a wagon of goods he got from the village. His family didn't live far, but three hours on foot was still a long walk alone. His father would be back from hunting now, and his mom would be in the kitchen, roasting up the daily catch for dinner while his younger brother played with his wooden toys.

A strong scent of fire caught his attention and he could see the black cloud trailing up in the sky. He knew his home was in that direction, but even his father never burned a fire that dense.

Panicked, he raced down the gravel road—leaving the wagon behind—his heart stricken with fear. The road led to a small cabin in the clearing, surrounded by thick smoke and ash. "Mom? Dad!" He called as he ran inside.

"Oh, Kio, I didn't hear you come home." The smoke cleared away around his mom, pulling a large bird out of the stove. Her dark brown hair was loosely pulled up and stray hair framed her warm smile. *"Have a seat; your father is just..."*

Kio stood in the doorway, *but... there was a fire. Flames... blood...*

He remembered coming home many times to his mom cooking, his younger brother running around the kitchen yelling as he played, and his dad lugging his furs inside and sitting around the table drinking ale with a big grin.

But this time, when he came back from the village and entered his home, the turkey was burning in the stove, causing a cloud of black smoke from the chimney. He peered inside the cabin and saw his mother sitting up on the back wall with her throat ripped out. Her eyes were full of fear as she held the limp body of his brother, both saturated in a pool of their own blood.

In the shadows, he saw the six red eyes of a creature—as large as a horse—with long fangs, a large snout and curled horns.

He stood in the doorway.

He saw large paw prints in the snow, trailing blood towards the house. His eyes followed them out and around his house. He could only see the woodpile where it came from and his dad's boots.

"...Dad." He walked away from his cabin towards the woodpile, but only enough to see the red stain of his father's torn chest. There was blood on the axe he clenched in his hand as he fell, but it didn't stop whatever this creature was.

"*Dragon's Breath.*" A soft whisper danced through the trees.

Then all that he knew roared into flames before his eyes. They consumed the cabin, the carts, and his family. The embers flared into the sky like tiny lights reaching for the stars.

Heavy rain poured down to control the fire. "*No one will see your tears in the rain, kid. So cry as much as you need.*" He was there with someone as he watched the flames engulf the simple world he knew. The fire continued, roaring strong under the wet clouds, and blazing bright as the sun...

Kio sprung up from his sleep, feeling hot and wet. It took him a moment to calm his breathing and realize he was in an elegant room, sleeping on a soft bed, and everything was just a dream... *a memory of the past.*

"Kio, are you okay?"

He saw Taemi watching him with worried green eyes. She touched his head and grimaced slightly at the dampness. "You don't feel feverish."

Calming his breath, he managed a small smile of reassurance. "Just a bad dream... Those shadow wolves, huh?"

The princess' eyes lit up, "You dream about them too!?"

Not exactly, but... Kio shook his head. "Kind of. Must have been the lack of sleep lately."

Taemi nodded. "Well, tomorrow we will continue our journey by ship."

"Oh *my*, do those Sandarians know how to throw a party," Nars swooned in the late hours and crashed on her cushioned thrown across from Reiji-Arashi and his crystal disc.

Arashi peered up briefly on her entry, but kept his gaze on the crystal, viewing the outside world, "I saw... But I'm sure you have taken care of our situation?"

"Well... I was a bit too gone when I got to her little soldier boy, but everyone that is part of her escort should be easy enough to manipulate through the mirror." Nars smiled amused, "It's a little trick of the magic. All I had to do is seep into their minds and they'll believe whatever I wish of them—and think it's precisely the truth."

He was pleased with that. While Arashi harnessed his magic through the use of crystals, Nars could cast spells on a whim. The simple ones were just a wave of her hand. *She was magnificent!* Arashi was sure that even most of the elves couldn't summon on her level. "Curious thing, that contortion magic of yours... You certainly have some remarkable gift... You sure you've never used it on *me*?"

The drunken sorceress gave a curt smile, "It wouldn't work on anyone able to wield a vast amount of magic. Our brains are imperative to any mind spells," She stated, poking at her skull, "otherwise, I'd already have you groveling at my feet like a *pretty* pet." She giggled while over-pronouncing the consonants on the last two words.

Arashi smiled to that—a small smile—and turned towards his selection of crystals and rocks he had shelved on the wall. He always kept them in this room, as there were no windows for sunlight to drain them of their color. He collected them over the years, studying which ones allow which spells. Orange aragonite for shifting earth, blue azurite for manipulating air, chrysoprase for forming illusions, and a large selection of healing stones. The bloodstone was the best of those as it rarely shattered when he used it.

He fixated on his prized possession, an aquamarine that was as large as a human head. It was polished smooth, but a shadow swam inside it. He lifted it off its stand and smiled. "They'll be going by ship to avoid the Forest of the Damned."

Nars nodded with squinty eyes, "They were hush-hushed down by the dock, so I wasn't able to locate the sailors that would be on their ship." She curled up on her throne; unable to keep her eyelids open any longer.

"That's quite all right; I have a better surprise for them." He smiled down at the stone, watching the shadow swim within.

CHAPTER 7

The Voyage

Gusty winds carried the musky scent of salt and fish of the Mythic Sea as Taemi peered over the rail of Sandar's *Zazen* to watched the waves and felt the mist from each splash. The air blew past her face as if she was flying over the ocean, soaring up and crashing down. There was never a need for her to travel anywhere by ship before—or anywhere, really—but this was exactly what her heart yearned for when she wished for adventure. From here on out, she'll actually see new places that she's only ever read about.

She glanced back at Kio to share her excitement, but he didn't express the same joy. He leaned over the rail, but clutched it for support and winced every time it crashed down.

"Not everyone is made for the sea, mistress." Taemi glanced up at the bulky man with a booming laugh. He was a tall, large, gruff man hauling rope over his exposed arms that were thicker than Taemi's head. "He'll be fine after we port, but there isn't much you can do for him till then." The sailor gave the sick boy a hearty pat as he walked away with a grin.

"D-don't worr...ry P-prin...cess." Kio's voice was weak as he still huddled over the rail, but he made an effort to smile at her.

"Kio..." *Perhaps there's something I can do with the moonstone...* Taemi held the pendant in her hand and thought about all the times she'd activated it. *It slowed the shadow wolf at the inn and I controlled light in the Dragon Cavern.* She knew that there was some way it could cure whatever it was that's affecting Kio. She placed her other hand on his head and tried to channel the energy. She closed her eyes and felt the pendant eliminate warmth.

She heard a thud on the floorboards and opened her eyes to see her soldier lying unconscious before her. *I suppose that... did help.*

Two men carried Kio down into the ship's quarters to rest, along with her team of escorts that she had met earlier.

Willis gave her eight *of his best* soldiers—so he said—all dressed in their own traveling clothes, but all wore the same forest green cloak with the crest of Sandar's three spears on the back. The most experienced of the group was Glenn, whose blonde hair was starting to gray in most areas. He had a hard face with a scar close to his eye. If it were any closer, he probably would have lost that eye. He wore expensive armor, both tough, but lightweight and was known to be Sandar's finest swordsman. She hoped that maybe he and Kio would have time to practice together over the trip, but it wouldn't be any time on the ship.

Nazoo was a large man with a shaved head and iron face behind his scruffy mustache that blended into his long, red beard. He didn't wear any sleeves on his uniform—and perhaps he couldn't—based on the enormous size of his bulging muscles of his painted arms. Taemi stared each time he flexed wondering if his biceps alone were as big as her head. His weapon of skill was a giant double-sided half-moon axe, and Taemi was sure only a man as built as him could carry such a beast.

Kaza, an energetic sort with his head shaved as well, but left a strip of red curly hair down the center of his head. He was the most excited of the group to go on the quest. At first glance, he looked like he was coming on the trip empty-handed, but he demonstrated his skill with a collection of throwing knives hidden amongst his sleeves. It was astonishing how he didn't prick himself while carrying so many blades in his clothes.

Zemire had dark hair and dark, sun-kissed skin—darker than most of the men on the ship—but he was very lean and quick. According to Willis, Zemire was the best at handling the Sandarian spear.

Tilly was the youngest of the group with shoulder-length blonde hair and green eyes on a boyish face; he probably was only a few years older than Kio. *But if Kio is capable,* Taemi thought, *then this kid could probably hold his own.*

When Taemi noticed the points of his long ears, Willis explained that Tilly was a descendant of the elves. He was only a small percentage of the breed, and even though he couldn't use magic like his great grandparents, he was just as nimble and a straight shooter with the bow as his ancestors.

There was even a woman among the team—Scarlet whose skin was dark as the night, with long, wavy hair to match. Taemi was shocked at her unique beauty, and even more so to find out she was a soldier. *But who says women couldn't fight?*

"She's as marvelous with a sword as she is beautiful," were the words Willis used to describe her. His eyes twinkled with admiration for the woman.

Taemi wondered if any of the women from her kingdom would want to join Adrienan's army.

Her breath caught when she was introduced to another swordsman. Lloyd—a tall, pretty man with high cheekbones, blue eyes, and hair so blonde—it was practically white! He had it parted on the side, but it fell down past his eyes and was kept short on the back and sides. He may have been older than her by ten years, but his smile alone was enough to consider him the future king of Adrienan.

Lastly, was Mel—with dark hair that fell into his slanted eyes—he kept the sides and back of his head shaved. He wasn't nearly as tall as the other men, but Taemi felt his presence unsettling with those dark eyes that clearly had seen too much. He wasn't one for words, either, as he merely nodded during introductions with his cloak wrapped around his body. Willis didn't say much about him, other than the brisk mention of his name, and avoiding eye contact. The man kept to himself within the group even after they boarded the ship.

All in all, she felt that they made a great team of ten. She was sure she'd have a similar team prepared by her father if they didn't have to leave so fast in the middle of the night.

To pass the time of the day, Taemi watched the sailors manage the ship. They were all barefoot, wore sleeveless shirts exposing their sun-kissed skin, and wore trousers knotted up to their knees. She thought sailing would be relaxing, but each man hustled around wrapping, carrying, or knotting ropes. The captain called orders from the deck and the responses would call overhead down to the bow. She looked upon the large mast with white sails that took on the wind, turning by the captain's command.

Sandar was long out of sight, and all Taemi could see now was a vast surface of dark, blue sea rippling in the sunlight with a visible horizon separating it from the airy sky. It was endless, and not once did the sea touch the sky.

Taemi frowned as the thought slipped past her mind. *Is that really what it's like? The sky being all the world of the lords and ladies, while down here, there's a vast flood of everyone else?* It felt more real down here, while her castle lifestyle was a constant coma of comfort, boredom, rules with no purpose, and actions with no consequences.

"Everything seems like that because you're young. When you're queen, everything you do will affect someone negatively, and another positively."

Those were the king's words whenever he overheard Taemi complaining. *But does he know he says that while still untouched by* this *world?* She looked up at the gannets circling the sky before diving down into the waters.

"When it rains from the heavens, it either nurtures the living or drowns them. When the sun shines bright, it either blooms the flowers or withers them to dust." Lost in her thoughts, she could still hear the vital question from her father, *"What kind of queen do you want to be?"*

But it wasn't just that that was bothering her. She knew somewhere deep, she felt cut off from something she needed... or just wanted. Something about the apparent horizon line sunk her heart into her gut. *I'm touching the world now, aren't I?*

"There's nothing more that clears a man's head than the silence of the sea," The captain of the ship shared the railing with Taemi and watched over. "Ladies too." He bowed, "We're at a fair sail now. It may get a little more rough depending on the weather's temper." The captain of the *Zazen* wore a long, emerald green coat that went past his knees, a matching hat with gold seams, and black knee-high boots. Other than that, his wardrobe was as casual as the crew's. His shaved face exposed high, gauntly cheekbones and a narrow nose. At first glance, he appeared to be as young as Willis, but there was something about his grey eyes that bid him a whole decade older.

"The sea never touches the sky, does it?"

The captain smiled at Taemi's question, "Ah, you are all kinds of troubled, ey?" Taemi wasn't sure if he knew something. *Did Willis give my identity away?*

"Oh, I didn't mean that in offense, my Lady. Just... you just seemed like something was bothering you."

"Oh," Taemi turned back to the ocean again, not really sure if she wanted an answer from before.

"I can tell you, though—the sea and sky are one universe together. The rain that falls from the clouds is originally from the sea." Taemi glanced over at him quizzically, "You can't physically see it, but on hot days, you sure can feel it. When it's cool again, the water falls back into the ocean." The captain shrugged, "It's more like a life cycle, really. One day you're swimming, then elevated into the sky... and when you're ready, fall back down into the waters."

"...So when the water is in the sky, does it touch the stars?"

The captain exhaled in defeat, and slid his hat from his head as he stared straight up to the heavens, "Well... sometimes I think that nothing can touch the stars, but I'd recommend that you come out here later tonight and see for yourself." He stood up, placed his hat back on his head, and bowed before he left.

Taemi frowned slightly. *That is a silly question; nothing can touch the stars.*

The sun was setting over the horizon, but all day long, Taemi was fascinated by how the crew always found something to do throughout the day. She watched men work on the ship—washing the deck, painting sealer on the rails, and replacing soggy boards. There were some who did their own thing; sharpening knives, carving wood sculptures from driftwood, or socializing over smokes around a game of cards, laughing over their mug of ale.

Their laughter was charming as the princess watched the bright, yellow globe descend slowly behind the sea, emanating its radiant, golden glow and spilling onto the ocean. Few clouds filled the sky, and their normal white pallet was now a burst of dark blues, purples, pinks and reds. They added a brilliant contrast as they drifted slowly across the light sky. Even though the bright globe looked still, it was eventually swallowed into the horizon line. The skylight still lingered, but soon it would all fade into a velvet shade of navy blue.

Taemi's stomach rumbled and she decided that it was time to eat dinner. She made her way down to the sleeping quarters to grab a small meal of bread, smoked sausage and cheese. She opened the door to a room big enough for two cots. Kio was sitting up on the bed to her left, running a stone over his sword to sharpen the edge. His messy brown hair fell over his eyes while studying the edge of the blade and wiping it down. His loose tan tunic was wrinkled and a little too big for him, but it was a fresh spare from Willis' castle.

She checked on him twice during the day and both times he was still asleep. It was a relief to finally see him up and functioning.

The boy peered up and smiled at the princess when she walked into the room, but stayed focused on his task.

"Feeling better?" Taemi asked while she pulled the small snack bag up from under the spare cot and sat down with it.

Without losing rhythm to the sharpening, the boy nodded, "A little. It's a lot calmer now than it once was."

"Want some bread?" Taemi dug in the bag and pulled out a small, wrapped loaf, a square cut of cheese—about the size of her palm and two fingers thick—and linked sausages.

Kio pulled out his small folded knife, "I just sharpened this one, so I can cut off a few slices of the loaf and cheese for us." He sliced two thin slices of bread—one for each—a few cubes of cheese, and two sausages off the links. The bread was still fresh and moist from the castle's bakery; even lords would rarely put butter on it. The cheese, however, was too sharp on its own, but paired well with the smoked sausage. These were the few items that would last without spoil during a week's voyage.

"This is my first time on a ship. I never thought it would be so relaxing and exciting at the same time!" The girl mentioned after a few bites of the cheese and sausage.

"I've not been on something this large, but a small boat when crossing the river."

Crossing the river? Taemi almost forgot that Kio was born south near Nishe. "Oh, that's right... you're not Adrienian."

The boy glanced up at her with those large, brown eyes slightly hidden by his hair, and shook his head, but smiled. "Not originally, but after swearing into the knighthood, I became your loyal, faithful Adrienian guardsmen—I'll protect my princess with my life!" He bowed his head and placed a fist on his chest.

His devotion made the princess flush, "I didn't doubt that; I just... forgot that you were from somewhere else."

"Not everyone who serves you will always be from Adrienan. Sometimes..." Kio hesitated for the words, "Sometimes people are forced to leave behind their homes to make a better living."

"Did you not like your king?"

He scratched at his face while hunched over the cot, slicing cheese bites for himself, "No, it wasn't that... I didn't have a lot of money, and it was a shorter journey to Adrienan than to the kingdom of Nishe. I figured it'd be easier to make money in the city rather than a village, and I was right."

"...What about your parents?" She wondered why Kio never mentioned them on their trip so far. *Were they merchants? Or did he leave home? At what age did he start then?* He wasn't much older than Taemi, and she just turned eighteen.

The brown hair over his eyes hid his expression, and he paused on his last bite, "My parents..." His eyes stared off at nothing, but for just a moment, and then smiled boyishly back at the princess, "They're just typical farmers on the outskirts of Nishe. I left... home because I wanted to see the world." He took his last bite and continued, "There's so much more than just staying at a farm, though; I never imagined running away from shadow wolves with the princess herself."

The sound of merriment began to rise from the other quarters beneath the ship's deck. Those who weren't tasked to manage the night watch turned in to enjoy ale with their dinner.

Kio shook his head, and sighed, "I don't know how these sailors can drink and hold it all down when the sea gets rough."

Taemi giggled, "Maybe they don't." Kio glanced back at her comment with slight confusion. "Maybe in the morning, they just purge it all over the side." She laughed more at her own joke while the boy just grinned, unsure if to be amused or sickened.

"Oh! Do you think the stars are out yet?" Her eyes lit up, remembering what the captain had mentioned earlier.

"Well... the stars are always out, you just can't—"

The girl grabbed him by the arm in a burst of excitement, "Let's go see!" and she led him up and out onto the deck. "I was told to come out at night to see if the sea touched the stars," she managed to say through breaths.

"I don't think you have to make an effort to see that they don't," but Kio's words were lost in the wind as the princess pulled him along the ship. The sun had been down for almost an hour or so; lamps were already lit around the rail to add light for navigation.

As the girl reached the front rail, she was able to see what the captain really meant. The night was so black, she could only see the shimmering specks of the stars that surrounded her like a dome. Their reflection faintly danced in the ripples of the black liquid below. The solid horizon line that taunted her in the distance was gone, and it felt like she was floating through the vast void of the celestial heavens.

She gazed up, lost in their magic, and began to feel the real distance between where she stood and home; idling in the vast void of darkness. Holding Kio's hand was all that kept her anchored to the ship deck. She peered up at him, and saw the stars sparkling in his eyes. His face showed pure awe.

Noticing her stare, the boy looked down at her, and raised his eyebrows in question, *"What is it?"*

She shook her head, unable to refrain the smile beaming on her face to where her checks were almost sore. *"It's Nothing."*

CHAPTER 8

The Storm

The princess' slumber ended abruptly when her body rolled hard into the wall and thudded back into her cot. Taemi was sure her eyes were opened, but the room was too dark to see anything. She could hear echoes of commotion and hasty footprints on deck, and wondered if the matter was serious enough to get up.

"Ahh… what happened?" She heard her guard moan somewhere within the darkness, but close by.

"…Kio?"

"Princess?"

Taemi grabbed her moonstone and illuminated the room with the white, glowing orb of light that she had summoned before when in the cavern. The other cot across from her was empty, and she found the boy lying on the floor in the walking space.

"Thank you, Princess." He slowly started to raise himself up from the floor, "I would not have figured this out on my own." But even as he rose, the ship jerked again, and sent a sudden rush of blood to Taemi's head—swelling with pain and dizziness—and then a sensation of chills tingled down her spine as if a cold wave washed over her. The toss left Taemi motionless while Kio's face was resting on the floor.

The ship continued to rock, causing three less-intense brain-rushes before it finally stopped. The girl lingered on the cot for a moment, but then pulled on her socks and boots, determined to see what was happening on deck. Feeling as if she had drank too much wine, she stepped around Kio, and stumbled up the damp stairs to the deck.

It was early enough to be dawn, but the sky was cloudy, and a hazy fog surrounded the ship. The air was wet with a thin layer of drizzle. Dark clouds spiraled above the ship, and the men hustled across the deck shouting while tying down as much as they could. The white, large sails were already wrapped up tightly to the masts. Cannons were fastened up against the rails, but men were still gathering supplies up from storage.

"Be sturdy; it's just a storm!"

A storm that appeared out of nowhere, Taemi thought, trying to keep her balance while walking towards the center of the ship. Men yelled orders near the bow and explosions flashed through the fog like lightning. Taemi speculated as to what they could be firing cannons at, but found herself staring at a massive spiked fin rising on the starboard side—towering over the ship's tallest mast—and fading in and out through the fog as if it was on the back of a large snake...

Sea serpent?!

The gruff sailor from yesterday ran up to her. "Ay, mm'Lady! Yer best safe below deck, but I'll give ya here a safety harness—so not to fall off yee ship." He was already looping the rope into a harness around Taemi as he talked, and then handed her a small knife. "In case the ship goes under, yer wanna cut yerself loose. You can keep it in yer boot." He shuffled off quickly.

The cannons ceased fire, and for a moment it was quiet. But it wasn't long until everyone noticed the serpent's tail with dark, red fins, looming over the ship from the stern.

It slapped down at the sea, sending the ship flying higher than the waves.

Taemi held on tight to her harness, experiencing another head rush. The ship crashed down, spraying salt water. The girl fell on the deck, drenched. The sailors recuperated from the tension as they continued to load and fire the cannons again. She hoisted herself up, but her heart stopped when the monster roared a piercing scream. She looked out into the distance where the creature appeared from dense fog.

It was a snake-like creature with a long narrow snout and long horns like a dragon. Small fins sprouted down its neck, and two larger fins that appeared to be like dark, red wings. It rose up from the sea and swam through the sky as if it was still immersed in water, and hailed a white, nova blast towards the ship before it dove back down into the sea.

The blast missed the hull, but took down the main mast, and Taemi regretted being on deck as she watched it damage the railing and surface, filling the air with agonizing screams from those who couldn't evade it. The men around her helped her up, but there wasn't anywhere on the ship that would be safe.

The creature arched over the ship with its large body and massive fins. The sailors attacked it with whatever swords or axes they had in hand, but barely scathed the creature's natural armor. Crossbows were loaded and fired with frenzy at the creature, but the arrows fell back down to the deck with bent shafts.

The head rose up from the port side—twice the size of the ship—and opened its large mouth to engulf all that were in sight. Taemi watched in disbelief that this was to be her end when a figure jumped over her head and slashed the creature's muzzle with his sword.

Kio landed softly in front of Taemi and paused in

a stance as the serpent rippled back into the sea with a piercing, ominous scream that echoed amongst the storm.

"*...Mmmagic ...ussssssserss.*"

Even with her hands over her ears to cancel out the monster's scream, she heard those words clearly in a low, alienated voice. She squinted her eyes to see where it would appear next from the sea.

Kio pivoted his footing and took off towards the front of the ship, and jumped past the bowsprit into the ocean as the monster's head rose up again—striking the beast's underbelly and kicking off to land back on the ship.

The creature crashed down into the sea from the strike with another scream.

"*Pain... it hurtssss!*"

Taemi felt its agony through the screams as if the creature endured suffering long before they encountered it. *Is that why it's lashing out?*

"*Yessss... but nooo....*"

Her breath caught. *It IS speaking to me!* Her mind flashed to when she fell down that strange hole where the fluttering lights talked to her. *If I can communicate with it, maybe I can tell it to stop.*

"*Can't... Must destroy... magic ussserrrr... destroy all!*"

Taemi couldn't believe that the storm could get any darker until a large, black shadow engulfed the ship's light. She peered up, expecting the serpent to rise from the sea, but instead, her heart sank at the massive wall of ocean rushing towards the ship.

She held on to her pendant and hoped for the best as the wave crashed down. It knocked the air from her lungs and nearly crushed her body. Her surroundings dissolved into chaotic currents, but it was over as fast as it came, and she floated in a vast vacuum of sea.

She wasn't sure if she was alive or thrown into the

stream of the afterlife. Taemi opened her eyes to an endless darkness. She looked up where she thought the surface might be, but couldn't see a distinctive light. Pieces of the boat drifted down from above her *...or was I sinking?*

"Are you... the girl it wants....?"

"Who wants?" Taemi shifted around looking for the creature that was speaking to her. Bubbles blocked her vision as she breathed out... *But how am I breathing in? The Pendant?*

"Magic... ussserrr..."

Something moved through the sea, and her heart pounded rapidly.

"It wants... more... mmmmmmagic!!"
She saw it breach the shadows in the distance before her, closing in faster than she could think.

"Let the moon be your light in the darkest of the night," The words echoed through her mind—*"cease from this cage that blocks you in, and fly to the sky of the heavens!"*

Hot Light spewed from the pendant—so hot— Taemi released her grip from it and surrendered. Her energy poured through the crystal and four spheres appeared—three nearly vertically aligned and a fourth off to the side. A thin thread from the top sphere connected the others with a flash of light. She closed her eyes from the blinding ray and felt a sensation release the creature from an invisible prison.

Taemi opened her eyes. The creature had stopped its thrashing and floated calmly before her. Taemi stood in awe of its giant head while the fins and long serpent body drifted in and out in the endless sea.

"Many thanks, Moon Child."
...Moon what?
His aura was different. Before he was a trapped

beast on the brink of insanity, but now he shared the same presence that she felt from her father—patient, calm, and comforting. *"It seems we both have lost ourselves in this world... but you've rescued me from a prison... My mind was unclear. I apologize for your suffering."*

Leviathan... His name slipped into her consciousness as if she always had known him from a recurring dream where they were once companions. She recalled sitting above that massive head and flying through the starry sky, just like she had last night on the *Zazen*. The memory from her vault felt as real as the creature before her.

I remember... Just like that weird prayer I said... what did I say? She felt conflicted as if she'd been living between two worlds, and now ashamed for forgetting everything about the other one. *...Moon Child?*

"I see..." Leviathan's low voice was filled with dismay. *"You've been reincarnated too many times to know. Perhaps we shall meet again, another time when you have all your memories?"*

She nodded, but tears began to pool in her eyes. *Can you cry underwater?* Leviathan's sadness swam through her as if it were her own emotion—like a whirlpool of overwhelming joy and shame. *Why do I feel such compassion for this creature?*

"I'll make amends now."

Her surroundings suddenly shifted through time, and the ocean dispersed into air and her feet stood on solid ground, overlooking the ocean from the cliff. The sun was already high in the now cloudless sky; with its rays sparkling on top of the ocean's surface in shimmers of yellow and orange.

Leviathan's head hadn't moved, but Taemi could see his whole body arched up on his tail with his large fins spread out like wings. His teal scales shimmered in the sunlight, changing colors from navy to light purple.

She heard coughing behind her and turned to see the surviving sailors, seven of the escorts, and Kio, all slowly coming to consciousness.

"Be careful here, Moon Child."

Taemi peered back to Leviathan, who was already fading back into the sea.

"The Behemoth still slumbers beneath the seal, but his wrath will soon come. The ground faeries will awaken the savior, now that you have arrived."

Blinding light illuminated the chamber and the aquamarine crystal shattered into dust before her beloved master, Reiji-Arashi, and drifted down to the floor like glitter—shimmering in the light of the flickering torches.

"I don't know anything about crystal magic... but that *can't* be a good sign." Nars spoke quietly, from her seat. She had no intention of getting close to him at this point. She thought she did a fantastic job leading them out into the sea; this couldn't possibly be her fault this time. She even had the Sandarian soldiers under her mind contortion, so they could view everything through their eyes, and control their actions if she had to. She kept them below deck to not interfere with the plan.

Humans and deities are just not dependable these days. She blinked. *...These days?* She wondered. *What days did I live to where I was comparing this to?*

Arashi stood in shock for a long moment of silence staring at what used to be one of his most valuable possessions. But Nars knew it was his silence before the eruption. A few seconds later, as expected, the sorcerer grabbed his goblet and threw it across the room—hitting the closest wall and giving it a splash of maroon.

That will leave a stain... Nars let him have his

tantrum, but contemplated if she should clean his mess or leave it well alone. *The room could use a little more color...*

The sorcerer continued his rampage, destroying anything he could get his hands on—potions, wine bottles, jewels—while he yelled, "She has *NO* idea how much *WORK* it took to capture *HIM*! Blasted Leviathan!"

Nars sipped her wine in silence. She watched him patiently and chose her next words carefully so that she didn't get caught up in the blast. "If you couldn't conquer the world with *that* deity, then he probably wasn't very powerful."

Her comment fueled his rage anyway—"GO! Go get her!! She's in the blasted Forest of the Damned!" He started stomping on the fragments of the glass pieces that were once bottles, but didn't turn his direction to her. "Get her for me *now!*"

The phrase sparked something in Nars' memory. *The Behemoth Forest...?* No one in this land called it that anymore. *Somebody used to call it that... but who?* Nars shook her head. Her bender in Sandar may have loosened too many screws. She started getting mild headaches and dreamt of bizarre places she had never been. *Even that soldier boy looks a bit familiar...*

"Forest of the ...Damned?" *Even the trees in there feasted on flesh.* She sighed and waved the offer off, "More like 'the perverted forest of the grabby trees'—ew, no thank you. I have no desire to have this perfect body molested by some rotted whipplet bark."

"If you don't want to look like you're asking for it, then wear a cloak," Arashi stated flatly while rubbing his head. His temper finally ceased into exhaustion and vexed as he walked over to his seat.

"She's in the Forest of the Damned," Nars sipped on her wine, bringing up a map that she copied from Sandar. "She ain't coming out alive in something named like that. I also still have contortion on the escort. I can easily have one of them slit her throat and bring you the —"

She was pulled sharply by the collar of her wardrobe and tossed to the floor. "You just don't LISTEN, do you Narcissus!" Arashi let the anger rage from his voice openly, "I need her *very* much alive! She's fully connected with the stone, and I need her in order to *use* it. She will be mine, and I shall control all the kingdoms through her!"

Nars pursed her lips, "Fine… I'll go get your *precious* princess." Her voice was soft, but the words still came out flat and rolled off her tongue with a hint of distaste, though, she was aware that she should have watched her words more carefully. *He always became rabid whenever I spoke about killing the girl.*

Normally, I would have kept my mouth shut and obeyed without resisting when his temper is hot like that but… Nars growled while leaving the fortress. The girl's very existence sickened her from the beginning and had only made her master agitated. She didn't know what plan Reiji had that involved the girl, but Nars preferred to keep it as the two of them, as it had been for the past ten years.

Besides, she snarled, *why does he even* need *her? There isn't anything she can do that* I *couldn't do… What makes this girl so damn special?*

CHAPTER 9

The Seal

The sun descended on the horizon as Taemi and the bravest of her escorts ventured into the Forest of the Damned. Alert, they walked slowly through the dark forest searching for the beasts. Taemi's escort was already down by two; Glenn was lost in the storm during their battle with Leviathan, and Kaza, who didn't dare to venture through the forest, stayed back with the sailors.

"No way, man! I'm not going in there! I didn't sign up for this, man!"—Kaza exclaimed earlier after following only a few paces in.

Scarlet grabbed him by the collar. "You signed up to be a soldier, didn't you?" She tossed him forward to keep him moving.

"No way! Forget this! You all can go die for some other kingdom's princess, but not me, man. I wouldn't even venture through here for our king!"

Nazoo was about to step in and carry Kaza with them, but Mel spoke up, quietly, "Let him go."

The team of soldiers stared back at Mel in bewilderment—Taemi wondered if it was what he said or just the fact he said anything for once. He ignored their looks and kept walking, "This forest will devour the weak. It's better that he turns back now instead of being a burden and getting us all killed." His words were unsettling. Taemi was glad that he didn't speak too often.

Kaza stayed at the cliff with the sailors to wait for another ship to get them. She hoped they didn't have to wait too long.

Mel took the lead and had them walk single file in the woods, stepping where he stepped. He had Tilly behind him to shoot any beast ahead with his bow and arrow. After Tilly was Scarlet, and then Lloyd; Taemi was in the middle of the group with Kio close behind; Zemire and Nazoo took the rear.

Mel was confident that Nazoo would be the toughest of the escort for a beast to take down. *"If anything attacks from behind, we'll hear it,"* he stated when he arranged the team.

The only noises within the forest were the soft steps of the group and their own breath. Birds didn't sing, small rodents didn't chirp, nor the clicking and buzzing of insects. She couldn't see the sky through the thick tree branches that loomed overhead, but even they didn't rustle. *...It's so quiet.* She could almost hear her own heartbeat.

It was completely dark in the forest. Taemi could barely see Mel leading the front. He led them over a mossy tree root and her footing slipped. Lloyd was already turned to catch her as she fell into his arms, "Easy there, Princess Equillis," he laughed charmingly. "We'll have plenty of time to get to know each other better."

Despite the darkness, his gorgeous smile and words made the princess' face flush. *He could* brighten *the darkness of night!* She smiled.

She barely paid any mind to the grumbling comment behind her, "*Pretty* boy..."

"Not unless something eats you for breakfast," Scarlet laughed up ahead, but immediately got serious when Mel stopped and looked back.

Unsettling! Taemi would never have expected him to gain so much respect from the team so quickly, but then again, he's probably the only one who has been in the forest before.

They continued on a bit longer, going over slippery roots and mossy rocks. Kio reached out his hand, "Here," he whispered each time to assist when Taemi had to step on or over something. *Probably to prevent me from falling again,* Taemi smiled at his sweet gestures.

"We'll set up camp here," Mel stated. "If we go further, we'll only encounter the bigger ones that come out at night."

How can he tell? It felt like night the entire time they were walking.

The soldiers set up camp per Mel's orders, gathering wood for a fire and setting up torches around them. "The beasts are sensitive to light, so fire will deter them from getting close." He explained quietly without emotion. "Tilly and I will hunt something to eat."

Taemi could see the whites in Scarlet's wide eyes, "Are you *kidding?*" I don't plan to eat *anything* from the Forest of the *Damned.*"

"Then don't." Mel's short response was quiet, but effective as he continued to walk into the forest.

"That guy gives me the chills," Kio whispered as he watched the two disappear into the shadows.

Taemi nodded. She was glad she wasn't the only one who felt that way as she continued to help gather sticks for kindle and move the stones to make a bedding area.

The fire was blazing and they had all the torches lit by the time Tilly and Mel returned with three bird-looking creatures—enough to feed the team—and handed them off to Zemire to clean. Taemi peered over the man for a closer look at their dinner as Zemire plucked off the black feathers from their black skin. The three creatures

FOREST of the DAMNED

resembled large crows, but each had six eyes—three on each side of their heads—and their beaks were lined with small razor teeth. The size of the creatures' talons was what frightened her the most.

The girl backed away quickly, bumping into Lloyd who was also checking out the food. He caught her gently, "Yikes! I wouldn't want to be the one coming across a flock of these!"

"They fly solo because they're predator creatures." Mel responded.

Tilly nodded, "Yea! We were able to pick them off one at a time."

Lloyd chuckled at Mel's comment, "So how much of the *Damned* cuisine have you had?"

The emotionless leader didn't notice the humor of

the situation, "Those are the only things that are probably the safest to eat here. Many of the beasts spew poison, so if you can take them down, you'll have to remove the venom sac. In most cases that is prone to be lethal." He talked so casually as if it was just a hunting sport.

There was a strong hint of discomfort in the pretty blonde's laughter as he held Taemi closer to whisper, "Man, this guy makes me feel…"

"Like spiders crawling down your spine?" He nodded to her question and shivered at the thought.

"Don't worry, Princess Equillis," Zemire flashed a smile, "Mel may give off an eerie vibe, but that's just his personality."

…Or maybe this place isn't as bad as everyone says it is.

"He's lieutenant of the field patrol, and has more experience within the forest than anyone else. He insisted on joining the escort, and I'm glad, too—it's almost like he knew it would dive him deeper into the forest."

Lloyd looked skeptical at Zemire and mumbled under his breath, "What kind of psycho would want *that* chance?"

Zemire continued with a smile, "If any of the creatures seem to get through the elves' spell and venture outside the forest, we're assigned to hunt them down and annihilate them for the safety of the villages. It doesn't happen often, but some of the smaller ones do make it past the marshes.

"Okay, this one is ready for the fire," Zemire handed the cleaned, black corpse to Lloyd to stake over the fire. The dark-skinned man continued as he started on the next bird. "I've even been keeping track of some of the beasts we encounter," He paused and handed Taemi a leather-bound book with crinkled parchment.

The princess scanned through the contents of

hand-drawn sketches of creatures; one was a long six-eyed insect with large claws and a hundred legs down its long body to a tail that curved upwards with a spear at the tip. Next to the drawing were notes on whether it was poisonous and how to avoid the creature's venom.

Scorapede
Poisonous: Yes
Attacks with its claws by pinching and stabbings prey with a venom stinger. Kill by slicing off the tail and pinchers or spear from a distance.

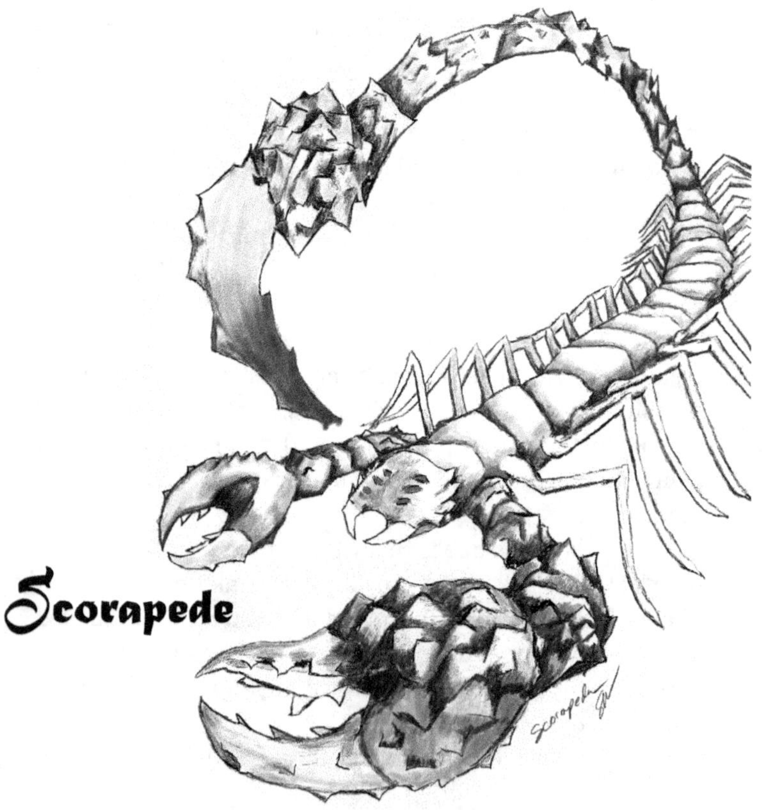

Scorapede

The creature on the next page resembled a small horse with a sharp spear spiraling out from the center of its skull, and rigid, sharp blades that ran down its back like a mane. It had the same six red eyes—three on each side—and six hair-less tails.

Xran
Poisonous: Yes
Attacks with its head down to slash enemies.
Avoid its blade-mane! Cuts or wounds from
it contain poison. Kill by surprise attacks
from behind or spear from a distance.

Xran

Fenir

Fenir
Poisonous: No
Attacks in packs. Kill with fire torches and swift attacks from behind or spear from a distance.

Taemi opened to the next page of a wolf-like creature with curled horns, a thick, black, mane, and large fangs and claws.

"The hell is *that* thing?" Scarlet asked while looming over the princess' shoulder.

Zemire glanced at the page that was open and nodded, "Yea, those are the most common ones that get out. We've been calling those fenirs. Ironically, not poisonous, but they're quite vicious and travel in packs. Mel and I have been here a few times hunting those ones down."

The dark woman's face coiled and slowly rocked her head side to side at the thought, "You *both* are insane."

Zemire smiled, "Another one is ready for the fire."

"I'll take it," Scarlet already had the stake to mount it.

Taemi handed Zemire back the book and he tucked it away under his cloak. "It didn't quite keep in the storm, but I can retranslate it again. Right now, we use it to train the rookies, but one day I'd like to have it published."

Taemi nodded, "That's a fantastic idea!" The forest bordered Adrienan as well; *if these monsters are getting out, I too, would like to know how to defeat them.*

"Hey, Princess Equillis," Lloyd waved over from the fire, "Dinner's ready. Come over and eat!"

"Like *hell,* she will!" Kio yelled with his fist up, waiting for a fight.

The princess sighed. *He doesn't trust anyone.*

"I'll eat first." Mel approached and took the stake from Lloyd. "This one will be for me, Tilly and Zemire. Lloyd and Nazoo will share the second one, and the third can feed whoever is still hungry." He looked at Scarlet when he said the last part. "I don't care if the princess eats or not—she looks light enough to carry if we have to, but the soldiers will need to be at full strength to get through this place."

Mel's commanding tone was enough to calm Kio's temper from fighting, but he still glared at everyone.

Maybe he could learn to trust that *one.* Taemi smiled.

The Damned birds didn't taste as bad as Taemi thought they would. The meat was dark and gamey, but it filled her rumbling stomach. After the group ate their meal they prepared for sleep. Kio and Tilly volunteered to take the first watch. Taemi was exhausted. She settled down to rest her eyes.

"Taemi-che."

Taemi ruffled in her sleep; there was no getting used to sleeping outside after her years of being in the castle—even if she was on the brink of exhaustion. The ground was covered in a thick layer of moss, but Taemi could feel the twigs and rocks underneath. It smelled of wet, musky soil, and tickled of barreling worms and long, crawling, segmented creatures. She imagined giant centipedes with thousands of little, thin legs and their smooth, slimy, bodies sliding beneath her. Slowly, they would rise through the moss, and their legs would crawl up her arms and across her chest.

Her skin prickled.

"Taemi-che."

Taemi sprang forward with a gasp. Her skin was tingling. For a moment, she felt that she was surrounded by night crawlers. But there was nothing.

The forest loomed overhead with high trees that blocked out the sky. It would be pitch dark if not for the fire and the circle of lit stakes around them, but even still, the stars did not watch over her this time.

Everyone was asleep except for the two men on watch. Kio was asleep up against a tree with his hand on his hilt. He had been on the first watch, but Taemi imagined that he would have kept watch the entire night if Mel hadn't forced him to rest. Nazoo and Zemire were on the second shift, and they were sitting around the fire chatting softly between themselves.

Taemi sighed. Her eyelids felt heavy and her body was starting to ache. There would still be a few hours before the sun came up, but trying to get to sleep was a difficult task. She had to stop imagining insects and night crawlers.

"Taemi-che."

Taemi blinked. The forest was quiet except for the crackle of the fire and the low humming snores from her comrades. Off in the distance, she could hear the leaves rustle through the wind, and the snaps of breaking twigs.

"Taemi-che."

It was like a whisper in her ears—quiet and subtle. *Was something... calling my name?*

Her body got up and swayed.

"Taemi-che."

There it is again. Towards the left...?

Nazoo and Zemire looked at her. Their lips moved, but she couldn't hear what they said. She turned away from them and started off towards the whisper.

"Taemi-che."

She followed, her body wavering and stumbling. *So tired... Where am I even going?* The woods were so dark; she couldn't see anything even if she touched it. Her eyesight drifted from black to speckled colors that flickered in front of her, and yet, her body continued into the woods evading the trees and exposed roots.

"Taemi-che."

Her vision returned as she came to a clearing—the only spot in the entire forest where the trees gave way to the sky. Taemi stared in awe at the light of the moon shining down and reflecting off the smooth stone surface of an unusual crest before her.

On the ground where there should have been grass or dirt was a giant labyrinth circle. It looked like stone, but

the smoothly carved symbols inset within the seal reflected like marble under the moonlight. Exposed roots from the surrounding trees weaved an intricate pattern with the stone towards the center of the circle. In the middle was a crescent moon surrounded by seven stars.

Seven. Seven stars. Seven generations... seven towers. She pulled out the knife Prince Willis had given her.

"Taemi-che... Come to me!"

Her body staggered forward to the middle of the symbol, onto the crescent moon. She held out her hand, and began to slice the blade across her palm. Taemi screamed inside her head at the piercing pain of her flesh peeling open. *What am I doing?!? Stop. Stop!!!!* Crimson blood flourished up from the exposed wound.

"What *are* you doing?"

The voice broke through Taemi's trance like chimes ringing in the wind above her. She looked up. At the edge of the clearing stood a woman up on a branch. She leaned against the tree, casually posed with her arms crossed.

The moonlight reflected off her strange, pink, inappropriate armor and the metal spikes entwined in her golden blonde hair.

"I would have never guessed a princess would be a masochist—mommy and daddy didn't give you enough attention?" Her voice chimed, mimicry.

Masochist? "What?!—No." Taemi shook her head and peered down at her hand. The light from the moon was shining down on her directly, and her pendant gave off a bright glow. The wound was already closing up without a single drop of blood left on her arm.

"Oh, *that's* interesting..." The woman smirked, "I suppose that's the power of the moonstone that everyone is *obsessed* with all of a sudden."

Taemi gasped. *Who is this woman?*

"It's very convenient that you left the others on

your own. I can't seem to even control my puppets in here, and it would have been such a bother slicing through them to bring you to my master."

Her master?

The strange woman casually looked down at her nails while she spoke. "At first, I wasn't even going to attack. Since my magic doesn't seem to work here, I'd have to drag your limp body out of this forest." She gave a light laugh, "But since your precious pendant still works, perhaps I could still batter you up a bit, and see if it takes us home."

The woman pushed herself off the tree and jumped down towards the clearing. She wore two long swords cross-mounted on her back with their hilts sticking up from each side of her face.

A double sword wielder?

As soon as her raised heels clicked against the rock-like circle, there was a *pulse* that vibrated beneath Taemi's feet. The woman in front of her staggered and grabbed her head, flinching with a cry as if she was suddenly in pain. The forest stirred without the flow of wind.

The roots outside of the circle twisted and tore up from the ground—attacking the woman before her. "Blast this forest!" She unsheathed both her blades and began to slash through the trees' roots and branches. She danced with those swords cutting each attack into splinters.

Taemi stood there mesmerized by the woman's speed and dodging flexibility. As she watched, she felt something wrap around her right foot, but she was pulled from under before she could react. After hitting the carved, marble ground, she looked back to see the forest slithering towards her as well. A root was wrapped around her ankle and others were reaching towards her arms and other leg.

With the dagger still in her hand, she tried to cut away at the root. However, it didn't slice as easily as the double-wielder made it look. A tree branch whipped at her arm holding the dagger and squeezed around so tightly, she lost her grip.

In fear, Taemi grabbed onto her pendant and the moonstone lit brightly as the sun. The forest flinched back from the light, and released its hold on her leg and arm. In her short moment, she grabbed the dagger from the ground and took off as fast as she could away from the trees that whipped their branches at her from above.

She ran into the darkness, with a mild glow from her pendant. She didn't know where her party was camped. *I wonder if Kio and the others felt that* pulse. *The forest came alive so suddenly—almost as if it was the damned forest's heartbeat!* She wasn't even sure how she got to the clearing without Nazoo or Zemire stopping her.

She slowed down her pace; the trees ceased their attacks as she got farther away from the clearing. She leaned against one of the trees to catch her breath. The pounding of her heart filled her ears. The moonlight barely pierced through the branches at this part of the forest. If it weren't for the dim glow of the moonstone, Taemi was sure it would be pitch black.

Taemi's heart jumped at a loud snapping noise not far into the distance. She could hear the soft crunches getting closer. She clasped her hand around the glowing orb to diffuse its light.

She peered through the dark to see a large shadow shift through the trees less than ten paces away. Taemi gasped; it was twice the size of the shadow wolves, a furred beast with curled horns and three red, glowing eyes. She ducked back behind the tree, dodging its sight when it unexpectedly turned its head—*Six eyes!*

It let out a low growl. She peered over again slowly to see its narrow snout open, exposing long fangs. *Yikes! It could probably devour me in one bite!* Something opened on its forehead that resembled a large, glossy eye—larger than its other six. It let out a loud roar, and crouched down, twitching its spiked tail to align its pounce.

Oh no! It detected me! Taemi darted away from the tree, only to slip on a root and fall onto the damp dirt. She turned swiftly to watch the creature jump with its huge clawed paws.

A gust of wind blew past and the beast landed with a heavy thud before her, practically throwing Taemi in the air from the tremor. The beast was only a lump in front of her with a twitching tail and dripping blood where its head would have been. There was a second thud further behind her. *That's probably the head...* She grimaced.

"That's enough play time." Recognizing the woman's voice from earlier—calm, but irritated—Taemi glanced over to the double-wielder as she sheathed one of her swords and grabbed her by her arm, "Let's go!" she snarled, only getting more frustrated. "Why isn't it working?!"

Taemi was confused. *Is she trying to use magic on me?* But the princess became more concerned with something else that slithered in the shadows behind the woman. Her eyes widened as a mass of slithery heads appeared above them.

The woman's eyes narrowed with a sniff. "...You gotta be kidding me," she mumbled under her breath.

"Behind you!"

The woman crashed into Taemi as the two of them were tossed into the shallow muck nearby. The sword wielder took most of the blow from the monster's attack, but Taemi felt as if she was dragged into the woods by a wagon.

She sank in the muck up to her elbows. Its stagnate stench was unbreathable. Taemi's pendant was glowing bright, illuminating the space and the slithering mass of the creature crawling towards them.

There were five—*no, six*—heads! Their swirling

heads made it difficult to count, but Taemi was sure of six. They constantly weaved around like a nest of eels, with purple and green scales with jagged fins. They each had narrow-finned snouts and their mouths were full of razor-sharp teeth all sharing one massive body. It had short legs with giant, clawed paws and a tail that thrashed around.

"I hate this blasted forest!" The woman was already up on her feet with her blades drawn, "I will destroy you!" She turned towards the beast and sprang into attack. "I will destroy this *entire* place!" The muck slowed her speed, but she was still able to dodge all the snapping heads as they attacked.

The pendant's light kept the heads from getting close to Taemi; it shined brighter, deterring their sensitive eyes. But she wasn't about to be a pathetic damsel. She had her dagger ready in-hand. *I can fight, too!* But... all she knew how to do was make her pendant shine.

A smoggy gas slowly thickened above the muck, clouding the pendant's light. *It's getting harder to see.* The fog made her dizzy and she coughed. She turned and saw that one of the heads was releasing gas from its mouth on them. *Oh no! It's poison!* She pulled the neck of her dress up to cover her nose and mouth.

Even the woman started to slow her speed and began to cough. "Blast this... I can't... use any of my magic here..."

There was another pulse, but more faintly off in the distance.

The double sword-wielder cried out in pain and fell to her knees, clutching her head from before. "Stop it! Stop it!!" Her voice transformed into a growl. "I *will* DESTROY ... this *ENTIRE* forest!"

A powerful gust blew through the trees, and knocked Taemi into the foul water. She felt the other woman against her back with her screams being drowned out. The strength of the eruption made it hard for her to breathe, but the wind continued to spiral around them, lifting the toxic smog up into the sky, and then releasing the poison to dissipate. The trees even flinched from the power and shifted away from the muck.

The moonstone glowed more blindingly than usual, but Taemi's eyes adjusted quickly to see the double sword-wielder standing calmly with her eyes closed. The woman was surrounded with a familiar aura—similar to the presence she felt from Leviathan—but that same energy was now being pulled from Taemi's crystal and spiraled into a cyclone around the woman. Taemi could almost see a thin thread of light, streaming the magic from her moonstone to a the surging power *burning* within the other woman.

How? ...Is she using my *magic? Was this what my father had warned me about?*

The beast coiled back, with all its heads hiding behind its tail and roaring helplessly for mercy.

Without opening her eyes, the woman walked slowly up to it, reached out, and the monster began to *melt* like a burning candle.

Its piercing scream rang through the forest. Taemi clutched her hands over her ears to block the noise as the monster pooled into the muck of leathery skin and...

Taemi gagged and covered her mouth from the foul stench of its insides spilling out. *How could the smell have gotten any worse?!*

As soon as the creature was nothing but a puddle, the woman released the power. She stuttered back, but her legs gave out and she fainted backward into the water.

She'll drown! Despite the monster's remains floating around, Taemi trudged as fast as she could through the water to grab the woman's lifeless body and pull her to the shore. *Ugh, why is she so heavy!?*

The double sword-wielder murmured incoherently

while clutching her head—"*Ah–Meh... Woa Ta... Ieshna, Ieshna...*"

Taemi pulled the woman up onto solid ground, rested her head on her lap and peered over her, "Hey, get up. Are you okay?" She tapped the woman's cheeks.

The woman slowly opened her eyes, but they were gazing off into the distance, "*Ah..mee Tru Vahts...*" she continued to speak gibberish. Taemi's pendant glowed dimly in the reflection of the woman's blue eyes and she blinked and looked up at Taemi—"*Tsuki-no musume...?*" Her eyes suddenly widened in realization "*Te Rah Ha!*" She clutched Taemi's head and pulled her down towards her until they were practically nose to nose and chanted "*Tr´u me Ah tare-os ess!*"

A white flash filled her vision and faded into the blazing fire of the camp.

Taemi blinked. *What? ...Was it some crazed dream?*

"Princess!" Kio rushed towards her, "You're wet and covered..." He clenched his mouth, "What did you sleep in?" He said with his mouth muffled behind his hand.

...It wasn't a dream, was it? She shook her head and instinctively summoned a purity spell through the moonstone. It washed the decay from her body and dried her clothes.

Kio smiled, "You're getting pretty good at that." "Thanks..." But kept the fact that she didn't remember *how* she was able to do that.

"Princess, Are you okay? All the others were passed out on the ground when I woke to a piercing scream." Kio explained.

"I'm..." she failed to finish her sentence as her body felt completely drained of energy. She slipped away into a dreamless sleep.

"*Princess?*"

Chapter 10

A Long Night Ahead

Taemi opened her eyes to the dark forest. She wondered how long she had slept and hoped that it wasn't the whole day. She rose up and saw that everyone was currently awake, enjoying breakfast. *They were likely eating the birds again.*

Lloyd smiled down at her. "Good morning, Princess Equillis."

Morning? "Then why is it so dark?"

"We're probably in the center of it," Mel stated calmly, looking up at the sky. "The forest is darkest here, but it'll lighten up as we get closer to the edge."

Kio wiped his mouth with the back of his hand and rushed to her side. "Princess, are you okay? You passed out so quickly last night."

"Oh…" she tried to think, "I must have used too much of my energy…"

"We'll need to head out soon. If you can't walk, Nazoo can carry you."

The princess shook her head. "No… I should be fine."

After packing up their camp, Mel had them file up as they did yesterday. "Again, we're probably in the center of the forest, so be on the lookout and let anyone know if you see anything."

The beasts were more aggressive than they had been yesterday. The group halted for a third time to wait until Mel, Tilly and Scarlet dispatched the monsters they encountered. Zemire and Nazoo kept guard behind. Taemi crouched down, with her hands above her head—Kio and Lloyd waited with their swords ready for anything that could get past the front line.

The creature screamed in agony as its body fell down with a thud, defeated. "Ugh, I hate these six-eyed bastards," Scarlet mumbled as she sheathed her weapon.

"Alright, let's keep going."

Taemi glanced through the trees to see the creature that they had taken down. It had the same long, black, claws, but this one had huge black wings. She wasn't sure how they could have supported its large body in flight. *Maybe it didn't fly?*

The air became foul as they continued ahead. Taemi and the others covered their mouths as the stench grew stronger. Mel halted the group again and sent Scarlet forward to investigate their path.

"We don't have to worry about this one," she called. "Looks like something else already took care of it."

The group approached to see what Scarlet was talking about. The furred head was the size of a horse, with curled horns, and long fangs from its narrow snout.

"Man! Look at the teeth on this thing!" Tilly exclaimed. "What kind of monster do you think could have taken *this* one down?"

"Ugh, is that what stinks?!"

The dark-skinned beauty shook her head, "I don't think so; it would have gotten stronger this close." She glanced around and slipped off into the shadows to find the rest of it.

"Maybe this was the roar I heard last night?" Kio said, staring at the head in disbelief.

Tilly raised an eyebrow in question, "You heard something last night?"

Taemi grimaced. *...No, it wasn't* this *one that you heard...* The creature looked a lot scarier up close in the light. *It would have completely devoured me in one bite if the woman hadn't been there to behead it.*

While Tilly and Kio were talking about the other night, Mel detected something in the shadows and asked Zemire to accompany him. The girl wondered what he could have seen; there was nothing left of the hydra from what she could remember. That memory alone almost made her gag.

Scarlet found the body of the beast a few paces away and called out to the group, "It looks like its head was sliced clean off," she stated, inspecting the smooth cut of where it was detached at the spine.

"I wouldn't get too close to that, Scarlet." Lloyd stated from his distance, "I'm sure its body radiates poison or—"

"Something will probably come out and eat the rest of it." Nazoo stated gruffly.

The dark-skinned beauty curved her mouth in distaste at his choice of words, but nodded and backed away.

Lloyd smiled, "Yea, that's probably it—right, Mel?" The handsome man turned to look towards his leader, but he wasn't with the group. "Mel?"

"He and Zemire went to check something out over there," Tilly pointed to the shadows. "He'll just be a moment, though."

Lloyd sighed. "Great. The only guy who isn't afraid of this place goes off on his own, leaving us behind."

Scarlet laughed as she returned. "Easy, pretty boy. He's with Zemire. They shouldn't be that far."

But Scarlet's words weren't enough to calm Lloyd down. "Oh, like you ever had nothing go wrong when your party decides to split up?"

Nazoo took a seat and pulled out a pipe to smoke. "You know what your problem is, kid," he took a drag before he finished, "you don't seem to trust your comrades."

The pretty-faced soldier crossed his arms, "I'm just concerned about the princess." He glanced over at Taemi and her face flushed. "Getting her out of here is my number one priority."

"I bet that's what it is," Scarlet smirked from the shadows. If it weren't for the whites of her eyes and her toothy grin, Taemi could barely see her.

The rustle in the trees above took everyone's attention off the situation. Tilly prepared his bow and shot an arrow towards the sky. It struck something that gave off a screech and fell to the ground with a loud thud. But the noise above them didn't cease.

Everyone pounced to their feet and pulled out their weapons, forming a circle around Taemi. Tilly shot another arrow towards the sky but backed away. "There's too many for me to take down—we have to get out of here!"

Nazoo was the first to lead, removing the giant axe he carried from his back. "Then let's go!"

"Wait, what about the others?" Taemi pleaded.

Scarlet grabbed the princess' arm and pulled her into a run, "They shouldn't have left the group!"

They ran into the dark forest with the rustling in the trees following them closely above. Tilly ran ahead to shoot more arrows, and even though he took another down each time, it didn't stop them. The creatures dropped down on them like spiders, and hung upside-down from the branches by their extended tails.

The princess screamed as a glossy, black, oval head of six red eyes dropped down in front of her. Her pendant illuminated and it hissed with razor-sharp teeth.

Scarlet pulled Taemi back while Kio slashed the creature in half with a two-handed front swing. Its insides spewed out as the top half fell to the ground. Scarlet began to weave the princess through the forest while Lloyd and Kio covered them.

They ran at full speed until the princess' comrade halted so fast, Taemi staggered out of Scarlet's grip and rolled onto the dirt ground. She peered up at the dark-skinned woman, wondering why she stopped.

A giant scythe-like blade impaled the woman from behind. Blood pooled out of her mouth as she gasped for breath.

The creature hissed from above at its kill and lifted Scarlet up into the trees by its demonic tail.

Taemi reached for her, "No!"

"Leave her!" Lloyd and Kio lifted the princess from her shoulders and carried her away as she watched Scarlet's body ascend into the shadows.

They caught up with Nazoo, who was breathing heavily and slowed down. Tilly scanned the trees overhead, but they no longer rustled. "I think we lost them..."

"That's because they're probably feasting on Scarlet." Lloyd said dismissively.

His comment was more unsettling than what Mel would have said. Taemi's stomach churned in agony and she heaved up onto the nearest tree.

"Oh, Princess..." Kio gathered her hair and held it back and away from her face.

Lloyd extended out a cloth. "My apologies, Lady Equillis." He turned away. "I'm sorry, I shouldn't have said that."

Kio gave her the small cloth and she wiped her mouth. "I'm okay..." She liked Scarlet, and the forest devoured her. She now understood Mel's dark eyes; *the Forest of the Damned is as terrible as they say it is.*

"We should keep moving..." Kio whispered as he rubbed her back.

She nodded. *I don't want to be here anymore...*

They aligned themselves with Tilly taking the lead and then followed by Lloyd, Taemi and Kio while Nazoo guarded the back again The sunlight started to peer through the trees, and the elfish boy was able to take out the creatures ahead with just his bow. As they continued, the forest became less dense and easier to see.

Taemi was finally able to see an opening out of the forest ahead, and they all hurried to get to it. They reached the exit that exposed the vast plains, and beyond that was the translucent shapes of the mountains.

Recalling the map she studied in Sandar, she knew Laquar lay behind those mountains. *Almost there...* And yet, she still felt as if she wasn't even close. *How will we get through the mountains? If they were like those that surrounded Adrienan, it would be a difficult travel.*

The sun was well into the evening and was about to set on the horizon. A flickering light across the plains caught her eye. *A fire maybe?*

Kio nodded. "It doesn't hurt to check it out."

There was a single figure sitting next to the fire, and as they got closer, Taemi was able to recognize his features.

"Mel!"

The short man rose to his feet as they approached, but he was alone. "I was hoping the rest of you would make it," He replied, but didn't express any type of emotion on his face or in his voice.

Lloyd stomped forward and grabbed Mel by the collar. "What happened? You completely disappeared back there!"

Mel looked up at him, but didn't change his expression. "I saw a woman not too far off—unconscious— so Zemire and I went to retrieve her. As soon as I got her on my back, we were attacked by these small, rodent-like creatures." He pulled out of Lloyd's grip and continued.

"When they bite, they really tear at the flesh." He lightly touched his arm to show a darkened bandage, "I couldn't fight with the woman on my back, so Zemire said to go on ahead and he'd fight them off." He peered over towards the forest, "...I've been waiting for quite some time, but I didn't see him come out, yet."

Lloyd stepped back and stared at the ground. Taemi's stomach sank, feeling that Zemire shared the same fate as Scarlet. She could hear Tilly and Nazoo shifting on their feet.

Kio glanced around. "Where's the woman?"

Taemi noticed a blanket laying on the ground, and a pack near the top for a pillow, but it was empty.

"Hmm." Mel peered around himself and then turned back to the group. "Who?"

His response surprised everyone, "...The ...the woman you carried out?"

Mel blinked and stared at the empty blanket, "Oh, she must have woken up and vanished home."

Vanished?

The others were troubled by his words and started whispering about whether or not Mel was possessed by the forest, but Taemi knew that he was probably telling the truth.

She frowned. *The woman was the sorceress from last night. Now that she was out of the forest, she was able to use her spells again. She probably used some sort of transporting magic... One that she intended to use in the forest to take me away....*

"I'm going to *burn* that blasted forest to ash!" Nars stormed into Reiji-Arashi's chambers unannounced, stomping angrily. She could see his calm, expressionless face begin to crinkle with vexation. "The damned beasts and cursed trees can devour them all and then I'm going to *burn* it to ash—"

Nars was cut off as a hard blow whipped across her face—she heard her jaw make a sharp crack—as she stumbled back.

Arashi sat back down on his thrown and drank from his goblet. He didn't speak a word, but his glare expressed his thoughts enough: *Useless.*

Nars cupped her jaw—the whole side of her face ached from Arashi's slap—and it even burned to the touch. Immediately, she cast the reverse spell to herself, locating her jaw back into place. "...If you want *her* for conquering then you can get her *yourself.* I'm tired." She decided it was time to retire from serving this man and finally return home to Eithsa. She turned to leave, wondering if Arashi simply presumed she was only going to lie down. She intended to leave without a word to him. *He'll have to crawl and plead on his knees if he wants my help ever again!*

"Narssey," Nars was a few paces from the doorway when Arashi teleshifted to place himself in front of her. The door closed shut as he reached out to touch her face where he hit so hard earlier. It was mostly healed, but the memory of the sting still lingered. "Let's not go to bed like this." The edge was out of his voice, and it was back to the serene, Narpal tone.

She gave him her iciest glare, but she could smell his intoxicating scent when he was this close, and her heart started to pound as his hand caressed her cheek.

"It would be no fun to conquer the kingdoms on my own. I'd get bored without someone like you keeping things... interesting." He slowly paced around her tracing his other hand around her waist.

I'm not really in the mood...

"Imagine the two of us; you have a couple of countries, I have a couple of countries—we make it into a little game, making them fight each other and see who's better at winning." He held her tight from behind and his free hand gently cupped her chin to turn her head to face him. "We will throw giant masquerade balls, dance all the time, drinking wine, and everyone will adore you as their queen."

A chill rushed down her spine and tingled throughout her veins. *...That does sound fun, I suppose.*

"You can have a whole army of tigers." He brought his face closer.

"...I like tigers." She whispered, gazing at the lips she longed to taste.

They curled into a smirk, "I know..." Arashi pulled her in to meet his lips and she melted into him as her head filled with a humming buzz.

In a brisk moment, she felt her back up against the door and his body was pressed up against her, crushing her just enough and pinning her arms above her head "...I'll adore you," he whispered in between breaths, "...I'll do anything you ask," Then he paused and caressed her chin. "...You just need to do this one simple thing for me, and I promise, to give you anything you ask." His breath was hot against her skin.

"Now," He released her from his grip, pulling back and turning away. "Get some rest," He sat back down in his chair, and sipped from his goblet. "I expect you to return with the girl and the moonstone, instead of another pathetic excuse this time. You're better than that."

The electrostatic buzz subsided, but she still breathed heavily. *He did that on purpose...* She sighed. *A short taste of a vintage bottle, but yet...* She contemplated his words. *If the girl's only purpose was simply to be used as a mere tool for Reiji and he really intended to deliver the future he promised... perhaps I could give it one more chance.*

She was disappointed, but satisfied. She bowed,

"As you wish... my Lord," and turned away towards her chambers. *This wouldn't be an issue if I could just teleshift the girl, but the same ward that protected her from the viewing crystal also repelled that spell.* Even in the Forest of the Damned, the girl's protection wards were still activated while Nars' contortion spell was temporarily disabled among the Sandarians. She hated that forest. *Why would the moonstone magic work and not mine? Could that be the only benefit of this crystal magic?*

She felt the headache forming just thinking about the blasted forest. *Maybe I'll lay off the wine for a while...*

CHAPTER 11

The Cloymein Plains

The plains were near freezing at night, and scorching hot the next day as Taemi and her remaining escort continued through the tall grass on foot. They stopped at a cattle farm to purchase food and to refill their stock of water. Taemi wished they could have stayed the night, or even a bath would have been appreciated, but they were already asking too much of the farmer's good hospitality.

"Most people don't travel out here on foot because of the prairie weevils. In fact, many at least have something to keep out of the sun as well. I don't have a spare wagon, but these scarves might help."

Mel bowed as he took the farmer's offering. "Much appreciated."

"What in hell's breath brings Sandarian soldiers and a high lady to *these* provinces?"

"We were traveling by ship, but it got wrecked in a storm. We are the only passing survivors." Mel explained.

The farmer nodded, rubbing his chin, "Ay, yes. I suppose you wouldn't want to hike back to Sandar with that blasted forest in the way. The screams of those creatures at night are enough to keep me out of there."

The tall blonde scoffed and mumbled under his

breath, "I sure as hell wouldn't advise it."

They continued on their way, all with their heads wrapped with the scarves provided by the farmer. Taemi was more than grateful, as it helped with the hot, beating, sun and dry wind. With her dark hair, she knew her head would feel like it was on fire without it.

As soon as the sun went down, the air dropped near twenty degrees and the wind cut through her cloak like an icy razor. The group halted their travels to build a fire and to hunt dinner. Taemi looked out towards her destination, but it barely seemed any closer than the morning.

"Damn, these plains are *endless*!" Lloyd exclaimed in exasperation.

"I've never ventured the plains of Cloymein. My scouting expeditions are only to the Forest of the Damned, per the king's orders. It could take weeks to get to those mountains."

The tall blonde sighed at their leader's comment.

"The fire seems to be good. Tilly and I will see what we can catch for tonight's dinner."

Taemi scrambled to her feet as Mel and Tilly turned to go. "Can I go with?"

"Lady Equillis, you should stay here."

"I want to learn how to use a bow and arrow... I... don't want to be just a helpless damsel." *...And useless while watching my comrades die.*

Her thoughts drifted to Scarlet and how she would have hoped to spend more time with the dark-skinned beauty to learn how to become a warrior like her.

The shorter man shrugged, "It's fine by me. Tilly?"

"Sure, Lady Equillis," The elf boy smiled. "I can show you the basics to get you started."

Kio got to his feet, "I'm coming with you!"

"You're on first watch, Kio." Mel stated quietly. "You'll stay here and rest up."

To Taemi's surprise, Kio obeyed and sat down when she expected the stubborn boy to protest. She smiled softly so he wouldn't notice. She never expected that the short man would be the one who held everyone in line when she first met him, but she was glad he could keep Kio in check.

"You two go on ahead then. I'll clean whatever you catch." Mel stated.

Tilly nodded and pointed out towards the grassy plains, "Let's head in this direction, Lady Equillis. I thought I saw something flying ahead."

"Right!" The princess smiled and followed the elf boy out to the plains.

"Over there," Tilly pointed to the sky, and just as he mentioned before, there was a small flock of winged creatures that were spiraling down to rest for the night.

As they approached quietly, they stopped twenty paces away and ducked down into the grass. The birds they hunted were colorful compared to those they ate in the damned forest; they had large, bright, yellow beaks, and purple feathers. Their tall, lanky legs brought them close to four or five feet in height, and they fed on the insects by reaching down their long necks.

The princess gasped at the sight. "Wow... they're huge."

"Yea," Tilly nodded as he examined them, "but not much meat on them. We'll probably need three to feed the group. They'll fly off as soon as I hit one, so we'll have to find where they land next."

Tilly took his bow off his back and strung it up. "I'll demo it for you tonight, and tomorrow you can practice shooting it."

"Okay!"

"First, you'll want to identify which of your eyes is the most dominant, for most it's the right eye, but some use their left."

Taemi already felt lost in his instructions.

"I'm right-eye dominant, so I hold the bow in my left hand. Next, I'll nock the arrow below the anchor bead on the string." He pointed to the bead and how the notch in the arrow clicked onto the string. "That's the easy part; what matters on whether you hit your target or not is the pose. You straighten your bow arm out, and with just the two finger-tips, you pull back to here." He extended his left arm out and pulled back on the string with his other hand until his thumb touched his face just above the corner of his lips. He took a deep breath to focus and then released.

The arrow flew—slicing through the air—and the birds rustled to a chaotic run, exposing their large wingspan and taking off in different directions to a safer feeding ground. But one stayed behind, lying on the ground with Tilly's arrow.

"That's one!"

Taemi observed the flock to locate their next landing destination as Tilly prepped their first catch to be easily carried. There was little meat on the legs, so he sliced those off and left them behind for other creatures to enjoy.

"Alright, this time, let's see if you remember the steps."

"Oh, um..." Taemi pondered for a minute. "You said something about the eye, but you hold the bow in your left hand like this." She motioned and then pointed to the bead on the string, "and then you nock an arrow here, on the string."

Tilly tilted his head and smiled brightly, "Sounds good so far!" He loaded the arrow and pulled it back to his cheek. "Watch my stance closely. It's important to keep your elbow up and your arm out."

Taemi nodded and mimicked his stance. He took a deep breath in and released his second shot. Again, the birds flew up to the sky in a frenzy, but left one of their own behind.

The young, elfish boy smiled as he held up the two fingers that pulled back the bow, "That's two!"

The birds flew further down the plains, and by the time they reached them, they were done eating and folding their long legs beneath themselves to sleep. They huddled close together for warmth.

Tilly held out the bow. "I think you're ready to give it a shot."

The girl waved the weapon away, "Oh no, you go ahead. We only need one more, and it'll get dark if I miss."

The elf boy dismissed her decline and smiled, "Nonsense! This will be easy." He handed her the bow and an arrow, "Here, look at me for a second." She glanced up and saw that Tilly held his hands in a triangle.

What is he doing?

"Great! You're right-eye dominant!" The girl frowned, feeling like he was speaking in another language, but the elf boy simply laughed at her confusion. "Don't worry about it. Just shoot exactly as how I did it."

Taemi went through the steps in her head, *one: hold the bow in my left hand—don't worry about that eye thing— two: notch the arrow below the bead. Three: ...pull back?*

"Just use your fingertips here," Tilly showed her on the string and she followed. "Great, now extend your left arm, and pull the string back to here," He lightly grazed the side of her cheek.

The bowstring was near impossible for Taemi to pull back, and even more so when only allowed to use her fingertips. *He made it look so easy!*

"Oh, I guess it's a bit heavy for you," He laughed as she struggled with it a few times and sighed in defeat. "Let's do it this way," Tilly came around her from behind, held the bow over her left hand and pulled the string back to her cheek. "Okay," He whispered in her ear, "You aim and let me know when to let go."

She looked over the arrowhead and aimed at the large mass of birds. They were huddled so close, she wasn't sure where one ended and another began. *But maybe that's why it'll be easy? No matter where I aim, I should get one?* Just as Tilly did, she took a deep breath in and was ready. "Now!"

The arrow flew and a piercing screech forced Taemi and Tilly to seal their ears. They watched in dismay as the birds ruffled to their feet, and those that were quick took off into the night sky. The others were pinned down by long tethering roots that sprouted out from the ground. Yellow, worm-like creatures, nearly as large as the birds, popped up and pulled the birds into their mouths with their long tongues. The birds squawked as the leachy worms clenched onto their bodies and devoured them.

While they were feeding, Taemi found where her arrow pierced the one that popped up at the wrong time. *That must have been what screeched.*

"Those must be the prairie weevils the farmer mentioned earlier," Tilly notched his bow and started shooting at the weevils. Each time he hit one, they shrieked in agony. "Slimy bastards, we were here first!"

Taemi watched him shoot, making mental notes of his stance and poses. *He always hits his target every time he releases. I bet I would have gotten a bird too if the worms didn't pop up.*

A painful pressure grew on her ankle and reached down to massage it, *probably not drinking enough water...* She felt something sticky and jumped away in disgust. Taemi fell as it pulled at her leg and dragged her across the grass. She looked back and saw a lump in the ground pulling her closer. *Ah—my ankle is caught in the weevil's gross, sticky tongue!* Taemi attempted to grab onto the grass and tug herself away, but the grass blades slid through her fingers.

The ground exposed the yellow, eyeless creature. Its wide mouth was a gaping hole, lined with small razor teeth. The princess screamed and clawed at the weevil's tongue, but it only clutched her ankle tighter.

She heard the comforting sound of arrows flying through the wind, followed by *thud-thud-thud* without a second in between. The creature gave off its high-pitched shriek as it was pierced. The girl felt her foot release and she coiled up, closing her hands over her ears to block the creature's cry.

She was embraced gently and rocked back and forth. When the scream subsided, she looked up to see Tilly's green eyes filled with concern, "My lady—I-I'm *so* sorry! I'm *so* sorry! I didn't hear your scream over theirs. When I looked back you were gone!" He continued to rock her, but Taemi started to feel that it was more for his benefit than hers. "I'm *so* sorry!" He trembled as tears weld up in his eyes.

"I'm okay. Tilly, I'm okay..." The boy sniffed as she consoled him.

"You trusted me to protect you! They all did—and I failed!"

She shook her head and petted his cheek, wet with tears, "You did just fine. See, I'm okay." She smiled up at him and he began to calm down.

He took a deep breath in and stopped rocking to examine the princess' hand and ankle. "I have a small bandage kit—I'll clean up your hands." The girl didn't even notice the scraps on her palms and wrists from being pulled through the grass. She held out her sores for him to clean and wrap up, and he began to mumble, "Shit! Mel's gonna kill me... Hell! Lloyd will *skin* me alive... I-I don't even want to know what *Kio* will do!" He glanced up at the princess briefly.

"We don't have to tell them about the weevils." She flinched as he cleaned her hand. "We'll just say... I fell! I was so excited to get my first kill and I *tripped* and fell." The princess laughed at her own plausible story.

Tilly shook his head, "I don't feel comfortable lying about this... you almost..." He frowned instead of finishing the thought.

It was *pretty close...* She decided that it was best to change the topic of discussion and maybe he'd forget what happened. "Did you shoot three arrows at once, or loaded them individually?"

"It's near impossible to hit your target with more than one arrow on the string, my Lady!"

There was barely a second between those hits! "You really can shoot them off quick!"

The boy gave a small smile. "C'mon let's head back before they die of hunger." He said as he finished wrapping Taemi's scraps. Tilly carried two of the birds while Taemi helped with the other one. They were able to get the third one after Tilly killed all the weevils. The poor thing was partially consumed and too wounded to survive, so they let it out of its misery mercifully and took the rest of it for themselves.

When they arrived back to camp, Kio and the rest were cleaning their swords, trying to catch their breath. "Whoa, what happened here?"

Mel sheathed his short swords and kicked at a lump on the ground. His dark eyes watched the carcass roll down the hill. "Looks as if we encountered the infamous prairie weevils."

"Their sticky tongues sprouted out of nowhere, damn it!" Lloyd yelled as he and Nazoo helped carry another one to toss down the hill. "It was a good thing you went with Tilly, Lady Equillis, otherwise you'd probably be weevil grub," Lloyd smiled, wiping the sweat from his forehead.

Taemi gave the elf boy a slight nudge.

"They gave us some trouble too—" Tilly began with a soft voice, shyly shifting on his feet.

"But Tilly got them all with his quick-shooting bow skills!" Taemi exclaimed as she reenacted the elf boy's fighting stance.

Mel walked over and ruffled the kid's hair, "Good work. We probably want to have two people on watch in case they... weevil back. We'll do two shifts—Kio and myself will take the first watch. Lloyd and Nazoo, you can take the second."

"Wait, what about me?" Taemi asked.

"Princess, you should get some rest. It's a long walk ahead."

Taemi shook her head. *They're doing it to me again.* "I can help! Why don't we do three shifts? I can sit with Tilly?"

The boy had his smile back and nodded, "She can use the crossbow! She has a good handle on aim."

Their leader shrugged his shoulders and took the birds to start cleaning. "Three shifts it is. Let's get dinner started."

The next morning started just the same as the day before, and Taemi watched the sunrise dry up the morning dew that misted the plains. Her and Tilly didn't see anything during their shift, but waited until it was fully daylight before waking up the rest from their slumber.

"Anything?"

"Nope, how about you?"

Nazoo shook his head, "Quiet as the dead."

"I guess weevils feed only at a certain hour before nightfall. We might not have to worry too much about them."

They trudged through the hot sun, wrapped up

in their scarves. They stopped when the sun reached the highest and hottest peak of the day to rest and eat lunch. They had enough water to get them through the rest of the day.

The wind chill came back as soon as the sun settled on the horizon, and once again, they decided to stop for the night. Mel had them split into two groups—one for the hunting party, and one for the cooking crew—in case the weevils attacked. Taemi used the crossbow and hunted the birds together with Tilly, while Kio watched for the burrowing creatures. They were able to get the three birds for dinner in half the time than it took the night before. The weevils didn't attack either of the parties that night, but to be safe, they still kept watch in pairs in three shifts. Taemi felt better being part of the group instead of being waited on.

In fact, she actually enjoyed seeing the sunrise and watching the plains slowly warm up by the golden sun. She enjoyed the melodies of the birds chirping, and the soft buzz of the grasshoppers. She'd never experienced such while being within the luxurious walls of her castle. The handmaids never woke her up until the sun was already out for hours, and then there was only the sound of the maids running through the corridors.

The group woke up early the next day to eat their leftover meat along with the last bit of rations. They hiked through the plains until the sun was high.

"Hopefully we run into another farm or something." Lloyd tapped at his water bag. "I think those are my last drops…"

Taemi looked towards the mountains to see that they grew in size. Her heart fluttered with joy. *We're getting closer!*

"You're sure cheerful today, Princess." Kio smiled.

The girl nodded, "We're almost there, Kio!" She

flashed him her biggest smile from the excitement.

"That's true, Princess; we are getting closer, but hopefully we find another farm or village that can spare water. It sure is hot in these plains."

...I wonder if there was a way to collect the water from the morning dew. They haven't seen any other sign of human life in the past two days, much less a village out here. *There should be water from the mountains, but...* They would have to get there first. Taemi felt a little pit of despair form in her chest.

As her group cleared over the next hill, her spirits lifted again.

CHAPTER 12

The Traveling Circus

Over the hill, there was a line of eight colorful wagons that crawled over the grassy plains like a rainbow caterpillar. As they got closer, Taemi was able to see the painted images on the side of the colored wagons of creatures that she'd only ever read about in books, but never thought existed in real life. Six large, dark horses with feathered hooves pulled the first wagon that was painted red with *Shemra's Traveling Circus* in large, white lettering. The other wagons descended in the colors of a rainbow: orange, yellow, bright green, turquoise, blue, and purple.

The bright green one had a wall of silver bars caging in two large, furry creatures. Taemi wasn't sure what they were, but hoped to get closer to examine them.

As they approached the first wagon, a short man with a black mustache, wearing a tall hat and bright red coat with gold embroidery, halted the large horses. "Whoa!" After tying the reigns, he hopped down to the ground to greet them. "Aye, what brings you folks all the way out here in the middle of nowhere? The nearest village is still another fifty miles south of here."

"If you're going east, perhaps we can travel together." Mel bowed to the gentleman and then the other soldiers saluted.

"Sandar soldiers, and a fine elegant lady?" The short, little man eyed them all up, rubbing his large mustache. "What interest would you have with our humble circus?"

Taemi shifted on her feet, "Well, we just... want to travel with your members. I'm afraid it's a long journey, and we only have so much. I'm sure I can do something to repay you."

Master Shemra took a long look at the group. He eyed the girl up and down. Taemi could only hold her breath—*We could travel a lot faster if we could hitch a ride with them*. She was exhausted having to go on foot the past two days. They were not prepared for this kind of journey to begin with.

"Well, as long as your soldiers," He pointed to Kio and the rest, "agree to be an accompanied bodyguard. You, my Lady, you're just much too pretty to be traveling out in these conditions. I'll let you tag along as long as you agree to tell me what is this quest you're going about, and how you ended up traveling on such light conditions."

Taemi started with a sigh of relief until the ringleader finished his sentence. *Another lie...* "Well," she swallowed. *Any woman who's to be queen should learn to come up with some white lies as well!* "I am indeed, a lady of the... Condor." She picked a name, hoping he was not familiar with, "I was invited to the grand gathering of Princess Equillis' banquet when suddenly—the castle had been under some sort of... ambush!"

Master Shemra flinched with a yelp as Taemi stepped forward with her fingers arched like claws.

"An evil presence—would be all I can say to describe such a tragedy!" The princess swayed to block the scorching sun from her eyes, pretending to nearly faint from the horrors she witnessed. "We took off in the night. I was separated from my escorts and... my other accompanies had not been so fortunate." She paused to lightly place her hand on Kio's arm. "I plan to go to Laquar to request their assistance on the matter, before… it's too late."

The ringleader pondered at her words, listening intently. "Evil, you say?" he said softly, stroking his mustache. "Well, at times like these, I wish I employed a bard to share your tale." He shook his head with a heavy sigh.

"Hey, Master Shemra, what seems to be the hold-up?" A voice called out from the orange wagon while the rest of the cirqueteers emerged from their colored cabins to see why they had stopped.

"Oh, yes, yes, yes—let me introduce you to the team!" Master Shemra stated hastily and waved them to follow.

Kio nudged Taemi softly with a smile. "Nice work, Princess." He whispered with a silent clap as the short man guided them to the couple that occupied the orange wagon.

"Here are the acrobats, Lenra and Luna."

At first glance, Taemi considered them to be brothers *…or were they sisters?* They looked about a few years younger than Taemi, but identical to each other with their brown hair cut short and dark brown eyes. Their round faces had boyish features, but they were also pretty enough to be girls. They wore matching jumpsuits with geometric shapes of blues and purples, covered in sequins that shimmered in the sunlight. They smiled and bowed their heads in sync. "Nice to meet you."

Master Shemra nodded and applauded them. "They are the dynamic twin brother and sister duo!"

Taemi wasn't sure which one was which gender, but smiled and applauded politely, "It's a pleasure to meet you two!"

"And over here," He guided them towards the yellow wagon, "we have our strongest man, Vlad, and his lovely wife, JoMila!"

The strongest man was bare-chested, wearing only ankle-high trousers. His skin was sun-kissed with arms bigger than Nazoo's, as well as the tallest man she'd ever seen. He had his head shaved with thick, black eyebrows and a long, thin mustache that was twisted into braids and then beaded at the end, leaving his chin bare. He nodded his head as a greeting, but other than that, he was a man of few words.

"We're also the cooks," His wife smiled with an unrecognizable accent that exaggerated the vowels. She was tall and thin, with ivory skin and vibrant red hair that bounced as she walked towards the group. "I suppose this means we have more mouths we'll be feeding, no?" She raised a thin, red brow towards the ringleader. She was neither mad nor excited about the new members.

Master Shemra laughed, "Oh, it's okay, we have plenty to share!" He held his hand up to whisper, "Plus, maybe we can gain a little more coin with the new recruits!"

JoMila had a slight smile, and crossed her arms looking at the group, "I could... probably use one for the knife throw, yes?"

The knife throw... Taemi wondered what type of act that might entail—she'd never really been able to watch the circus before—but one glance at the ringleader who nervously rubbed his hands together made her less curious to volunteer.

"Oh JoMila!" The little man laughed, "She's a fantastic juggler, you should see what she can do with fire!"

JoMila looked down at her fingernails, pretending not to be flattered by the compliment, "Yes, yes, but I do grow bored at such things. My new thing is knife throw now, but nobody helps me practice."

"Well, we'll get you someone, my dear JoMila! Come now, just one more person to meet," Master Shemra ignored the glare he received from the juggler and pushed them to the lime green wagon with the exotic creatures.

Taemi peered through the iron bars to see the two lounging creatures. They were enormous black and white striped beast-like cats. Their heads and paws were massive, *like the creatures that resided in the Forest of the Damned, but they loafed about just like any lazy cat would!* Taemi's heart dropped when one of them yawned, exposing the size of its teeth and unbelievable jaw range. *They're just like the creatures from the Forest of the Damned! Yikes!*

"Don't worry, 'bout them—they're just really big kitties." Taemi looked over to see a girl not much older than herself from appearance. Her clothes were just as odd as the other cirqueteers; she wore baggy, multi-colored trousers where the crotch hung low and connected down by the knees with two deep pockets at the sides clasped with wooden buttons. They cuffed just above her ankles, displaying pink slippers underneath. Her solid pink, tight top outlined her curves underneath and exposed her slim midriff.

Master Shemra nodded, "Ay, yes. This be our tigress tamer, Morlisa."

"Oh, are you traveling along with us? The circus has its pleasant of adventures, indeed." The tamer's voice was like chimes in a summer breeze. The girl had long, gorgeous, curled locks as bright as the sun that rounded her oval face and high structured cheekbones. If her hair was the color of the sun, her eyes were certainly the sky— all in all, Taemi would admit she was as beautiful as any sunny day.

Those curved, pink lips formed a smile. But it was far less than innocent that it would allude to. *There was something familiar about her smile...*

She placed a painted nail over her lips as she looked over the group. "Hmm, I wonder what we should do about the sleeping arrangements?" She smiled at Kio and Lloyd, but quickly averted away from Mel. The princess didn't blame her. *It's probably because of those eyes of his.*

"There is a vacant wagon, but... you won't all fit. But us girls can share my wagon." She grabbed Taemi's hands and held them up in hers tilting her head with a big smile. "We can have a girl's night!" She got close and whispered, "...and you can tell me all the deets with these cute boys you're with."

Taemi blushed, *That sounds really exciting!*

"The prince—Taemi isn't sleeping anywhere with a random stranger!" Kio stated hastily, pushing his way in between the girls.

Morlisa giggled, "I have room in my bed for you, too," Morlisa pressed herself up against him with a smile— her face nearly touching his, "if you don't mind getting close."

Taemi's breath caught, and she blushed at the idea—*sharing a bed with Kio?!*

"You can even be in the middle," Kio took a step back, but the frightening look of shock got bigger as he looked over at Taemi, *likely thinking the same.*

Lloyd laughed at the display the two put on and made his way closer to Morlisa, "I'd take you up on that offer," he didn't hesitate putting his arm around the girl's waist, touching her skin, and pulling her close. "It gets pretty cold at night here."

"Lloyd!" The princess propped her fists on her hips. *He might be charming, but he just met the girl!*

Mel calmly stepped in to pull Lloyd's hand away. "We don't need you to make special accommodations on our behalf, my lady." Morlisa tried to avoid Mel's eyes since they arrived, but now her blue eyes stared wide-eyed into his as if lost in a maze. She swallowed hard as he continued, "Lady Equillis will get the empty wagon, and Kio and Nazoo will take turns guarding as necessary. The rest of us," he looked up at the blonde soldier, with almost a glare from his dark eyes, "can continue to camp outside."

The blonde grimaced down at Mel, but turned and stomped away.

"Tamm...mei, is it?" The princess looked back and Morlisa was just inches away from her face, her blue eyes studying her. They were like crystal pools welcoming her to a long, overdue bath.

She gets this close to everyone! "Heh- yea, you can call me that."

"Princ—I mean..." Kio leaned in to whisper, "...shouldn't you be using a different name...?"

"It's really cute that you call her *princess*... Are you her *suitor*?"

"I'm... uh... I..." The expression on Kio's face as he backed away from Morlisa's question made both of the girls giggle.

"Princess?" The tiger tamer grabbed Taemi's hand, "It certainly suits your beauty, but..." She made Taemi blush, "Your clothes... seen better days."

Her blush reddened in embarrassment. *She's right...* "Yea... they have been through a lot." *I might be able to dry them and remove... the melted insides, but they were still stiff from the ocean salt and smudged from the moss and mud of the forest.*

"Come to my wagon; you can borrow some clothes of mine." She began to lead Taemi, but Kio reached out to stop them. The tamer smiled up at him, "Why don't you come too and... pick out her outfit?"

Mel put his arm around Kio—whose face was red as a setting sun—and eased him off Taemi. "Sorry about him, he's like an over-protective brother." Kio's eyes widened at Mel's comment, but refrained from being thought of as too possessive.

Morlisa led Taemi by the hand up the steps to her

wagon. The inside was snug with a cozy interior of simple walls made of plain wood. She had a small table to the side with two chairs, and cabinets mounted near the ceiling that held ceramic plates and cups. In the back, there was a bed with drawers underneath, next to that were the washbowl and vase. A brass framed oval mirror above the washbasin reflected more light from the windows. But its style was the only item that didn't seem to fit within the rest of the room.

"Why don't you take those clothes off and wash up for a bit." The wagons began to move as the blonde shuffled through her drawers for clothes, "Hmm..." She glanced back at Taemi frequently as she compared each outfit before tossing it aside and grabbing another. Her blue eyes already made Taemi feel as if she was naked as she continued to mentally dress her up and shook her head. She went through an entire drawer and then moved on to the next one before she slowed down. "You have such pretty eyes, I think these would go well—"

"Nothing skimpy, I hope!" Taemi blurted out and then quickly, covered her mouth.

The girl only laughed at her reaction.

"I mean... nothing too... what you have on, I guess."

"Oh! You're too funny!" Morlisa laughed again and finalized her decision on the outfit for her and laid them out on the bed. "Need help with your dress?"

"Um... N-no, I got it."

"Well, hurry up and get washing!"

Taemi shuffled on her feet, shyly.

Morlisa's face just brightened even more, "Oh, it's fine, we're both girls." She got up to help Taemi with her dress by gathering up her long, black hair. "I can help wash your hair if you'd like."

"Um..." The girl made Taemi feel uncomfortable. She's never really been around other girls like this. The servants that poured her bath, washed her hair and dressed her had done so since she was a child. But to be around a commoner her age felt... too exposed.

"...I can get naked too, if that would make you *more* comfortable?" She asked slyly as she caressed Taemi's collarbone.

"N-no, that's okay. You're plenty naked enough!" She said the words before realizing she didn't mean for them to be said out loud.

The other girl exploded in laughter, "Haha! You're *so* sheepish! Haha. Ahh... Fine, I'll just wait outside then."

Morlisa let Taemi wash up alone, but came back in to help her with her hair after she dressed in the undergarments. They giggled over sparkling sweet wine and she wrapped her wet hair up in a towel. The outfit Morlisa picked out, fitted comfortably. Her top was an emerald color that matched her eyes and the trousers were a loose brown material that felt light and breezy. A clasp made from wood served as a sash belt to keep them tight to her hips.

"See, it's perfect!"

Taemi blushed at the tamer's compliment. "T-thank you for letting me wear them. They're really nice." She wore the finest dresses at the castle, but she never thought boy's trousers could be so cute on women.

"C'mere; let me brush your hair." Morlisa reached out and pulled Taemi to the bed where she sat cross-legged.

"Why would you want to do that?"

The tamer guided Taemi to sit on the end and pulled her close to whisper, "So we can talk about boys!"

Boys?! Taemi blushed. *Talk about them...* how? This sort of thing was never in her adventure books. Not even the servants gossiped about it. *...Or at least not when they were around* me.

"So, is the one that calls you *princess,*" Morlisa began to untangle Taemi's dark hair, "*Is* he your suitor?"

The hair stood up on Taemi's back, "W-what? N-no… I don't have a suitor!" She hid her embarrassment with laughter, "He's just a… soldier my father hired."

"Your daddy has great taste!" The girl's choice of words was unusual. "That tall blonde sure is handsome—what do you think about *him*?"

"L-Lloyd?" Even hearing his name made her smile. She thought back at the time when he caught her in the forest and she was looking up at his sweet face. *He's the knight in shining armor from all my fantasy books.*

"Well, that *look* says it all!"

Taemi's face blushed, forgetting she drifted off in thought. "Stop! He's just… another…" She couldn't finish her thought… *What was I going to say?* She peered down at her glass that was still full and wondered if it was starting to get to her. *My head does kind of hurt a little bit. Maybe I should have some water…*

"Hmm, you sure like him a lot, I can't imagine how much effort it will take for you to fall for someone else." Morlisa's voice seemed like it was off in the distance.

Isn't she… right behind me?

"Jeez, this is a lot more work than usual… These strings are stubborn."

Is she talking about my hair? Yea, she must be. That's probably why my head hurts a little bit. I have such long hair…

There was a knock on the door, but it pulled open abruptly, and Kio stepped inside, "Princ—I mean Taemi, dinner is ready."

Taemi wasn't even aware that the wagons stopped for the night.

Morlisa giggled at his entrance. "All right, let's go eat before JoMila throws a fit. She won't cook anymore if she's upset."

The meal was simple rolls of bread with a stew of tender meat chunks, and hearty vegetables of corn, peas, carrots and potatoes. While they ate around the fire, Morlisa went around to refill everyone's drinks with a white, crisp wine.

Kio made sure Taemi's cup was refilled with water, but every time she took a sip, it tasted like sweet wine. She looked back at Morlisa who only gave her a smile and quick wink. Taemi peered into her cup, shocked. *Maybe she's a magician too?* She watched each time as her cup was filled from the water pitcher, but each time it tasted like wine.

She watched Morlisa refill Kio's cup from the same water pitcher, but his expression wasn't out of the ordinary after a sip, so she knew that wasn't the trick.

After the meal, the circus performers practiced their set for Taemi and her team. Morlisa and JoMila drummed on sheepskin buckets, playing different sounds to a consistent rhythm. The acrobats rolled out, practicing their tumbles and lifted each other in the air. They flexed their bodies into exotic poses that Taemi couldn't believe were possible.

After them, Vlad, the strongest man, came out with his large, metal weights to display his strength. Nazoo got up to join him and it turned into a competition of who was strongest. They each twirled around the large axe Nazoo carried and then they lifted the heavyweights, one after another, adding more weight each time. They were neck-to-neck in strength until it came down to a simple arm wrestle. Nazoo bowed his head in defeat, but Vlad was a worthy opponent.

JoMila switched with one of the twins on the drums and came out with a simple juggling routine of colorful balls. There were three, then six, then ten and then so many more that Taemi lost count, but was sure no more than fifteen. The juggler tilted her head back, and a great flame from her mouth singed the balls into ash.

Even Kio jumped in his seat with a yelp of "Dragon's Breath" as he watched the balls burn and their ashes drift down around the artist like snow.

She then advanced onto a rolling sphere and rolled it from left to right, juggling three knives—growing to six—as Vlad tossed her three more.

The last bit, the tiger tamer played a fast, beat on the drums while both the acrobats and Vlad came out to join JoMila. Vlad balanced on a contraption of a plank of wood on top of a small sphere. He held up the acrobats who then lifted up JoMila and she blew the flame of fire from her mouth once more to light the three torches in her hands to juggle.

It was an excellent sight to watch JoMila juggle and hold her balance on top of the acrobats as Vlad rolled the plank side to side on the sphere. Taemi sat on the edge of her seat, holding her breath with anticipation that any moment they could fall...

The torches went out and they all jumped down to their feet with a bow.

The tamer walked out next with her tigers. Without whips or verbal commands, the tamer danced with the tigers, holding up hoops for them to leap through to the intricate rhythm of the drums played by JoMila and one of the twins. Morlisa spun around and threw the hoops up in the air and the tigers circled around and jumped through them as they came down. JoMila lit the hoops on fire and the tamer continued to dance through and over them without a singe to her hair or outfit. She had the tigers jump through the three blazing rings before the fuel gave out. The tamer and her tigers bowed before walking off to feed each beast a large piece of flesh to gnaw on throughout the night.

Morlisa came back to sit next to Taemi asking how she enjoyed the show. "You were magnificent! All of you were, actually! I've never got to enjoy the circus show before!" *When I'm queen, the circus will perform in Adrienan at least once a year!*

"Oh stop!" She smiled, "I bet you could do something pretty great too!" The compliment made the princess flush. "And then we can travel around the world together." She put her arm around Taemi and took a deep drink from her cup before she leaned in close and whispered, "and the boys can be our bodyguards." She giggled.

That doesn't sound too bad either. Taemi smiled, unable to take her gaze away from the girl's brilliant blue eyes that shimmered in the light of the fire. She could smell the sweet scent from her glossy, pink lips and for a moment Taemi wondered what flavor she wore... *and does it taste as sweet as it smells...?*

She watched those pink, curved lips move, forming words, but didn't pay attention to what she said. They smiled, they laughed, her tongue lightly licked her upper lip right before she flashed her teeth and bit her lower lip.

Suddenly, they formed into a pout, and the girl got up to sit on the other side of the fire. Her icy eyes scowled at Kio who took her place next to Taemi.

"You should keep your distance from her, Princess... She reminds me of someone I think I encountered in Sandar..." Kio gave her a light nudge when she didn't respond to his comment. "Princess, are you alright?"

"What?" Taemi glanced at him briefly, but continued to watch the girl across from her.

"You're acting like... a lovesick puppy..." the boy grumbled and glanced over at the tamer. "Princess... you're not one of those who likes..." His voice trailed off.

What is he trying to say? Taemi turned to her soldier perplexed, "What?"

He opened his mouth, but Master Shemra spoke first, "Drink up everyone! We have plenty to share! In two nights, we'll be at the next town near Laquar to put on another show!"

They all raised their drinks in a cheer and knocked

their cups back to be filled again. They continued on into the night sharing stories of humorous events that occurred within their travels.

"So when did you join the circus, lady tamer?" Lloyd asked as he refilled her drink.

"Hmm..." she put her painted finger to her lips as she thought, "I think they picked me up somewhere near *Belsa-Hidé*. The tigers didn't care for their previous owner—if you know what I mean—" She winked as she nudged Lloyd, "and I guess I fell in love with them ever since." She giggled.

"*Belsa-Hidé* is the old elfish translation for the 'Bell's Hide'..." Mel stated quietly as he sipped from his cup. "They stopped calling it that a few hundred years ago, I don't think even the elves still use that name for it."

Lloyd's drink burst from his mouth as he laughed, "Whoa! History buff!"

"Ah, she's from Eithsa." JoMila explained, "They probably still use the old maps there."

Morlisa stuck her tongue out at JoMila's comment, but her smile came back so quick, she didn't seem offended.

Mel nodded, "*Ta-ishka o shi-gutstu nay-no wa?*"

Without skipping a beat, Morlisa answered him with a smile, "*Tesh-kat noba.*" But her eyes widened in shock and cupped her mouth with both of her hands. Her flushed complexion glowed bright red.

Mel shrugged, "I doubt a country north of the sea would be fluent in ancient elfish. You must be a descendant..." he stated casually, taking a long sip of his drink.

"That's impressive!" Tilly exclaimed. "Of course it's a little different dialect than what I remember." The boy took a moment to ponder the translation, "*Ta-isha ji-gutsu no wa* translates roughly to *you're significantly skilled* and *Te noba* translates to *you cannot fathom*—or *you have no idea*—would be something *we* would say." The elfish boy smiled brightly towards the tamer and Mel. "You must have studied the language intensely to know the older versions."

Taemi blinked. *Mel knows almost everything about the Forest of the Damned AND speaks* ancient *elfish*! Each day, she found herself being more and more fascinated by the man.

The glow disappeared from the tamer's smile as her face reddened from embarrassment. "Oh no," she shook her head and peered down into her cup, "The wine is probably just making me pronounce things wrong." Morlisa yawned. "Well, I think it's time for me to turn in." She looked over to Lloyd and reached out to grab his collar, "Hey, pretty boy," she pulled his face towards hers and her lips curved in a foxish smile, "will you help me get something from my wagon?"

The tall blonde soldier grinned with a nod, "Oh, absolutely, Lady Morlisa."

"Actually," Mel stood up, "I'd like to offer my assistance." He unhinged Morlisa's hand from Lloyd and held it in his.

Through the orange glow of the fire, Taemi saw Morlisa's eyes widen when he touched her. Her face flushed bright red as she took a hard swallow and stared up at him, speechless.

Mel raised her to her feet. Her eyes examined him from head to toe, and then back to his eyes. "...Are you... sure? It's..." She forced another swallow, "it's stored pretty deep..." The last part was mostly a whisper.

Lloyd jumped to his feet and leaned over their leader, "You heard her, Mel." He shoved the shorter man back, "I think I should help her out." He smiled down at the tamer, but her eyes were locked on Mel's.

Both Tilly and Kio put down their drinks and shifted in their seats with concerned looks as the energy became hostile. Kio and Tilly waited, but they were ready to spring to their feet if needed.

Lloyd wrapped his arm around the tiger tamer with a grin, but shifted in disquiet under Mel's glare.

Mel paid no mind and addressed the tamer, caressing her chin, "For you, I can get it... *twice.*" Taemi didn't understand his answer, but he flashed a smile that even made her heart skip.

Did he just... smile?

She felt her own face redden as she watched Lloyd back away timidly for Mel to escort the tamer to her wagon.

The pretty blonde fell onto his seat in defeat near the fire, and Kio let out a heavy sigh as if he'd been holding his breath the entire time. He spoke softly so that only Taemi could hear, "I'm glad the responsible one put *her* to bed." He eyed Lloyd with a frown. "She drank quite a bit..."

He really doesn't trust Lloyd. She doubted that a charming, blonde gentleman would be the type to hurt a sweet girl like Morlisa. *But Tilly looked uneasy too...* She smiled realizing something comforting, *Kio may not like Morlisa, but even* he *would have defended her.*

Taemi left to turn in for her night's rest shortly after. She yawned from the day's excitement and her head buzzed from all the wine, but she was certain Mel return to the fire. *He probably just went to bed as well...* she thought as she laid her head on the pillow.

CHAPTER 13

A Delay In Travels

The wagons started moving around early dawn the next day. Taemi woke up briefly to the rattling vibration, but it was still dark. She smiled and lay back down in the comforting travel. *Well, in comparison to what I had earlier on this trip...*

She drifted off to sleep in a warm bed, dreaming of a warm bath.

The wagons halted violently and woke her up again. The horses screamed outside along with something else that screeched at a higher frequency. Master Shemra yelled, "Kill it—kill it! Over there!"

Taemi rose to her feet and ran to see the commotion outside. The wagons were stopped in a line and Master Shemra and Vlad held onto the horses as they huddled together in a circle. She saw lumps in the ground circling around them, and the giant, yellow worms exploded from the ground with their loud, screeching calls. Their tongues whipped out from their mouths in an attempt to grab the horses and Master Shemra for their meal.

"Stay off the ground, my Lady, we got a pack of prairie weevils." She looked up to see Nazoo sitting on top of her wagon with his axe ready if needed. "We must have rode right into their nest, but they seem to be handling them well."

Taemi followed his gaze back to the field to see Kio, Mel, and Lloyd racing with their blades unsheathed and slicing through the creatures that were harassing the horses and ringleader. Arrows flung overhead from the wagon tops—piercing the weevils that were overlooked by Tilly's comrades. The weevils screamed, shriveling back down into their dens.

Mel was, by far, the most entertaining to watch as he danced with short swords in each hand and flailed them across the field. Taemi thought he was a mage as she watched the blades zip back into his hands—catching them by the hilts like a skilled juggler and hurling them back out like spears—before she noticed the metal cables connected to the handles. There was a contraption attached around the short man's waist that whined the blades back into his hands. He was well-equipped for both long-distance and close combat.

His forest green cloak of Sandar floated around him like wings as he fluidly sliced and pierced through the weevils with both blades. His fighting style was similar to the woman she encountered in the forest. *He must have trained longer in the Forest of the Damned than he'd admit to in order to master such skill with unusual use of equipment.*

The event came to an end as the remaining weevils burrowed down and fled off to the distance.

The swordsmen wiped the beaded sweat from their brows as the hot sun hit its peak.

"*Ay-Yay!*" The tamer clapped her hands and led the tigers out into the field to feast on the slain weevils.

Lloyd's face twisted in disgust, "Ew... they like that?"

The tamer shrugged with the same look of repulsion on her face, "What can I say, they're really big cats..." She watched them graze before turning away with curled lips, "and cats love eating bugs..."

"My–my, do I have no regrets having you fine

gentlemen join our travels!" Master Shemra gave the horse's reins to Vlad to lead them back to the front wagon. "Those pesky weevils would have devoured our horses if it weren't for you! Many thanks! Many thanks!"

"Master Shemra..." Vlad returned with the train of horses. "The front axle of the red wagon is shattered. Do we want to leave it behind and hook up to the next?"

The short man burst out in rage, "What?! No, we can't leave the red one behind! That has the great circus name!! How will the village know it's the *Great* Master Shemra's *Circus*!!" He quickly turned to the Sandar soldiers. "You lads! Please! Help me fix the front axle—I'll make sure to treat you to extra wine at the next village we stop at!"

"I don't know anything about fixing wagons." Mel replied, slowly wiping his swords with a cloth as he watched the tamer feed her tigers. He hadn't taken his gaze off of her since she pranced onto the field.

"Ha! So there is something that you don't know!" Lloyd laughed, sheathing his sword.

"I don't comprehend. I'm sure there's lots of things I don't know..." Mel stated casually in his monotone voice.

The blonde man sighed and shook his head, "Uh, you're so strange, it's annoying." He wrapped his arm around the short man's shoulders and turned him away from the tamer and towards the red wagon. "All because you don't know, doesn't mean you can't help."

"Fair enough."

The three men and Vlad went over to the front wagon to fix the axle while the acrobats and JoMila stayed in theirs. Taemi didn't remember seeing them even come out during the commotion. *They must be really deep sleepers...*

"Well, I guess it's just us girls this afternoon," Morlisa smiled brightly up at Taemi with her hands resting on her hips. "The acrobats are probably playing a game among themselves, and JoMila will use this time to meditate before preparing dinner later."

"Oh, I see... What do *you* usually do?"

The tamer shrugged, "Anything to pass the time. I have a deck of cards in my wagon if you're interested."

The girl's face beamed with excitement. *A card game?!* She didn't know how to play any, but this would be the only chance to learn. She looked over towards Kio helping with the repairs. *He wouldn't mind if I went to play a little game.* "Okay, I'll come over."

Taemi sat with the tamer on her bed as the blonde gathered the cards from one of her drawers. One fluttered down to the floor and as Taemi picked it up, she gasped. Each card was hand-painted with either a mystical creature, or had script for spells. "Oh... I thought these would have numbers on them."

The other girl stared at Taemi with disbelief, "What? You've never played *Spells & Monsters*—it's the latest rave in these parts!"

Spells and Monsters... Taemi felt more and more out of touch with commoners every time she was introduced to something new.

"I got these at one of the markets near Narpal," she continued as she began to shuffle the set of cards before handing out five to Taemi and to herself. "The illustrations are hand-painted and the game itself makes the players feel like real mages! You use the spells to eliminate each other's monsters." She placed three cards down, each with a creature. "You roll the dice to see how many spells can be cast or support cards you can use per turn. Some cards require crystals that you have to buy, but each monster rewards coins upon their defeat." She continued to talk Taemi through the process and rules, pointing to how many spells are needed to defeat each creature and how much money is rewarded. She set up an assortment of

small, colorful rocks—crystals she said they resembled—
and took the first turn. "The end goal is to eliminate ten of
your opponent's monsters first. I'll guide you through the
first couple of steps, and help you with any questions until
you get the hang of it, okay?" She winked. "You can only
place down up to three monsters, but can always place
another down if you have one in your hand when one gets
defeated at any time." Morlisa had a Faerie Fox, a Spingle
Spider and a Swamp Leach.

Taemi had only two monsters out of her hand of
five cards—a Desert Griffin and a Mountain Ogre. She placed
them down and waited for her turn as Morlisa rolled the die.
Its face displayed three dots.

"So I have three moves during my turn. I can either
draw a card, cast a spell, or use any of the support cards if
I have them—which I don't." She chose to draw a card and
then cast two spells on Taemi's Mountain Ogre, taking him
out of the game. "Your turn."

Taemi rolled the die to gain a six. She had three
cards in her hand; two of them were spells and the third
one was a potion that she could have used if the ogre was
still in play. She sighed and drew three cards—a Flock of
Ravens, a strong spell card that required a crystal to use,
and a Lake Kelpie—an aquatic creature that was half-horse
and half-fish. She placed down the monsters that she drew
and used two of the weaker spells on the Spingle Spider to
remove it from the game. She drew another card for her
last move.

"Good, looks like you're getting a hang of things."
Her opponent replaced the spider with a Swarm of Bees.
She then rolled a five and began to draw cards, her face
forming a frown after each one until she drew all five and
sighed, "Ugh, you gotta be *kidding* me!"

Five cards and nothing?! *I wonder what she got...*
Taemi rolled for her turn, only to get one move out of it. She

drew a card and that was the end of her turn. She watched Morlisa roll a four and draw another card, but this time she smiled.

"Well, now it looks like things will get interesting!" She showed Taemi her support card. "The thief card! I get to take any two of yours!"

"What? Why? Can't you just draw two more?"

She shook her head, "Nope, I want yours—but you don't have to show me which are which. It just says I get to take two." Morlisa had two more turns after taking Taemi's cards—at least Taemi knew what the two cards the blonde *did* have—she played another support card, "This one allows me to sacrifice two of my own monsters and take their coins." She removed the leach and Swarm of Bees and replaced them with a Dark Unicorn and Poisonous Centipede. For her last move, she bought a crystal.

Oh... she's going to use that high spell for her next turn... Taemi rolled a three for her next turn. She only had the one potion card in her hand, and the new monsters that Morlisa placed all needed three spells to take out. *So I guess I'll have to draw some spells...* She drew three cards but sighed.

"Hmm... we're missing something..." Morlisa pursed her lips looking down at the played cards. "Oh, that's right." She got up off the bed briefly and came back with a bottle that contained a pink liquid and two small cups that literally would hold only enough liquid for one quick gulp. She smiled and poured the strange drink into the small cups. "Much better." She peered up and giggled at the confusion on Taemi's face. "Every time I kill one of your monsters, you take a whole cup of the grapefruit liquor, and vice-versa for me."

"A cup? It's practically only midday!"

The blonde tamer nearly shrugged at Taemi's comment, "Then I guess you better not lose any monsters!" She covered her mouth to muffle a laugh.

On her next turn, Taemi rolled another three. She picked up Haste—a support card that skipped her opponent's turn—and the second card she drew was another monster. The illustration for Triplet Chick was three, identical, magenta birds that shared a single body— three heads, four wings, and four legs.

When Taemi saw that it would take six spells to take it out, she read the creature's description. She would have to sacrifice three of her monsters to summon it, but once played down, it would allow her to cast any of her spells three times.

"I can tell you got something good there." Morlisa smiled with her deep blue eyes peeking over her hand.

Taemi gave a start, "What?!—No!" but she couldn't hold back her smile. *How could such a card exist?!* "I'm sacrificing my three monsters to play this one—any spell I cast with it on the field will times the attack by three!"

The other woman smirked and welcomed the challenge. She rolled and drew her cards, but didn't use the strong spell to attack. Instead, she equipped her Faerie Fox with a mirror.

"You can equip them?"

Morlisa nodded, "Certain support items work that way. The mirror reflects your magic attacks, but the monster using it will still receive damage, but only a fourth of the spell's power. Meaning, instead of needing two regular spells to kill my fox, you will actually need to attack him eight times."

Taemi's eyes widened. *If I had* that *for my Triplet Chick, I'd be unstoppable...* It was her turn now, and she didn't hesitate to use the Haste spell in her hand, which gave her a total of three rolls before Morlisa could do anything. She used a thunder spell to take out the Dark Unicorn.

Morlisa took her first drink, poured the next and laid down a weaker monster from her hand. Taemi drew another spell card and used it to take out the centipede.

Morlisa took her second drink and played another monster. From there, Taemi continued to draw spells and slaughter what was left of Morlisa's monsters that she had in her hand. By the time she ran out, only the Faerie Fox was left, and the tiger tamer had taken five drinks.

Taemi hesitated. *If it takes eight spells to take him out, I would have to attack him three times, but since it reflects magic back, my Triplet can only take the counter-attack up to two hits.* She'd have to use potions on her monster after each spell. She went to draw cards as she thought up a new strategy and picked up a cure spell—a spell that can be used on her own monsters to heal them.

"Alright, Triplet! Time to take out the fox!" She had three moves left and chose an attack spell, healed her Triplet, and another attack spell. By the end of her turn, the Faerie Fox would be defeated by two more spells, but Taemi would have to wait till her next turn.

"Finally, my turn." Morlisa said as she picked up the dice. The effects of the drinks slowed her movement, but she didn't need time to think about her next move. She used the potion card on the fox, which made Taemi grimace.

I'll need another cure spell before I can attack it again.

"And then I guess I'll use this." It has been so long since Morlisa got her turn, Taemi forgot about the high-level spell and crystal the tamer possessed. "Bye-bye Triplet Chick..."

With a frown, Taemi discarded her powerful monster. *She probably wouldn't have used that if I hadn't made a second attack on my last turn.* She was too greedy.

The game continued, but after five more of her monsters were killed, Taemi felt her moves becoming more sluggish, and had a difficult time remembering what she wanted to do each turn.

The tiger tamer wasn't any better; she was constantly distracted by her own stories and forgot to take her turn entirely. Eventually, they came to a stalemate, as they were both too impaired to form a strategy, much less to keep track of who was winning.

Before long, the tamer was back to playing with Taemi's long, dark hair, wrapping it into complex weaves, while the two of them drank sweet white wine that sparkled across the princess' tongue like a twinkling night sky. It felt strange that the blonde was unusually fascinated over her hair, but perhaps it was because she had blonde coils, while Taemi had dark, midnight hair of silk.

"That sure was quite the show your men displayed, dispatching all those gross, prairie wormy-thingies."

"The prairie weevils?"

"Sure... I thought the sun here was hot, but just watching them felt like I was *standing* on the sun! Oh, and the way the blonde danced with his sword!"

Taemi nodded, *They were quite skilled.* "You seem to be really taken with Mel, seeing how you both can speak in ancient elfish—Ow!" Taemi stopped as she felt a hard tug on her hair.

"Whoops—sorry! Got a little tangled," The girl laughed. "I was hoping to get to know the cute, uptight boy, but he seems to have eyes only for you."

"Kio? N-no, he's just..." Taemi searched for the words. She knew he's just paranoid about her safety, considering their journey this far. It seemed like every turn was a surprise attack. *And it's his duty for his kingdom to keep me safe.* The others—she was sure the Sandarians would receive a generous compensation when they returned, but Kio was different. "He's just... the really cautious type."

"Mmhm, you're so lucky to have someone who cares a lot for you."

The words caught Taemi off guard, but a soft smile formed on her lips as she thought about all the times Kio had come to her rescue. *Yea, it's nice that he's been there for me.* She couldn't imagine if she had to be on this journey alone.

Morlisa leaned in close and whispered in Taemi's ear, "Do you wish that it was *Lloyd* who cared for you like that?"

The princess' breath came to a halt and she felt an icy touch tingle down her spine. *If Lloyd liked me…*

"He *is* really cute… Have you kissed him?" The tamer's face was flushed from the wine and she no longer filtered her words in a coy manner.

Taemi felt her face grow hot and she tried to hide her expression behind the goblet of wine. She didn't know how to respond and avoided eye contact with the tiger tamer.

But the woman stayed close, speaking softly as she slowly placed her hands around Taemi from behind, "Do you want me to show how?"

Taemi jumped ungracefully away, and stumbled back on the bed to face the blonde woman, "W-what do you mean?!"

Morlisa brushed Taemi's hair gently out of the way and smiled, "I can show you how to kiss, so it's not so awkward when *he* kisses *you*." Her index finger lightly tapped the tip of Taemi's nose.

The princess' face beat red, but she was paralyzed.

The tiger tamer put her glass down and caressed Taemi's head in her hands. She watched Morlisa's soft lips speak words she couldn't hear, but they never got close to her. Her head became dizzy and started to ache.

The wagon door opened suddenly and Morlisa pulled away. Taemi shook her head and felt like she woke up from a strange dream. *Was she* really *going to kiss me?*

Mel came up the stairs and nodded with his apology, "Sorry ladies," He turned his attention to Taemi, "but Kio was looking for you."

Morlisa put her arm around Taemi and hugged her close, "He can wait till tomorrow—we're having a girl's night," she replied snarkily, tapping Taemi's goblet with hers.

The man turned to the blonde with his composed, blank expression, "That's a shame for him, but what if I was looking for you...?" Taemi swore that one of his eyebrows rose slightly as he asked his question.

Morlisa forced a swallow and took Taemi's goblet to drink it down before finishing her own cup next.

Taemi blinked and was standing outside of the wagon in the cool air of dusk.

...She just kicked me out? Taemi shook her head. *No, I must have left...*

Taemi walked around to her wagon and saw Lloyd sitting at the campfire warming up a snack on the stick.

"Mind if I join you?"

Her words gave Lloyd a start as if he was lost deep in thought, staring into the fire. "Oh! Lady Equillis," He threw aside the stick and stood up to bow, "How can I serve you?"

"Oh... I was just wondering if I could join you."

"Absolutely! Have a seat. Here, are you hungry?"

It occurred to her that she didn't remember eating all day. *All I remember is waking up and drinking wine...*

It was well into the dark evening now, but she must have eaten at some point. "Um... I guess I could use a snack."

The blonde nodded, "Here, I have some treats from Mr. Shemra for fixing the axle."

Taemi took her seat and glanced around. "Where's Kio and the others?" It was odd that she hadn't seen any of the other circus people other than the tiger tamer since yesterday. *Maybe they don't help with maintenance because they're performers?*

"The others? Oh, well—I think I saw Nazoo around your wagon. He took up his guard post for the night, and *Mel...*" He said the name scornfully as he glared over at the turquoise wagon. "He found himself a warm wagon to nuzzle into..."

"He said Kio was looking for me; have you seen him?"

Lloyd picked at something in his hand and threw it into the fire. "'Doubt it. He probably was just trying to get you out of the way."

Taemi frowned. "You really like Morlisa that much?" Her own heart sank as she said the words out loud. She couldn't blame him though. *She's intoxicatingly gorgeous...*

Lloyd shifted, vexed, "It's not that, Lady Equillis." He stared into the fire. "It's just that, I thought I'd like being a soldier—the money is good for the taking and I enjoy sleeping under the stars, but... Well, we lost Glenn, Zemire and Scarlet so quickly... It made me realize how short our lives are. I'm glad I got to spend all this time around a gorgeous princess..." He turned to face her, and brushed the dark stands of her hair behind her ear, "with beautiful green eyes and a smile that lit up even the Forest of the Damned."

Taemi's heart began to race as he spoke.

Lloyd turned back to the fire, "But I know she's out of my league... and it just feels so lonely. Don't get me wrong," he laughed, "that Morlisa gal sure is pretty, but I was just trying to get my mind off of you." Taemi was lost for words as he turned to her, holding her hands and looking down into her eyes. "After all of this, I'd be honored to serve you... as my queen."

Her face flushed under the night sky, but she hoped her smile blazed brighter than the flame of the fire as she stared into his blue eyes. *I'd be your queen if you be my—*

She watched his eyes close as he leaned in and

kissed her lips softly. She felt her heart flutter following the motions of his lips. It only lasted for a few moments before he pulled away to breathe in deeply, resting his forehead against hers.

He caressed her cheek, brushing another strand of her dark hair behind her other ear. "It's late; we should get you to bed." She nodded quietly, unable to shake the red smile from her face or the pounding rhythm in her chest. Lloyd raised her to her feet and escorted her to the wagon where Nazoo slept silently with a sharpened stick in hand.

Taemi climbed up the steps and paused. She turned around to whisper quietly to the blonde, "Did you... do you want to rest inside?" *What am I thinking?* She quickly shook her head and corrected her words, "I mean, there's room on the floor and enough pillows... and it's warm inside."

The blonde man smiled, but shook his head. "I'm sorry, my lady," he took Taemi's hand and gave it a kiss, "but a wolf like me belongs outside. I'll be fine by the fire." He wished her goodnight, and Taemi went inside to get ready for bed.

Her heart raced, unable to calm her breath as she rested her head down on the soft pillow. She wished she could run to Morlisa and tell her what happened. *But that can wait till tomorrow.* She giggled as she pulled the covers close. She smiled brightly, glancing up at the small window where the moonlight spilled through. *I'll tell her at first light!*

Kio wiped the sweat from his forehead and finally started to feel the cool breeze of the dusk sky. They finished repairing the axle and Vlad began to prep the horses so that they could leave the next morning.

It was hot working in the sun and Kio noticed that the blonde Sandarian became unusually quiet. Earlier he was complaining and cracking jokes, but after a few hours, he became somber and dazed. There were numerous times Kio had to repeat himself or nudge Lloyd for his attention. *It must be the sun.* They were out in the hot sun for days. He was glad that the princess was able to stay in her wagon.

Tilly hadn't come down from the wagon tops since the weevil attack. He waved at Kio earlier during a short break, but then continued to stare off into the distance. He could understand if the elf boy just wanted to stay on the lookout while they were stopped, but Kio watched him from afar, and noticed that he rarely turned his attention to any of the other directions. Every time Kio looked back at him, he was staring towards the mountains.

The Adrienian soldier walked back to the fire pit and saw Nazoo in front of the princess' wagon, carving a piece of wood with his knife. *He's been doing that all day.* They had enough hands to fix the axle between Mel, Lloyd and himself, so Nazoo stood at his guard post the whole day, whittling. Kio wasn't sure if he even ate anything, and it was a surprise that the large man wasn't enjoying his pipe. *Perhaps he lost it and is whittling a new one?* That would make sense, but he still couldn't shake off the eerie feeling that he was also acting strange.

Kio nodded towards Nazoo as he knocked on the princess' door, but there was no answer. He let himself in, hoping he wasn't intruding. The dimly lit wagon was completely empty. *I guess she's in someone else's wagon...* He hoped it wasn't that seductive tiger tamer. *The princess shouldn't be hanging around such a girl—putting soiled illusions through her head.* His face still colored at her comment of the three of them sharing a bed.

He walked out of the wagon to search for the princess. He thought he'd check with JoMila's place first. The other cirqueteers kept to their wagons all day as well, but he at least expected that they'd all come out for dinner.

Not even JoMila has come out to start dinner. He felt his suspicion growing all the more.

Mel was hunched over a dark pile of kindle, preparing the fire for the cold night as Lloyd sat nearby on a log, waiting to roast his meal. He could hear Mel saying something to the blonde and then looked up to nudge the man, and repeated himself.

Kio approached the short man, "Have you seen the princess?"

"Not of late." His response was short, but as expected, now that Kio adjusted to his character and mannerisms. Mel's face illuminated as he finally got the flame to ignite. "I'm sure she's in one of the wagons, though they've all been unusually quiet today." He gazed over the front wagons without expression, but Kio could detect a hint of concern in his flat voice.

So he senses something odd with them too… Kio nodded as he matched the short man's gaze. Master Shemra hadn't been out of his wagon while they were fixing the axle, and the twins' was dark, though it was too early for them to be sleeping. Vlad was still minding the horses and getting them tacked up to leave at daylight.

"Morlisa's and JoMila's lamps are still on, I'm sure she's with one of the two, but it's odd that the twins would be sleeping by now."

It was as if Mel could read Kio's mind, but the Adrienian soldier knew he wore his thoughts on his face. *At least Mel seemed to be acting as normal—Well… at least his usual self.* That alone, though, was disturbing since the man was far from normal.

"Yea, I'll go check on them…" *I have a bad feeling that something happened…*

He had to be sure for the princess' sake.

He went to JoMila's wagon first. *Maybe she'll even cook the dinner as promised.* But when he knocked, there

Mel
Kerstin Park

was no answer. The door was unlocked, but the wagon was completely empty. *Maybe she's drunk in the tamer's wagon...*

He went to check on the next wagon where the two twins stayed. Despite that they didn't have a lamp on inside, he still knocked on the door, but didn't receive an answer. He tried the latch, but their door was locked from the inside.

Kio grimaced. *Are they inside?* He knew no one came up to the red wagon while he worked on it. *If they weren't inside, then where could they have gone?*

He went around and climbed up the side to peer through their window, but without a lamp lit, he couldn't see anything.

I have to be sure though... Kio winced as he smashed the windowpane in with the hilt of his sword. After the crash, he hoisted himself through. He felt around the hard surfaces and found a lamp. Once he lit the small flame, he looked up and nearly dropped the lamp at the sight of a face.

"Ah, jeez—you frightened me for a moment... sorry about the window." There was no answer, and he shined the light up to illuminate the twin's faces. "Lenra? ...Luna."

They both sat up at the table as if having a nice conversation together, but their eyes were as lifeless as dolls. Kio felt for a pulse and their skin was still warm to the touch. They both were breathing but their eyes didn't blink and their bodies didn't move a muscle.

They're like... like puppets! Kio backed away and placed the lamp down, *I have to warn the others—there's something not right about this place!* It made sense to him now, everyone was slowly turning into lifeless dolls as the hours went by.

A glimpse of the princess caught his attention outside the window as he turned to leave, but a second look halted his steps with his blood boiling and rushing through his veins. The beautiful lips of his princess touched those of the blonde Sandarian soldier and it nearly made him sick. Their kiss lasted for an eternity to Kio, but all he could do was watch and wait till his strength drained from his legs.

The blonde soldier pulled away, but he still touched her. Kio's fist tightened in pure rage, and yet—he couldn't bring himself to do anything about it.

She kissed him back... He managed to take a step back and force himself to look away. His eyes burned. His chest ached. He reached out to the door of the wagon and unlatched the knob.

A large shadow stood in the doorway. "Vlad, the-the twins, they're—" He felt a harsh blow to his abdomen and his vision filled with darkness as his body thumped to the ground.

The blonde tiger tamer laid awake next to the man who exhausted himself on her. His performance was nothing like she was accustomed to. He held her tenderly with deep kisses. His movements were both gentle and stern. She liked the way he intertwined her fingers with his, and how his lips made her head feel like a shaken bottle of sparkling wine. Even with contortion, she could never achieve the fluid passion from her puppets.

She gently stroked his dark, damp hair as he slept. She knew she'd have to twist his brain like the others to complete her assignment.

The princess would have been under my full control tonight if his cute, handsome face didn't just waltz in and...

She blushed replaying the event that happened earlier.

This was the second time that she fell victim to his hypnotic face, one that seemed too familiar to her, yet she knew she'd never seen him before. She was star-struck every time he came near, and he acted like she'd belonged to him for years.

Even those eyes of his were filled with years of a past she felt she once knew. She could see herself as a child, running through lush, grassy plains and this boy caught up to her and pinned her down.

"Now you have to do whatever I say!" He laughed as she stared into the deep pool of his eyes anticipating his request. *"You have to do ten push-ups and run around the fountain three times!"*

Morlisa smiled to herself. *If only he knew all I wanted was a kiss*, but when it was her turn, she was never able to catch him. She shook her head. *Impossible...* She had no recollections of her childhood, but she had already lived twice as long as a normal human's life span. It was certain that she never met this man as a girl in *his* lifetime.

You're getting too close... The pretty blonde would have been easier to deal with. Even without contortion, she'd have that tall blonde on a leash and could send him away on a whim. *He* was simple.

Maybe this was what they called love at first sight *...or maybe he's using contortion on* me? She smirked at her own joke. *No...* She knew better than to think such a ridiculous thought. *This is merely the consequence of my own unsatisfied lust.*

The Sandarian soldiers likely suffered from the same overwhelming desire for affection. Even the tall blonde was intrigued by her offer the other night with only a hint of her control. It was no wonder their actions would come with so much compassion.

The fact that I didn't have to control him is an added bonus. She smiled, wondering what the man next to her thought about the situation. She brushed his dark, damp hair and peered into his mind.

From all her experience with the mind-altering spell, this man's head wasn't anything she'd come across before.

For being only a little over three decades old, his memory archive was as large as someone who lived to be eighty!

Hmm, not even the princess' mind was this complex... She didn't recall seeing that many threads back in Sandar. *In fact, I'm sure that most of his memories were broken fragments—nothing out of the ordinary before—but now...*

She wondered what he had hidden beneath...

"Narssy..."

Reiji-Arashi's voice broke through the night silence.

Damn. She looked around the dark room to see where he could be spying on her from. She assumed he was probably watching her through one of the mirrors with his fancy crystal. She got up and was able to see a faint reflection of his face in the oval mirror above the washbowl.

"Oh, Nars," Arashi's eyes glazed over her bare body, "you look so dazzling with those curls of yours..." He commented as she approached the mirror, "But what's taking you so long?" He had a hint of vexation in his voice.

She glared at him. "The princess' mind is weak enough to where I can use contortion on her, but it's taking more time. It's hard to pry her away long enough from that soldier boy of hers, but I'm getting closer."

"...Or perhaps," the sorcerer scowled, "you're too distracted by your own puppets."

Nars' heart skipped a beat. *What does he know?* "You've been spying on me?" She crossed her arms and tried to give him an icy glare, but she could feel her face begin to flush from embarrassment.

Arashi rested his head on his fist, swirling his wine. "I don't care what you do with your toys on your own time," he stated placidly as he peered down into his goblet, still swirling the contents, "but I don't have the patience to wait." She could detect his frustration as she watched him sip his cup. "I just wanted to make sure that you're staying... focused."

He doesn't even seem jealous. Nars pouted her lips, "It's your own damn fault. How can a girl stay focused when you've sent her to bed prematurely?" She pressed herself closer to the mirror and circled her finger. "Look, I need more time to get full control. When I do, she'll be putty in your hands."

The sorcerer still wore the glare on his face as he sipped his glass, "Like the way you are in someone else's hands?"

His stark words clenched her heart tightly. Her lips curled involuntarily into a smile... *Maybe he* is *jealous.*

"Don't disappoint me, Nars." His voice was flat. "Bring me the girl tomorrow." His reflection faded from the mirror, and Nars was left looking at herself.

She peered back over to the bed reluctantly and sighed with dismay, "...Yes, my lord."

Kio woke up in the damp field of morning dew to the sound of birds and grasshoppers stirring early in the morning. The sky was dark blue with a light glow of gold as the sun slowly rose over the horizon. Kio winced at the pain in his stomach as he pushed himself up, wondering how he ended up passed out in the field.

He lay near the smoldering embers of the fire, trying to retrace his steps. *Mel built the fire and Lloyd...* The name alone made it difficult to breathe as his thoughts replayed last night's vision without consent.

Did I... did I drink? He wouldn't have put himself past it, but he couldn't taste liquor on his lips.

He heard Taemi's wagon creek open and glanced over to see her greeting Lloyd with a smile. The very sight of her pained him as he shied away.

But... there was something I had to tell her...

His mind flickered to the lifeless looks of the

twins. He glanced at their wagon and Lenra and Luna were sitting outside quietly enjoying their morning drinks and stretching their limbs.

The boy put his hand up against his head and stared down at the soil. *Was it just a dream…?*

"Hey there, gorgeous!" He heard the voice of the tiger tamer approach, but hoped she'd leave him alone if he ignored her. "What's the matter? Your beautiful face looks so glum."

She didn't.

Morlisa invited herself to sit next to him with her morning cheer and fluttery temptation. She glanced over in the direction of Taemi and Lloyd, analyzing their close behavior, "Oh, is that what's bothering you?" She repositioned herself to be in Kio's line of sight and smiled up at him. "You know… I have something that can fix that."

The woman's presence alone felt like she was prying into places she didn't belong. She was like a siren sending off a piercing frequency through his head.

Her seductive expression slipped from her face, "… How… how come it's not working?" She pushed his head up and stared into his eyes. He watched her stormy blue eyes study every inch of his conscience. "That's odd… it usually would be working by now…"

Prying in places…

She blinked, noticing Kio's blade drawn below her chin and her face fell to complete bewilderment.

The Adrienian soldier glared down at her as he spoke. "Something weird is going on around here," he lifted the sharp edge closer to her throat, "and I have a feeling that you're behind *all* of it."

Morlisa's pink lips curled into a smile that made Kio's palms sweat. She closed her eyes and laughed. "Alright, fine. Forget this charade anyways."

The moment she flashed open her crystal blue

eyes, Kio was flung hard into Taemi's wagon by an invisible, powerful force. He heard the princess scream his name as the impact knocked the air out of his chest.

CHAPTER 14

Unraveled Illusions

The tiger tamer's illusion dissolved and the colorful caravan faded away as if they were never there. The appearance of the young Morlisa transformed into a tall, slender woman, and Taemi found herself standing in the vast, empty plains. Even the cirqueteers disappeared, and it was only her, Kio, the Sandar soldiers, and this strange woman.

The woman's clothes shifted to the familiar magenta outfit of baggy, satin trousers that hung at her hips and tucked into her magenta knee-high boots with raised heels. Her armored top only covered her chest, exposing her deep collarbones and toned midriff. She had armored cuffs that covered her forearms where drapes of satin hung down from the wrist end and clasped up at the back of her neck.

She pulled out a thin rod from within her right cuff and twisted her golden curls up—coiling her hair up and stabbing it into place—to expose her cool face of brilliant blue eyes and curved, pastel lips.

"You're… you're that witch!" Without hesitation, Kio raised himself off the ground and charged at the woman with sword in hand. Keeping her gaze directed at Taemi, a blade appeared in her hand and she disarmed Kio effortlessly with two swings of her sword. She sent him back down with a kick while wearing a soft smile on her face.

"Rude... I prefer being called sorceress."

A loud roar sent Taemi's heart racing. She muffled her scream as she turned to see the large white and black striped feline beasts appear and circle around her.

"My, my, it must be nice being a *princess*; look at all these gorgeous men." Taemi watched the woman prowl around Tilly, Lloyd, and Mel who stood like statues.

"What... what did you do to them? Why aren't they moving?"

"These are my puppets. All your Sandar soldiers were under my control as soon as you left the forest. I used a little contortion on them at the docks, but now it's just you and me."

Contortion...?

The woman paused in front of Mel, "This is the one, here." She stroked his cheek, but hers colored. "He pulled me out of that *blasted* damned forest." She gave him a kiss and he vanished. She turned to Taemi with a smile. "He's my favorite, so I'll let him go. Contortion takes a toll on the memory, so don't expect him to remember you if you see him again."

Kio slowly pushed himself up with a mumble. "... Princess."

The sorceress grimaced and without a word, Lloyd and Tilly grabbed Kio's arms.

"Tilly! Lloyd—what are you doing?!"

They lifted him up to his feet while Nazoo hoisted a punch towards his gut. The Adrienian soldier's body went limp with a grunt and the Sandarians tossed him back down onto the grass.

"Kio!!"

The woman's smile returned. "Now... it's just you

and me, *Princess.* Would you like to accompany me to see the great grand sorcerer, Reiji-Arashi? I know Kio is ecstatic to meet him." She glanced back at his unconscious body. "I hear he's been looking for him for quite some time now," she smirked.

Taemi stood speechless. *Her master is another sorcerer? How am I supposed to defeat two sorcerers?*

The woman studied the girl's shocked reaction and continued, "Alright," she shrugged, "I'll make an offer. You come with me and do whatever my master asks, and I'll let you keep the blonde." She cupped Lloyd's chin in her hand, "and *he* will do *anything* that you ask of him. Deal?"

Be together with Lloyd… The idea crossed her mind as she stared up at his beautiful, lifeless face. She thought back on the kiss they shared. *All I have to do is go with her and Lloyd and I can be together…?*

"Come with… and I'll be yours forever…" Lloyd's words were a soft whisper inside her head as she imagined him extending out his hand towards her. *"I promise to always catch you if you fall."*

"We can travel the world together." A faint illusion of Morlisa's round face and blonde curls suddenly appeared by Taemi's side. The dazzling tamer's soft hands stoked her cheek with a bright smile. *"It'll be the adventure you've always wanted… Just come with me…"*

The sorceress waited for Taemi to answer, but she only received silence. "Don't let the tigers intimidate your decision." She clapped, "*Ahy-Ah*," and the tigers walked towards the sorcerer to sit by her side. She petted them both on their heads with genuine love.

The brief illusions faded from Taemi's head as she looked up at Lloyd. *N-no… He'd tell me not to go, wouldn't he?*

"Don't do it, Princess!"

Taemi gasped and peered over at Kio's unconscious body lying on the grass.

His voice rang the loudest in her head. *"You must get to Laquar no matter what."*

The princess frowned. *It's no wonder he didn't want me to get close to Morlisa...*

If he were conscious right now, he'd smile at me with those brown eyes, ensuring that he'd be fine... He'd tell me not to go.

"You must get to Laquar no matter what!"

Yes... Taemi clenched her fists. *No matter what!* The princess shook her head and fell to her knees with a yell, "No. I'm not going *anywhere* with you!"

The pink smile slipped from the woman's face and she sighed. "Typical. Even after I orchestrated your first kiss with the man you desire, I'm still seen as a threat..."

...What? Taemi stared at the blonde soldier, still as a statue, *she was controlling Lloyd even then?* Her heart shattered by the very thought... *Does that mean his feelings he confessed... it was all just a part of her act?*

The sorceress shrugged. "Very well, I don't have the energy to force you to come, so I'll just take the boy and be on my way. But, if you do change your mind," She pointed to the Sandarian soldiers, "well, just let one of them know. *Ta-ta.*" With that, the woman, tigers, and Kio *vanished* away—just like Mel did earlier.

Tilly, Lloyd and Nazoo were seated, but stood still like stone statues. Taemi got to her feet and ran to the pretty blonde, "Lloyd! Wake up, Lloyd!" *The woman said she used* contortion *on them?* Taemi held Lloyd's head in her hands and closed her eyes to examine him with the stone. As she peered into his brain, she saw illuminated threads that were his thoughts, memories and feelings, but they were all entangled into an enormous cluster of knots.

She didn't know where to begin to untangle it enough for him to snap out of the stillness, but she trusted her pendant and drew on the energy, guiding it through to him. The illuminated cluster glowed brighter as it absorbed the energy and then all the threads *snapped*. In an instant, the light vanished and instead of the cluster of threads, it was an empty, black void.

Confused, Taemi opened her eyes to Lloyd's lifeless stare, "Lloyd?"

Blood slowly streamed down from his nose. Taemi pulled away, and his body fell forward to the ground. She gathered him up into her arms, but there was no pulse or breath from his lungs. "Wha-what kind of magic *is* this?"

"Unless you want to kill the rest of your comrades," she heard Tilly's voice answer in monotone, "I would advise leaving them alone. I doubt an infant like yourself will be able to untangle the strings even if you practiced for weeks."

He's... He's dead. Taemi stared down at her own hands feeling both guilty and helpless. *I... I killed him...* A chilly breeze picked up and blew over the plains.

"And you came back with*out* the girl?" Reiji-Arashi was agitated. His body stiffened when the sorceress returned to their fortress empty-handed again.

Nars shrugged dismissively, "I invited her, but she didn't want to come, so I like to think I brought you something better downstairs." Nars smiled and teleshifted to the basement. Arashi followed moments later.

She had the princess' young soldier chained to the wall near the staircase in simple metal shackles around his wrist. The boy was awake, but didn't look up upon their arrival.

"What am I looking at here, Nars?" Arashi stated impatiently.

She smiled, "You can't tell, Reiji? Contortion doesn't work on him, and all the times that he *conveniently* arrived to save the princess, you sure you can't tell what he is?"

The silver-haired man snarled, "I don't have time for your games, Nars. Where is the girl I asked for?!"

"*Reiji... Arashi...*" The boy growled and looked up at both of them with daggers in his eyes like a rabid wolf.

The sorcerer looked down at him in distaste.

"You're the bastard that's been cowering behind those shadow wolves? ...I'm ...I'm going to kill you... Arashi you bastard—you killed my family!"

Arashi's lips curled, "Nars, I don't have time for this!"

"You're serious? He's a born sorcerer—just like us. We could train—"

"Liar!" The prisoner cut her off, "I could never be one of you monsters! Your demonic magic killed my family! I'll never be one of you!"

"So what if I did." The platinum man's cool response silenced Kio. The blood drained from the boy's face as he looked up at the sorcerer. Though enraged, he was stricken with fear. "If your family is dead, it's their fault for being in my way." Irritated, Arashi waved his hand. "Nars... get rid of him and meet me in my chambers." The bitter man teleshifted out of the dungeon.

He does that way too much. Nars grimaced. *Would it kill the man to discuss his feelings instead of storming out like a child?*

"Well, that was a disappointment," Nars stated solemnly. "I had this whole thing where I convince that you killed your own family in some bizarre fire explosion," she twirled her hand in a circle to indicate the chaos, "and then you would cry, we'd laugh, and once you realize you belong to us, you'd go out and get that princess for me."

"I'd never admit to being a monster like you." Kio's response was quiet as he glared up at her.

"Oh, but you are." She knelt in front of him and held his chin to keep his gaze to her eye level, "Maybe you didn't kill your own family—I don't know," she shrugged, "but I'll find a way to break you down and unleash that power you so deny that's burning within you." The prisoner pulled his face from her touch and turned away. With a sigh, the woman raised back to her feet.

"Guess I'll see you later." She peered down to the boy and smiled. "Those are normal chains that hold you. If you embrace that you're a sorcerer, you can focus on using your power to escape and help that little princess of yours." She instigated. Reiji doesn't believe her about his power, so it would be amusing if he *did* escape. "But if you want to believe you're just an average human, then you can stay locked up for as long as you wish… I'll be patient."

Nars left the dungeon and made her way up to Reiji's chamber. The sorcerer had wards around his room to keep mage assassins from teleshifting in while he slept, and he didn't trust Nars enough to be an exception.

Once she reached the doorway, she turned the knob and entered his room. "Reiji, my lord?" The room was quiet, and his bed and desk were empty. Nars walked in slowly, light on her feet, feeling like a small girl waiting to be disciplined.

"Over here, Nars." She turned around to see Arashi standing near the doorway, leaning against the wall with two glasses of wine in his hands. "Here, have a drink."

She eyed him up and down, wondering if he was still mad or not. But she couldn't tell from his calm, emotionless expression as he handed her a glass. She accepted it and swirled the contents around, releasing a sweet, spiced aroma with a hint of a citrus berry.

Strawberry, likely She guessed. Arashi watched her take a sip of the wine—*It IS strawberry*—and looked at the glass in astonishment. "It has a nice touch to it."

The platinum-haired sorcerer smiled, "Good, drink up." He walked around her to gaze into the fireplace and spoke softly, "Nars... Why did you bring me the boy instead of the girl as I asked?"

Yep, right on cue. She sighed—*he is still upset.* "I wasn't able to teleshift the girl—there's a protection spell on her." *Probably the same spell that made her invisible from the crystal mirrors,* She figured. "—So I took the boy instead."

He turned back to look at Nars, "And you think she'll just waltz in to save the boy all by herself?"

"Trust me," she drank down half her glass, "she'll walk right through the front door to get him back." She set up wards in the basement to block others from teleshifting in and out, so that if either the boy or girl learned that trick, they'd still have to walk in and out the main entrance. "And she'll be yours... for the taking."

Suddenly, Nars felt dizzy. "Oh... what proof is this, a port?"

Arashi tilted the cup to help her drink the last drops, "It's good isn't it?" He then took her glass and placed it on the side table next to his. "So you're telling me..." Nars tried hard to pay attention to his words, but they faded out to dribble. Her breath was restricted and she panicked to breathe.

She reached out, touching Arashi's hand on her throat and her feet dangled in the air. He kept squeezing, "...Wait ...Reiji ...Stop." She tried to teleshift out of his hands, but hit his wards that kept her in place. She thrashed, kicking her legs and hitting his arms to pull free.

Her head began to ache—starting with the same high-pitch frequency that pierced her ears when she stepped on that weird, stone disc in the Forest of the Damned. For a moment she lost all sense of feeling other than the growing pain in her head and ringing in her ears.

She dropped to the floor with a thud. She clenched her throat, gasping for breath.

It took her a moment to fully regain consciousness while Reiji was screaming in the distance, "My Hand! You Monster! What have you done with my hand!? You blasted—" His voice cut off as he stumbled into his crystals. There was a loud crash of glass shattering across the floor.

As the pain in her head resided, Nars slowly lifted herself up. She was still dizzy from the wine. *He must have laced it with something... so I couldn't use magic.* Yet, she *did* something. She looked up and saw Arashi lying on the floor, unconscious from the loss of blood that spilled from where his hand and part of his arm were.

She forced herself up and crawled over to him. His arm looked as if it was blown off by a cannon. She tried casting a cure spell on his wound, but the drug still kept her nauseous and unable to focus. She found a wrap and tied it around his arm to slow the bleeding, and placed the iron poker into the fireplace to sear the wound.

While waiting for the metal to heat up, she peered around, hoping she could reattach his arm with reverse magic, but there wasn't anything in the shape of a hand— just piles of unrecognizable flesh and shards of bone shattered around like the broken glass across the floor. *Even if I* could *collect all the pieces, no amount of healing would fix* this. *What... What did I even do?*

Nars stared down at her hands. In all her years, she's never cast a spell like this.

CHAPTER 15

Journey to the Mountains

The warmth of the fire was comforting on the cold night where the stars twinkled overhead in the vast opening of the plains. The peaceful night was quiet and cozy as Taemi stared into the flames, smiling and holding a hot cup of cocoa.

"It's a beautiful night, isn't it?"

Taemi thought she was alone, but when she glanced over, her heart leapt at the sight of him—*Lloyd!* He sat next to her with a bright smile on his face. He brushed his blonde hair away from his gorgeous blue eyes that twinkled the reflection of a million diamond lights.

It was only a dream that he died, but he's really here! Yes, that's right. I was able to fix his contortion and he's traveling with me to the rest of the mountains.

"Yes, it is... beautiful." She said the words while staring at him, but she wasn't referring to the night.

Looking at his face with bliss in her soul, she didn't notice the fire slowly burning out. She shivered at the piercing chill that came suddenly, and looked down towards the black hole where the flame had been. The glowing, red embers slowly faded to darkness. Even the stars that illuminated the sky began to drift further into the shadows.

"Lloyd, it's getting..." She looked up at the blonde

man—his gorgeous features still in focus even without the light of the flame. She lost her words looking at him, and the panic eased into comfort.

"It's all right, my love." He smiled.

My... my love. Her heart swooned.

But it only lasted for a moment as his face grew pale. His blue eyes became a glossy grey. The muscles around his eye sockets sunk in, becoming dark, empty pools.

Taemi stepped back, watching his face decay and melt towards the ground.

What... what's happening?

The hard, uneven ground shook beneath, and she peered down at the smooth, entwined pattern circle that she'd seen in the Forest of the Damned. The roots of the trees peeled back, unraveling the intricate marble seal, and opening the depths of the world.

"Taemi-che."

Taemi ran off the seal as it all crumbled away into a giant hole. She heard a low thunder of a creature dwelling within. Taemi stared at the opening, frozen, and her heart pounded in fear. The head of a large beast rose up from the crater with curled horns and a short snout. Its eyes were massive pools of spiraling lava. He crawled out with enormous paws—bigger than a carriage—and his long, black claws clenched the earth, rippling up the dirt and stones with ease. The beast bellowed a roar, forcing Taemi off her feet and hitting the ground with a bounce.

"Taemi-che... come to me!"

She gawked up at the demonic devil as it roared her name, wishing for Kio to be by her side more than ever before. *He... he would tell me to run.* But as simple as the thought was, she couldn't.

"The moon can't shed darkness on its own; it shines so bright because of the flaming light of the blazing sun..." Leviathan's deep voice echoed through her head. *"You can't*

defeat the behemoth on your own. You must find the Sun before he awakens..."

Taemi sprang awake from her sleep, panting and covered in cold sweat. Her heart still raced. The fire she built was long dead. She pulled Lloyd's cloak close to block the freezing wind of the night. She lay awake until the morning and rose when she saw the glow of the sun.

It took two days before Taemi reached the incline slope of the mountain. She traveled with Tilly's crossbow for hunting and Nazoo's knife. Lloyd's sword was too heavy to have been of any use to her, but she wore his cloak while the other two she bundled up, and used as additional warmth at night. She felt bad for taking them. No one would know that the men were Sandarians, *and Lloyd... he should be buried with it.*

She found a small path, likely traveled by the animals, and followed it up the mountain through the brush. It was a steep hike, but the path winded around trees and cliffs. As she continued to climb, the dirt path became the smooth stone of the mountains' surface. Slabs of rock were strategically cut to function as small steps. They were polished down with the obvious appearance that they've been traveled on frequently.

I guess this must be the way to the city? She wondered. *Where else could the path lead, but to the Laquar?* The path stayed on the side of the mountain where she could see her distance when there was a clearing. As she hiked, the clearing became steeper with short vegetation and fewer trees. She hugged against the ledge of straight slab rock that dripped with cool, refreshing water.

She took many breaks as she climbed, feeling more and more exhausted each time she stopped to rest. The air gradually cooled, and the gust of wind became stronger.

The sun reached its point where it cast an orange glow over the plains while sinking further into the horizon.

She rested on a boulder and sighed up at the sky. *Should I stop and make a fire for the night?* She frowned, looking at the narrow path of the mountain. *No, not yet. I have to keep going... get there as fast as I can.*

A large, dark shadow drifted over her, and she gasped, hiding close to the side. She looked up, but there wasn't a cloud in the sky.

...But it was too large to be just an ordinary *bird.* She loaded an arrow in the crossbow and hoped it wasn't a dragon. *Don't be silly... dragons don't exist...*

The shadow drifted across the mountain again, but as she scanned the sky, she didn't see anything above her.

Something crashed into the path ahead, and Taemi lost her footing as the mountain rumbled. She slid downhill to avoid the falling rocks that broke loose from the tremor. The ground trembled as the creature moved.

She held up the bow to aim, ready to take the shot as soon as the creature rounded the side and appeared into view. But she lost confidence as soon as it came into sight.

Its smooth, white head rounded the corner with a skull of a deer that had been cleaned and mounted. Two long black antlers twisted up from the sides. A red, spiked mane ran down the creature's long neck and down the spine of its bird-like body. It crawled around the corner with its black, webbed, wings folded, gripping the ground with long talons. Its short hind legs helped it to keep balance as its thin tail whipped around.

The winged beast sniffed the air and let out a roar, exposing rows of its sharp, white teeth and forked tongue. It locked its gaze on her with its human-like eyes, and the girl's hands began to shake.

The arrow shot off, but shattered into pieces as it hit the creature's deer-like skull. *Oh no...*

The creature roared and jumped into the air as Taemi turned to run down the hill. She loaded another bow and turned to shoot, but the creature knocked her down. She heard a snap, and the crossbow fell out of her hands as she slid across the smooth stone. She raised her head only in time to see the beast land on her only weapon and shatter it into pieces. The beast was as large as Nazoo or Vlad up close.

And its creepy face was just as ugly! Taemi rolled to her side, avoiding the creature's monstrous jaw. She sprung to her feet, grabbing and throwing loose rocks at the creature.

It expanded its large wings and blew a gust of wind that blocked her vision. The beast tackled her down. Taemi thrashed under her cloak while the creature clawed at her legs and thighs.

Screaming from the pain, she grabbed for her pendant. The energy gathered within her in an instant and shot out like a cannon—exploding in a blinding light. The creature screeched and flew off into the sky. Taemi's muscles trembled at the release of adrenaline running through her veins.

The creature didn't let up as it circled the sky, waiting for its moment to attack again.

It wouldn't have another chance... Taemi grinded her teeth and forced herself up. She could feel the energy dance in her palms. *Bow... I need a bow.* She imagined the form in her head, and it began to gather light in the shape of a recurve, similar to Tilly's, but longer. She began the stance—the proper form that the elf-boy taught—and the energy manifested into a long, slender shape, ready to be slingshotted out by her other arm. The light was blinding, but her eyes grew used to the hot, white flame. Her focus was the winged creature.

The creature roared overhead, and Taemi closed

her eyes, listening for its flapping wings. *Be still, and it will come to you...* She focused her aim based on the sound. She heard it circle again, lowering its elevation. It soared in a tighter formation. *Closer... from downwind...*

Her eyes shot open and released the arrow; the creature was halted in mid-air—only paces from in front of her as the arrow slashed through its body and set it aflame with the white, burning energy. Its body tumbled down the mountain screaming until it dissolved into ash.

The princess released the energy as she watched the creature burn to nothing. The bow vanished along with the power that filled her, leaving her drained to exhaustion and the throbbing pain of her wounds. *Oh... I forgot.* Dizzy, she stumbled back to the wall and sat.

The day quickly turned into dusk, getting darker by the moment. Taemi rested and examined her burning legs. Her clothes were torn, covered in blood from the gouging marks on her legs and thighs. Less-deep ones covered her arms, but hurt just as much. She pulled out one of the extra cloaks, and sliced the fabric into straps to wrap her legs. She wrapped the worst ones first, and then moved onto her arms.

She didn't want to think about how she was going to climb the mountain the next day. She didn't want to think about the additional creatures she'd run into. She didn't even want to think about what she would do if the blood never stopped.

I made it this far. So close. She held on to her pendant, holding it for comfort and protection. She couldn't stop the tears from streaming down her face from the pain, the cold, and the loneliness.

The stars slowly populated the dark sky and the moon shined, despite it being so cold. Her tired eyes slid down as her thoughts began to drift, *I'll never make it...*

"Don't give up, Moon Child..." The wind echoed,

carrying a voice of a little girl. *"You're not alone..."*

Taemi fell asleep against the mountainside.

The bright sun rose over the horizon and its blinding rays made difficult for it the princess to continue her sleep. Her arms tingled with a strange numbness as she stirred to drink from her water bag. The water from the mountain was cool and it eased her aches as she drank.

She glanced down at her stained bandages, but the sound of her empty stomach reminded her that she didn't eat most of the day before. *I have to eat first...*

She adjusted her seat and reached for her travel sack. A sharp sting pierced her skin and she dropped the bag to clench her hand. She inspected the plant nearby; underneath the leaves was a bustle of sharp thorns, and dark, purple berries. She covered her hand with her cloak and picked all the ripe ones, creating a small pile that would suffice.

She ate half the portion and saved rest for later. When she grabbed for her pack, a cloth item fell out. It was a large, unfamiliar leaf, enfolded around a small portion of cheese and smoked meat.

Where did I get this from? She took a small bite of each. The cheese had a sharp, smoky taste, but was otherwise smooth and flavorful. The meat was also smoked, but with a different taste of wood, and was heavily seasoned with garlic and spices. They were both rich and fresh.

After her breakfast, she eased herself up and was surprised that the pain in her legs had subsided enough to walk. They felt sore, but no more than from her constant travel uphill. Along the path, she found a sturdy stick to help support her. The mountain was lively with songbirds and the rustling of chipmunks and squirrels. The sky was a brilliant blue with the occasional large mass of cloud covering the sun and opening again—adding colorful contrast to the red bushes, pink flowers, and bright greens of the short vegetation with long, narrow leaves. The sound of rushing water filled her ears for paces as she scanned the path for more berries.

She was also alert this time, constantly peering up to the sky to see if there were more bird-like monsters. She intended to get them first before they even landed near her.

She rounded the next turn where she found the crashing water that cut across the mountain path with channels of a small stream. The water poured down from the peak through a small crevice, and pooled in a shallow pond before spilling over the side.

The princess stopped, placing her things down to undo her cloak and remove her boots. She stepped into the shallow pool and gasped from the freezing chill of the water. She refilled her bag first, and then removed her cloth bandages to rinse the dried blood from her arms. She was gentle at first, but couldn't see where her cuts were.

She scrubbed at her arms, but felt no ripped flesh, nor marks to indicate that the beast had ever even touched her skin. She removed the bandages from her thighs and legs where the cuts were deeper, but even there, her skin was untouched. She traced the areas where there was still a phantom memory of the pain. If it weren't for her bloodstained clothes, she'd never believe she was attacked the night before.

Did I... did I heal myself in my sleep? She was certain she didn't do anything but hold her pendant.

The loss of feeling in her toes brought her back to reality and she slowly got out of the pool to dry off and redress. After she re-tied her boots, she continued up the mountain. She took a few breaks on her way, but the sun was already setting into the shadows once again.

The path stopped at a ledge near the top where it opened to a vast view of the mountain scenery. Taemi awed at the gorgeous sight of the Cloymein Plains, and beyond that was the black shadow of the Forest of the Damned. The ledge was the end of the path, dropping down into a cliff of a hundred paces in all directions except for the small slab of earth that aided her climb up.

The girl leaned up against the slab, staring out at the end. Her tired legs gave out and she slid down to her seat. *This... this can't be it. Had I taken the wrong path? Was there another way through the mountain range?* Four days had already gone by, but if she had to turn back, *how much longer before it would be too late for the others?*

And Kio... The sorceress captured him easily because of her—her weakness for getting close to Morlisa even though Kio suspected something.

It's all my fault... I should have stayed in my wagon.

But the sorceress... she was so strong; would it really have made a difference? She had all the Sandarians under her command from the beginning. *All of them except Kio...* He was the one she should have trusted.

Her guilt pooled in her eyes and streamed down her cheek. *I can't do it anymore... it's too hard. It's too much...* As she cried, the overlook was nothing more than a dark shadow under the night's speckled light.

Susia was right... "Be careful for what you ask for." I want to be back home... I want everything to be normal again—I never wanted anyone to die because of me... because of me and my stupid *dream of an adventure!*

She looked up towards the sky. "How..." she whispered to the stars, "How am I ever going to protect Adrienan, if I, Taemi Lor Equillis, can't even protect those around me?"

She waited for the stars to reply as they had done before, but the night was silent. Her heart sank and she decided it was time to rest for the night and rethink her steps the next morning. She shifted in her seat and rested her head back against the stone.

Instead of being supported by the hard surface she was laying on moments before, her body fell back across the polished stone and the night sky faded from her vision as she continued to fall down the mountainside into darkness.

There was plenty of time in the dark dungeon for Kio to work on his breathing skills and to ponder his situation. He'd heard the whispers of a sorcerer in Narpal who controlled wolves on his travels. He discovered his name and trained under the best swordsmaster to learn how to fight. Now he sat in the basement beneath the bastard that caused him such agony even before this journey.

His mind drifted away from time to time—slipping off into a daydream about the past.

It was two years ago since he arrived in the grand city of Adrienan. As he passed through the gate, he went to the first inn he saw. The bar was small and quiet with only a few travelers sharing stories among themselves over pints. Two men who sat in the corner were at least on their second pint as the innkeeper had yet to take the empty cups. At the bar sat an older gentleman with white streaks in his dark hair and leathery skin, but still very much in shape by the look of his build. He wore a sword on his belt.

Kio took a seat at the bar near the men in the corner to overhear the news they shared with each other. Men spoke freely in empty inns and Kio learned that these were the places to seek out what information he needed.

"So, how's been Narpal? Few men speak of good news, but I hear the wolves have disappeared."

The other man laughed, "Haha, yea. Those were a pain. The council removed Reiji-Arashi from the king's advisor some years back. Say he wasn't right in the head and wanted to start wars with other nations." He had the soft accent of Narpal.

The other man shook his head, "I still can't imagine why any king would even make a sorcerer his advisor in the first place. I know they got them mages in the north doing whatever they wish, but I'd never trust a man that can talk to animals—much less control those beasts."

"During the times, it made sense—I suppose." The man took a long drink from his cup. "But Arashi and his shadow wolves been long gone for years now. Some say he went north, but I wouldn't put it past that he'd be back with an army someday. Trades for their oranges..."

"Shadow wolves..." Kio whispered to himself. The vision of his family flickered across his mind. His blood boiled at the large shapes of the dark wolves with red eyes.

Kio rose from his seat so fast that the stool fell to the wooden floor. He threw down his pint and grabbed the man from Narpal at his collar. "You said a sorcerer is behind those shadow wolves?!"

"Calm down kid!" He heard from the man behind him, but didn't obey as his blood raged.

"Where can I find him?! Tell me!"

"That's enough." A stern grip touched Kio's shoulder. "Quit disturbing the peace, kid." The old man tugged lightly at Kio's shoulder, but he was too close to his answers to listen.

Kio released the Narpalian and grabbed the old man's wrist—ready to charge—but the older gentleman was just as quick on his feet and used the Nishe kid's momentum to throw him across the room.

Kio tumbled into a table, but pushed himself to his feet when he slid across the wood floor. He aligned his footing and sprung back at the man before he could pull out his sword. Kio's first swing was inches from hitting the man's face until he was grabbed by the wrist, spun around, and thrown back at the same table he had hit before. But he didn't let that despair him. He pushed himself back up and continued to throw punches at the old man who either dodged them or slapped them away. The man defended each of Kio's attacks, waiting out the kid's temper.

Kio flared his teeth as the man deflected each of his hits. He eased back to focus for an opening. He found his path, took a deep breath and got an upper-cut punch to the man's hard jaw.

But just as quick as he got him, the man got him back hard in the face. Kio stumbled back, tripping on the table and fell to the ground. He was hoisted up and thrown out of the inn. The brick pavement was cold as he hit the ground.

Kio sat on the curb. His right eye began to swell and his ribs throbbed each time he spat up blood.

He heard footsteps from behind, and he looked up at the old man who handed him a cold cloth, "Here, this is for your eye."

Kio accepted it to relieve the pain.

The man took a seat next to him and continued. "You have a lot of anger kid, but you threw in some good punches back there. We could use a spitfire like you on the royal guard. The princess is a bit of a troublemaker herself."

"The princess?" He didn't know much about the royals of Adrienan.

"Tell you what, you join the royal guard and train beneath me—control that temper of yours—and I'll look into this Arashi guy for you. Is there a reason why you're looking for a sorcerer? They're not the folks that I'd like to get involved with."

Kio never told Master Gallanver any details about why he even came to Adrienan or why he was looking for the sorcerer. He kept that to himself, but the swordmaster never pried. He trained with Master Gallanver for three months before being acquainted into the royal guard.

That was when he first saw the princess. *He was on the day shift and she ran into him while running to her lecture. A leather-bound book slid across the floor as she fell. Her dark hair spilled over her vivid green eyes as she looked up at him.*

He felt his throat dry up and his heart pounded like a drum. He was unable to breathe as he watched another member of the guard help her up. He was paralyzed by her beauty. He wanted to grab her book, but his palms were sweating. Awkwardly, he looked away from her and bowed with his apology.

He requested to be on the night guard to avoid her during the day. But as Master Gallanver said, she did have a habit of causing trouble and occasionally enjoyed sneaking out at night.

His mouth formed into a smile just thinking about the girl.

He would have stayed on the night guard, but Master Gallanver was impressed by his sword fighting skills and intended to appoint him as one of the princess' guards once the celebration was done. He never expected that he'd be her primary guard after the shadow wolf attack. *Who would have guessed that was all it took to cure my nerves around her?*

"Hey, little sor-cey, are you hungry?" The dungeon was dimly lit, as the sorceress, Nars, descended down the stone staircase. Her heels echoed lightly as they clicked on the surface. She approached where Kio sat with his arms chained up, and she sat down on a soft cushion that appeared on the ground.

Kio looked up at the woman who held a plate towards him of deep-red sliced meat, slightly braised on the outside.

Its rareness made him cringe, but the scent reminded him of his hunger.

"No?" The woman frowned and started feeding herself. "I thought for sure you'd be hungry." A goblet appeared, hovering in the air at first, until Nars grabbed it and took a deep drink. Kio curled his nose at the strong scent of vinegar that rose from her goblet. "You won't be able to summon your magic and escape if you don't eat..."

She took another bite for herself, but the next she held in front of Kio. The red juice dripped from the fleshy piece. He was able to smell the spices of pepper and garlic. His stomach grumbled and he caved, devouring the steak. It melted in his mouth like butter and every bite burst with flavor.

The woman smiled, "That's a good boy."

Kio took down every slice she handed him like a starving wolf. His body responded on its own without thought. The rareness didn't even bother him.

Another wine glass appeared, but on the other side of Nars. "Here, try this one."

Kio didn't want to, but he couldn't control his primitive actions and drank down the liquid. *It* was *good!* The sparkling drink had a sweet flavor of raspberry; it was the finest juice Kio ever tasted!

Nars wiped his face gently after he consumed both the goblet and the plate of meat.

She might be feeding me, but she's still the enemy, Kio thought to himself. He looked up at the woman and glared. "Where's your master *'Arashi?'*" He was disappointed that he didn't see much of the sorcerer. *It would be difficult to take him without figuring out his weakness.*

...This woman, however... Even after all this time, Kio couldn't really figure out *hers* either.

Nars grimaced. "He's upset that I brought a boy home," She crossed her arms and looked away from Kio, "and didn't bring a toy for *him* to play with."

The soldier's blood boiled. *The princess isn't a toy!*

"She'll never come here…" He growled and glared up at the woman. She shrugged and started her way back upstairs. *Is she ignoring me?!* She was already halfway up the stairs when Kio exploded, "She'll go to Laquar and find a way to defeat you, but you'll never have her!"

Nars paused and looked down at him. With the dim-lit torch lighting, he couldn't read the expression on her face, but her voice, for once, was hollow as she responded. "Honestly… I couldn't care less."

CHAPTER 16

The Laquar Forest

he air held the scent of fresh, fallen dew atop of moss and damp pine as Taemi slid out of the dark tunnel and landed on a soft brush of lush, green, grass. The stars still shimmered above her in the open sky—illuminating her surroundings, but tall trees with their vibrant green branches blocked much from where she lay. The mountain range extended high beyond them.

She looked up in disbelief. *It took me two days to climb up to that ledge, but it only felt like moments to slide to the bottom. Did I slide to the bottom?* It didn't matter; she arrived in the forest on the other side.

She pushed herself up to her feet and looked around in awe of the enchanted elf forest. It was dense with trees of various species—some, she recognized—grew straight, and others grew with thick trunks, covered in knobs that twisted around to stay in the light. Despite it being night, a strange blue glow illuminated the forest in shades of green and purple. Small white flies fluttered like specs of glowing dust, and twinkled throughout.

The uneven mountain surface was thickly covered with ferns and moss-covered boulders. Fungi grew everywhere—up on the trees like white, little shelves, and in small openings—reflecting light that made them glow.

It was the most beautiful place she'd ever seen, and she couldn't imagine the elves having any reason to leave.

From where she landed, shrubs were cut away, creating a narrow mulch path into the forest. It wounded around the trees to avoid strenuous climbs as she followed it, but she had to step carefully around the mossy boulders and the thick roots of the trees. The forest was quiet except for insect chirps and the low hum of a bird's coo echoing throughout the forest.

Further into the lush, she started to hear the babbling stream of a creek and when she reached it, she stopped to rest and refilled her bag. She watched the water pour down over the large rocks, spilling over smooth pebbles of red, orange, and dark blue with yellow speckles. Fascinated by the colors, she reached in and picked up the brightest red stone to pocket it in her cloak.

She watched the small brook for a few moments longer, allowing it to fill her soul with peace. She took a deep breath and got back to her feet, but she jumped at the sight of a large, white creature that appeared out of nowhere.

It sat near the creek, holding the appearance of a massive cow with thick, long antlers that branched out from its head. The antlers resembled the smooth shape of the creature's surroundings to keep it camouflaged. She would have missed it if she didn't stop for a rest. Its ears perked and it turned its head slightly as she continued on the path, but the creature was passive and left her well enough alone.

Eventually, the mulched path became wider and was populated with large slabs of gray granite. She reached a clearing that had a large stone fountain in the center. It had a statue of two large, winged fish with long snouts pointed up towards the sky. The water poured out from their mouths and into the surrounding pool of colorful lilies. The trees nearby were illuminated with strings of blue lights. She saw the shelters of shops and homes, built with the harmony of the trees and stones. The tree roots intertwined in an intricate pattern and transitioned into the smooth silver marble.

It reminded her much of the seal she saw in the Forest of the Damned. *Perhaps it was an elven forest before it became corrupted.*

The behemoth...

She shook the remembrance of that nightmare and continued on into the city. More homes were inside giant trees—thick as her city's buildings—with fungi growing out of the bark, functioning as staircases that spiraled up the tree. Vine bridges connected the trees for ease of travel. The knots were hollowed out with large openings for windows. She saw the shadows of elven families enjoying the evening in their homes before turning in for the night's rest. But, there were also a few still drinking wine at the outside pubs near the trunk of the trees.

"Lady Equillis, we've been waiting for you."

Taemi turned around to a bowing man with long, pointed ears. His long, silver hair shimmered with a hint of blue as its silk texture reflected the light. When he rose, he loomed over Taemi. His complexion was fair, but Taemi couldn't ignore the unusual purple color hue of his eyes. "We're glad to see you arrive safe. Our hunters have been tracking down a dar'rakar that's been lurking on the main path, but we haven't heard from them yet."

The princess was lost on formalities with elves and lowered her head to a bow. "Yes! Thank you! ...Um ...I'm here on a special re-request."

She heard the light laughter of a woman's voice, "There's no need to address us as so." Taemi rose and she saw that the male was accompanied by three others. They all wore silver cloaks with a gold leaf for a clasp.

The elves were a tall, slender race with fair skin

and high cheekbones. They all had long, straight hair that varied in color. Those with silver hair had tints of the blue, but some looked more purple or pink. Those with brown hair reflected various shades of gold or red. The dark-haired ones had tints of maroon or navy blue.

Another woman stepped forward—her hair tinted pastel pink. "Yes, we've been expecting you for the past *eighteen* years—waiting for the time to teach you the ways of the stone and the history of the Moon Daughter." She was shorter than the others, with vibrant, red eyes. She wore a long, pastel-green tunic with brown linen trousers.

The woman with bright gold hair nodded. "Yes. Allow us to introduce ourselves to ease your mood."

The princess flushed, "I'm Sorry!" *Oh no! I probably have been staring at them like some frightened child!* She didn't expect their appearance to differ so much from Tilly. *But he was only a small percentage of elven.*

The woman's laugh was the last thing Taemi expected. She put her hand to her heart and waved off Taemi's apologies. "Oh, my goodness." When she composed herself, she continued, "I am Era, the Head Elder of the Council. It is an honor to greet you into our city." Era wore a long, red, silk dress that fitted snuggly over her curves with a gold rope belt wrapped around her waist

"This young lady is Coral," Era addressed the shorter woman with the pink, pastel hair.

"I am Madeem." The silver-blue male with the purple eyes placed his hand over his heart. He wore a long, blue tunic with white trousers.

Madeem! She felt the shower of reassurance for finally completing the mission her father had sent her on. *I found him!*

Era went on to introduce the fourth elf, who wore a plain white dress. "And this is the Oracle."

"It's an honor to meet you." The Oracle was a shy

young girl and her greeting was a forced whisper. Taemi couldn't tell any of their ages based on the lack of their wrinkles, but the Oracle was clearly a young child who stood shorter than Taemi and seemed only a few years over a decade. Her hair was a dark, navy-blue in the light, but shifted to black when she moved. What startled Taemi were the girl's glossy, white eyes with mere remnants of pale irises.

"Don't be alarmed," Era stated, "She still may be a child, but she can see better than the rest of us."

The Oracle gave a start at Era's comment and stared down at the ground timidly. "I'm sorry to frighten you." Her voice was barely audible.

Taemi immediately felt remorse. *They can read my every thought plastered on my face! I have to relax!*

"Why don't we get more acquainted inside over tea." The others all nodded with Era. "Please follow us."

"Wait!" Taemi alarmed. She should have said something right away, but wasn't prepared to be in shock when first meeting the elven race. "Um, well... actually—I also came for your help! A sorceress used contortion and— "

The elves hissed at the word before she finished, "Contortion is a sinister art!"

The Oracle grabbed Taemi's head on an impulse, and she could feel her scanning through her head. "She's ill with this magic, but it is weak." The Oracle spoke softly.

The princess gasped, *She used that magic on* me *as well?! How? When? Why didn't I go with her if she did?*

"Quick, let's get her in our healing well." Era called for more of the elves to serve.

"Wait, what about my friends? She has them sitting like statues in the plains!"

"How long has it been?" Madeem asked

"Four... four days."

The elves' faces fell solemn, and Madeem lightly

bowed his head. "I'm afraid it's already too late for them."

"No—please!" Hot tears pooled in her eyes at hearing the news, "Isn't there anything we can—"

The Oracle began to stroke Taemi's hair and she stopped her pleas. Madeem continued on, "I will send out scouts to check, but dehydration may have gotten to them first—especially if the controller doesn't allow them basic functions of drinking and eating."

Taemi felt hopeless. *I failed them...*

"You didn't stand a chance..."

The voice shocked her and she looked down at the Oracle.

"The... the sorcerer is Reiji-Arashi... they also took Kio as a hostage... Can we..." She swallowed, "Can we save *him*?"

"Let's get you in the healing bath first. We need to be sure that you're not being used to someone else's means, even if it's weak."

Sounds of harps chimed like crystals as Taemi floated in the hot healing spa. She was in a dome room with white, sandy walls that sparkled in the reflection of the teal-blue pool. Strange lamps that looked like orange, hollowed rocks surrounded the room. Their dim-orange glow brought a calming atmosphere.

The pool was shallow, but came up to the princess' shoulders when she lay down. It was scented with oils of lavender and eucalyptus. Herbs of rosemary and lavender petals floated on the surface. The white, sandy surface that surrounded the pool and covered the bottom was actually salt.

"It's a special healing salt, just like the lamps," is what the elf woman who led her into this room said after she discarded her clothes.

Taemi breathed and smiled. *It did soothe all my aches though...* She longed for a hot bath for days and allowed the water to spill over her. *I can be here forever...*

"It looks like your wounds from the dar'rakar healed well." Taemi awakened to the young girl's voice. The Oracle sat on the edge of the pool—her legs immersed in the water as she swirled her feet. "I was worried about your wounds after you defeated the dar'rakar, but I'm not able to leave the forest. I'm glad that my trick to heal you through the crystal worked just as well." The girl smiled.

The princess stared at the girl and remembered that it was *her* voice she heard on the mountain, *"Don't give up, Moon Child... You're not alone..."*

"Oh... that was you." The girl nodded with a smile. "...Thank you," the princess remembered the leaf package, "Oh! And thank you for the cheese and meat."

"I'm glad you were able to receive them. How is the bath?" Without waiting for an answer, the Oracle walked towards Taemi. She let her white dress soak up the water as she placed her hands on Taemi's head. "It looks like the contortion is completely removed. You should be able to think more clearly now."

"Thank you... again. Any word on Tilly or Nazoo? They said they would send out scouts..." The Oracle's expression was enough to answer Taemi's question, and she decided she didn't want to hear the answer.

"I'm sorry about your friends; I was informed not to cause you additional grief." The child turned away.

She was told not *to tell me... Would* they *have told me?*

"If it comforts you at all, all three of their bodies have been buried."

The princess brushed the tears from her face. She didn't tell the Oracle about Lloyd. *So they did at least send out scouts.* The princess swallowed her sorrow and nodded.

"Yes, yes, that does comfort me. Thank you again."

The Oracle walked out of the pool. "You may stay here for as long as you need. A bed and fresh clothes has been accommodated for you when you are ready to rest." The Oracle left the room.

Taemi rested her back against the wall and hoped the pool could heal the pain that gnawed inside her.

The sorceress, Nars, sat straddled on Kio's lap, combing through his hair and petting his cheek. "You see, I want you to use it; I want to see how strong you can be. Any amount of effort could break these chains—fire, water, earth." She shrugged her shoulders with a smile, "your choice."

If she leaned in any closer, I'll break her face with my head... The boy watched for an opening to attack, but the sorceress stayed just out of his range. All Kio could do was clench his jaw and fists.

"I even brought your sword for you," she gestured to the blade, sheathed and up against the wall nearby. She raised her hand to his throat, holding his head back forcefully, but was careful not to choke him, and pressed her face against his cheek. "You can throw me across the room by utilizing the air around you," she whispered. "Unless..." she pulled back with a grin, "you're actually enjoying all this attention?"

Kio turned away from her. "Do what you want." From the corner of his eye, he could see the woman frown.

She sighed and folded her arms beneath her breast. "Looks like I can't get a rise out of you unless I'm insulting your *princess*."

"It doesn't matter. She's safe with the others... that's all I care about."

"Oh my! Is that what you think?" She shook her

head with a giggle as if she had transformed into Morlisa again. "No, no. She left her poor comrades to die of dehydration out in the field."

"You're lying; she'd never abandon them!" *Not Lloyd, at least...* Kio stared down at the ground, thinking back on their kiss, and the ache began to swell in his chest.

"Oh, and the pretty blonde that she had a crush on," she nodded, "she killed him too, but under *unfortunate* circumstances. The poor thing died in her arms on accident. I intended to let them all live if she had come here with me." She traced her fingers up his chest as she continued, "But I'd consider that's good news for you. You can use some magic, escape my little prison, and run to her side now that she's all for the taking." She paused, but Kio didn't say anything. "Trust me, kid..." She went back to combing his hair and letting it run through her fingers, speaking softly, "if you don't get out and take her, I can assure you, my master will." She was on her feet before she finished her sentence—leaving a sudden, cold draft where the warmth of her body used to be. "And he's not a gentle lover..."

Kio pulled at the chains, angered by her implicated comment. "That bastard! He'll never have her! He'll never lay his hands on her!!"

Nars laughed as she climbed the stairs, "There you go! Keep working at it." With a wave, Nars left Kio alone in the basement.

"Arashi..." Kio's growl echoed through the empty dungeon. "That monster will never touch her—not as long as I live." *The moment I see his face again, I will* destroy *him...* His rage sparked the cold embers from the void within.

CHAPTER 17

Crystals & Incantations

Taemi woke up the next morning feeling well-rested on the down mattress. The sun was already peeking through the large leaf that covered the window of the knot-hut—the living quarters within the trees. The air was already vibrant with songs of birds harmonizing with harps and flutes. A light breeze blew through the open crease and caressed the girl's face, carrying the sweet fragments of flowers.

The princess stepped out of bed onto the soft, moss rug that cushioned the wood floor, and brushed open the large leaf to peer out at the city. The elves populated the stone walkway as they went about their daily tasks, causing a quiet buzz around them. Elven children ran down the vine bridges hanging from the trees, laughing as they chased each other in play. Music filled the air from those who played their instruments up on the mushroom balconies as they perfected each note.

Not far above the forest city, beyond the branches of the tallest tree, was the light shadow of the mountain range.

I finally made it to the forest city within the mountains! It was a sight she wished she could have shared with Kio. She still expected to wake up from a dream and still be out on the Cloymein Plains.

She turned and saw that the elves already brought a clean outfit for her to wear, displayed on the bed. It was a simple, green gown made of chiffon. She slipped it on and finished the clasps at her neck. It left her shoulders bare, but the tulle sleeves hung down like long drapes. Gold embroidery decorated the bodice and around her elbows. She fastened the gold sash and glanced at herself in the mirror.

The last time she saw her reflection like this, she was dazzled in jewels and gems with her hair stacked upon itself like an elegant doll—a gorgeous, naïve princess who had no idea how that night would unfold before her.

Now, the mirror illustrated a woman from her fantasy books. She was a traveling forest mage who hunted her food with a bow and arrow, and cooked it on an open flame under the stars. She'd summon a white bow to defeat terrifying monsters and heal those in need! She would only wear the crystal pendant around her neck as she had no other need for any other jewelry—*just like the woman who only wore the star-shaped earrings and matching necklace.*

She recalled the woman's appearance as the thought crossed her mind and she frowned. *That was the same woman... the double sword-wielder in pink. She was the sorceress who took Kio!* She remembered her from the dragon cavern too... *She's been hiding in my shadow the whole time and stalking me like a helpless lamb.* Taemi's fist shook as she clenched her dress.

That sorceress' was powerful enough to take down the mydrallchobria like it was a common garden snake. She sliced through the heads of the damned beasts as if they were dandelions blowing in the wind.

And the hydra...

A knock on her door took her mind off the woman. "Lady Equillis," A young elf entered. Her blonde hair was pinned up and she carried a tray with a smile. "Good morning. I hope you don't mind that I brought you breakfast."

"Oh yes, please." Taemi bowed slightly as the girl placed the tray down.

"The dress is really becoming of you."

Taemi held up the large sleeves, "Yes, it is quite lovely."

"Would you like me to do your hair?"

Taemi's heart skipped a beat.

"C'mere, let me brush your hair," Morlisa laughed as she reached out, pulling her onto the bed.

"Why would you want to do that?" Her own voice echoed through her head.

Morlisa's smile was the sun, "So we can talk about boys!"

"Uh... no, it's okay." *I can't let her get that close to me again.* But it wasn't the deceit that upset the princess. *I really did like her... I'm such a fool.* "I'll just weave it into a braid myself. Thank you."

The young elf bowed. "When you're ready, I'll take you to Lord Madeem for your lessons."

My lessons? Oh... that's right. That's what I'm here for, after all. But it was the circumstances of *how* she got here that kept her from feeling relieved.

Breakfast was a plate of fresh, assorted berries on a bed of greens, and two sweet cakes with a spiced tea. Afterwards, Layla, the young servant elf, escorted Taemi through the city and across the courtyard to the large fountain of the two fish. In the daylight, Taemi could see the gold and silver fish that swam beneath the pads of the pink and purple lilies. She paused for a moment to watch them swim below, and Layla stopped to join her.

"The sky fish is what brings us the fresh, filtered rain down from the mountains," Layla smiled, addressing to the two large statues where the water spilled out. The young elf gave a small laugh, "We know now that the change in temperature is what really brings us rain, but it's cheery to imagine mystical creatures swimming in a blue sea above."

The girl nodded, looking up towards the blue sky, imagining that the clouds were the white caps that they'd jump over. Their scales would reflect the same colors as her pendant and catch the light as they dove back into the blue sky.

Layla gave her another moment before they continued on their walk. They entered the forest on a mulch path, opposite from the side Taemi came through the night before. There were fewer trees in this part of the forest that allowed for more light to shine through, growing grass on the smooth terrain. The trees opened to a field of tall wildflowers where colorful butterflies danced and fluttered.

"This way," the young elf continued, gesturing to a path through the field.

Down the path was another giant tree, but shortened to only a stump and re-purposed into a house with windows and a doorway. Moss covered the rooftop and toadstools grew on the sides. Fairy flies drifted through the air as Lord Madeem sat, cross-legged in a small clearing, enjoying his morning tea.

"Here she is, my Lord." He gave the slightest nod and the young elf bowed and turned back to the city.

"Come join me, Taemi."

He called me by my first name... She thought as she sat with him, arranging her dress to sit in the same style as him. A slab of rock was between them, holding two cups and a ceramic pot of tea that gave off a soft, floral aroma.

Lord Madeem poured the tea into the second cup before Taemi even had a chance to refuse, and she felt the obligation to take it. *Just accept the behavior of new cultures rather than risk offending.* She took a sip of the flower-scented tea. She didn't hate it, but it was strange to her taste palate.

"Alright, let's get started." The elf pulled out a purple satin pouch and placed the contents on the rock slab before her. Various colors of rocks—some polished smoothed with shiny surfaces, and the rest left with rough ridged edges—laid out on the slab.

Taemi breathed as she examined them, "...Crystals?"

"Correct. Just as you use your moonstone, other crystals can be used to wield magic and cast spells."

Just like... the game? She allowed Madeem to continue. *He probably isn't even aware of that game.*

"Elves are born with the ability to generate magic energy from our own natural existence, but we also use crystals to enhance our power as needed. There are others that can draw out the magic from crystals to cast similar spells."

"Oh! Like me!"

"Correct. However, I think you'll need the moonstone to channel the energy of the crystals, but we can certainly test that in your lessons. The larger the crystal, the stronger the magic we can summon. But, if you draw too much—reaching the crystal's limit—it will shatter. It is useless afterwards.

"Taemi." Madeem's face was serious as she looked up at him. "If your crystal shatters, you must immediately stop casting to avoid chaotic energy."

"What's chaotic ener—"

"Almost certain death." His stern voice cut her off. "You must guarantee me this before I continue."

Taemi held her pendant. *If my crystal ever shatters... it's useless.* She nodded. "I promise. I won't absorb its power if it shatters."

"Very good. When a crystal shatters, its power becomes unstable and most often kills the wielder. Even among our own kind, many thought foolishly that they were powerful enough to try to harness chaos magic, but each one of them perished in agony.

"I will tell you, since you're likely to find out eventually. There has only been one single instance where the wielder lived… and actually, without traumatic injuries as it was written. They were the first of our knowledge of what will happen when a crystal shatters, but we don't know anything further about this person. Therefore, many try to follow in their footprints and attempt to achieve such strength, but since the scripture is more than a thousand years old, many of us think it's a fluke and that the crystal or wielder wasn't very powerful to begin with.

"Now, let's begin. Your first lesson is learning the basic elements and common crystals used for them." He continued and held up a purple crystal that was smooth like glass. "This is amethyst. It aids with air-type magic." Madeem held an open palm to it, and the wind picked up around Taemi, blowing her hair. "Many use it to move objects and to levitate." The stone hovered out of his hand and back down to the slab as he picked up the next one—a brilliant, blue stone with white streaks and earthy gold speckles that shimmered in the light.

"Lapis Lazuli is also an air type, but if you master your air magic adequately, you can use it to cast electrostatic magic, similar to lightning strikes." Taemi flinched as the stone flashed a blinding light. It was short, but still took a few seconds for her vision to align. "We classify this as light magic, but it can take on many forms."

Next, he grabbed a translucent crystal that reflected colors of pink, blue and purple on its surface, much like her moonstone. "Would you like to guess what element this one is?" He held it out for Taemi to examine closely.

The stone was polished smooth. The colors shifted like light reflecting off a bubble. *But unlike air, it's something that reflects light… Like the blue ocean matching the color of the sky.* "Is it... water?"

Madeem smiled, "Correct, opal will aid with water-type magic. There are many other water crystals, but opal's translucent character allows it to replicate the various forms of its element—liquid, frozen, and steam.

"Like water, the right spells can cause great destruction. An aquamarine crystal, if big enough, could move the ocean and take down a nation."

Madeem placed the opal down and gestured to two stones that were left in their raw form as if freshly cut from the ground. "These next two are earth elements." One of them was brown with striped layers like the walls of the dragon cavern, and the other one was a pastel blue-green with grey spots. "Tiger's eye and amazonite can be used to create formations of the ground or enhance plant growth. These were used to design many of our elven housing. It can also petrify—or harden—objects to create armor or strength."

So that's how they intertwine their city with nature. Taemi glanced towards Madeem's house and smiled, *that's amazing...*

"This one is what we call our passion stone."

The elf's next stone was a dark red—too much like the color of blood *...and the shadow wolf's eyes.*

"One must be cool and serene when using the red garnet as it can easily ignite spells based on emotions."

Ignite like a rage... and bleed like sorrow..., "That means it's the fire element..." The princess felt disquieted by this stone. It was familiar, but in a sense that she knew to respectfully avoid it. Unlike the pure tranquility she felt from the moonstone, the garnet gave off a violent vibration of determination and resilience. *How could one be serene when holding* that *thing!?* Taemi eyed the stone wearily and looked up at Madeem, "It makes me nauseous."

The elf's expression was peculiar as he raised an

eyebrow, "It is strictly reserved for those who've mastered their emotions. There are other fire element crystals that can be used instead." He put the stone away in the satin sack to ease the princess' mood.

There was one final crystal on the stone slab that he had yet to introduce. It was black with a metallic sheen. Taemi thought maybe she could guess, but could only think of the five that he already spoke about. "Is the last one... does that aid with dark magic?"

The silver-haired elf glanced at the last stone with a light laugh, "Haha, no, my dear. There is no such thing as *dark* magic—just magic users with *bad* intentions. Most of the black crystals are associated with earth-type elements, but I brought this one because it's a little special, as it could be considered as a shadow-type."

The girl's eyes widened, "Shadow magic?!" *Like the shadow wolves?*

Madeem shook his head, "Hmm... Maybe that's not the right way to describe it..." He pondered for a moment and continued, "It's more like... *lacking* an element—like an all-consuming void—and acts like an anti-magic. This black hematite nullifies magic energy. It absorbs magic attacks directed to the user, but also the energy cast from the user. In which case, it's mostly useful to those who *can't* wield magic and wear it as a talisman against those who can. It's a special ore we mine from the mountains and trade it well with the northern continents that struggle with rogue mages.

"Now that you know the elements, we can work on creating spells that derive from each one—"

"Wait—what about mine?" Taemi held her pendant up, "What element is *my* stone?"

The elf sighed and sipped from his cup. "You and the female descendants of your bloodline are the only ones who are able to use the power of the moonstone, so we can only speculate on what you're capable of. It is known that your ancestors were healers and purifiers. If you can cast *all* elemental spells with it, then I would say it possesses *all* the elements."

Taemi thought about the support spells from the card game she played with Morlisa. "Can I do spells like Haste and Mirror?"

Madeem nodded, "Those are both water-based magic, so you should be able to summon them without any of the other crystals. I will teach you those two today while learning the incantations for summoning.

"It's important for beginners to learn the basic incantations—or magic commands—in order to cast a spell within your capabilities. You can still summon magic on instinct, however this always leads to drawing more power than you can physically handle and could lead to hurting those that you did not want to, or passing out from the extreme exhaustion."

The princess shifted in her seat. *I've been* over-*doing it almost* every *time...*

Taemi suddenly thought of the sorceress in pink glaring at her while in the Forest of the Damned, *"Ugh... why isn't it working?!"*

She *never says anything... and yet, the wagons, cirqueteers, the tigers, and Kio simply* vanished *away...*

"What... what about a sorceress who doesn't chant *anything*? She just... vanishes all the time."

"Then she must have practiced for many decades. When familiar with a casting, commands become second nature, and then merely a thought. Many can familiarize themselves with simple tasks, but... *teleshifting* on a whim takes even *our* kind years to master without incantation..." He drifted off and then caressed his chin, raising an eyebrow. "This sorceress you're referring to—is she the same one you mentioned the other day—the one that did the contortion?"

Taemi nodded in response.

"Interesting... She must be a rogue mage from the north, but I doubted their self-learning skills could get them *that* far..."

"Do you know what... uh *Tr'u me Ah*..." Taemi took a moment to recall the rest of it. "*...tare ...ess* means?"

"You mean, "*Tru-me Tara-mess*?""

"Something..." *Not quite, but...* "Something like that..."

Madeem sat back and pondered it for a moment, "It has the elfish root word for safety... But that's all I can say about it. I'm not familiar with the ancient language."

It's ancient *elfish?* Taemi blinked.

Of course, the woman is fluent in that as well...

She should have asked Mel... *If I* knew *it was ancient elfish... But how would someone like* him *be able to speak it when* even *the elves themselves don't know...*

"Let's move on, shall we?" Madeem continued her lessons and taught her the basic elvish incantations for the air-based magic types. He had her sit cross-legged in the field, holding her pendant in one hand and the amethyst in the other. "We'll tackle one magic task at a time. Try to focus on levitation."

Taemi closed her eyes and channeled through the moonstone and the crystal in the same manner and practiced the commands. She was quick to summon air-type magic that utilized wind. She was able to move light objects to a short distance and use air to block weak attacks.

"Good. With practice, you'll be able to strengthen your hold on objects and neglect stronger attacks."

The next lesson was with the opal and water-type magic. "Since you brought up Haste, imagine time as a stream. It can be slowed when there's less water moving, and it can be sped up in the rain. To cast Haste—or Slow, even—you're actually sending or drawing energy from the object you want to add speed to, or slow down.

"Let's practice with the butterflies around. Focus on one and send it energy to quicken its pace."

"It's not going to hurt them, right?"

Master Madeem laughed, "They'll be fine. You can't cause physical damage with these particular spells. Haste is used as a support, it will only make them move and think on a faster level than average—enhancing their ability to evade attacks. But, if you slow them down," He motioned to one that almost stopped in mid-air, "You're sabotaging them to be easy targets for their predators." Master Madeem released the butterfly and it fluttered at its normal pace.

That's what happened to the shadow wolf that attacked at the Country Rose. I didn't stop time for everything... just slowed the wolf. Already a little familiar, Taemi used the command to speed up one of the butterflies. "*Tah-Meo!*" She sent her energy through the opal, and the large butterfly with the black pattern on its orange wings jumped from flower head to the next, sucking the nectar from each in seconds. She released the energy of the opal, and it fluttered at its normal pace.

"Very good. If you wanted to slow it down, the command would have been, *Tah-Ma*. To better remember this is that *Tah* is the root word for time and *Meo* rhymes with *go*—from your language—and *Ma* means *to halt*.

The girl nodded. *That makes sense, but it would still help if I could write everything down.*

"Let's see, you said you wanted to learn Mirror too?"

"Yes—or the one that reflects magic attacks."

Master Madeem nodded, "Yes, that is correct, but it only reflects one attack after it's cast. It's more of a temporary water shield that dissolves once hit with a spell, and sometimes—depending on the strength of the attack—it can dissolve too fast and leak damage.

So it's kind of like the game... but I'll have to remember to repeatedly cast it, and it might not protect me from the strong spells. She had no intention to get hit with *any* spells, but it would be better than nothing if she couldn't evade an attack.

"The incantation for Mirror is *mirra*, but we'll work on just the casting part. We'll practice how well it counters tomorrow."

When she summoned Mirror, she didn't feel that she wore a shield, but she could see a faint line in her vision where the light reflected off a thin layer of glass in front of her.

They continued on with the other crystals, learning how to work with each element. With the amazonite stone, the incantations she had to learn were the elvish name of the plants and the elfish command of what she wanted them to do. She was able to make a small lavender sprout grow buds and blossom, but with more work, she would be able to generate a specific plant and use its abilities. The tiger's eye shifted the soil and opened rocks into a passage. She also learned that the crystal could mold dirt and rocks to create building structures and form the steps that she used to climb up the mountain.

The fire magic was by far the easiest for her to master. She practiced with a ruby instead of the garnet, working with the commands for heat and flames. But as easy as it was with the ruby in her hand, Taemi struggled to produce a simple spark without it.

"I guess you'll need more time with that one," Madeem examined, "but that's enough for today."

"But wait—I need to..." She was so focused on learning and mastering each technique Master Madeem taught, she didn't even realize that the day had slipped away and the night flowers were beginning to bloom. She realized how light-headed and exhausted she had become from her practices.

"It's well-past time for dinner. Why don't you stay and join me for the night? We can begin again tomorrow morning."

CHAPTER 18

Battle Magic

The next morning smelled of pine and fresh dew as Taemi followed Master Madeem further into the forest. They crossed a wooden bridge that led outside into the mountain valley where Madeem referred to as the practice area. When the bridge finally came to an end, the forest gave out to a clearing on the other side of the mountain range. The field was vast with luscious, green, short grass that shimmered across the hills when the wind touched their blades. Beyond was the teal-blue ocean where the light flickered across its surface.

They walked towards a leveled surface where nine, large, clear quarts were laid out in a circle with several herbs set in between.

"What's this?"

The elf smiled, "Well, you've mastered the smaller spells, so now we're going to see if you can enhance the strength of your magic. Consider this more endurance training, and then, in the afternoon, we'll go back to perfecting commands and techniques.

"Stand in the middle of the grid," He gestured towards the center, "and hold both the amethyst and opal. You only need the moonstone to touch your skin to activate its power, so you don't have to hold it all the time."

Taemi nodded. She took a seat within the grid and collected the two crystals from her satin pouch. The moonstone rested on her chest.

"Focus on wielding the magic from both stones to create a ball of water and throw it as far as you can. This will get you more accustomed to using the elements all at once before hindering yourself."

Madeem stood off to the side to supervise. Taemi focused on drawing water from the opal with the commands she was taught to summon water. The air changed and the water pooled in her hand, but as she shifted to draw air from the amethyst, the water steamed away. Taemi tried it again, but each time she transitioned from one stone to the other, the water faded from her hand.

"That's a common habit of the self-taught and they never find a way to advance to spells that use multiple elements. Think carefully, as it's important to remember how they all have to work together to become something."

"Oh..." She glanced down at her hands. *I have to use them both at the same time!*

She closed her eyes and drew power from both stones. In her mind, she became aware of three glowing orbs: one white, one blue and the last purple. The blue and purple orbs were connected to the white light—the moonstone. She knew that the blue one had to grow and the purple one had to maintain its growth all at one time. She moved the air first into a circular spiral, and then in the middle pulled the moisture out of the air. *Grow...* the tiny blue light sprouted and was pulled into the center, *Grow!*

She took a deep breath and opened her eyes to a floating reflection of herself. Holding onto the air and spiraling it around she gathered more into a single focal point and pushed the water off into the distance. It flew past the field, over the edge, and into the sea.

"*Very* impressive." Master Madeem praised,

"Beginners usually either form a water ball that's too big to toss, or a small water ball that they can throw at that distance. But to throw a large ball at *that* distance on your first time clearly shows your strength! There's no doubt you'll master the rest of your lessons quickly."

The next lesson circled back to using Mirror, where Taemi cast the spell as her shield and Master Madeem tested the strength with his magic attacks. The first few attacks, she didn't feel anything and he was able to diffuse the counter-spell, but then the elf's spells became a little stronger each time, and he had to use a spell himself to shield the counter-attack. When Taemi felt a strong wind push her down to her back, they stopped and moved on.

"Good. Your ability can ward off the basic spells before they slip through. The reflection spell will grow stronger over time as you continue to strengthen your endurance in magic." Madeem smiled as he assisted the girl back onto her feet. "You'll be able to withstand most of the strong attacks soon enough."

Throughout the day, Taemi's lessons advanced in difficulty where she had to use more elements at one time. Master Madeem had her form a bowl out of stone, generate water, heat it up, and collect the steam into a pocket with air. If she wanted to cool it, she had to pull air from above and the mist formed into white frost that drifted down from the sky.

"This is just the foundation of understanding how the elements all work together," he stated, "but there's a shortcut for when you do want to summon mist or ice. Water has to be hot before it can be steam or mist, and the air has to be cold to transform it to snow or ice."

Again, Taemi was able to master creating ice formations, but struggled with developing a fog. It wasn't just enough to focus on hot water when it came to the fire-type spells.

"That's okay, you'll get it within time."

Why is it so hard? The pendant is always hot in my hands and the dar'rakar even caught aflame when I attacked it! "Master Madeem, I created a bow of light once... to shoot something out of the sky. What element is that?"

The man was perplexed by her question, "A bow of light? Are you able to show me now?"

The girl gathered energy from her pendant and tried to pull enough to form the bow like before, but now it felt like a strain. All that she was able to develop in her hand was a small white spark before letting go in defeat of exhaustion. *Why can't I do it?*

"When you made this bow, what was the situation you were in?"

The girl hesitated, "I was... being attacked."

The man nodded with clarity, "I see. That form looks like a combination of electrostatic and fire? That must be the pure energy of the moonstone itself, an ability that your emotions can possess. However, you're not able to do it now because you're not skilled enough and no longer wielding with emotion—which, as I indicated yesterday, has the danger of overdrawing your limits."

Even though Madeem didn't have the tone of lecture in his voice, the girl still felt a swelling of shame harden on her chest.

"Don't worry, though. With more practice, you'll be able to use it again and control your emotions better."

The lessons ended early in the evening as Taemi became drained from drawing energy from multiple crystals at one time and casting difficult spells. She fell to her bed more exhausted than the night before.

Master Madeem had her make dozens of giant water balls and see if she could throw them faster and farther each time. After that, he taught her how to use both water and air to make a shield from magic attacks. It took all her strength and focus to pull the power from the stones, but Master Madeem ended her lesson as soon as she could no longer grip the energy.

"They get tired, too." Master Madeem said as she struggled to draw more energy from the stone. "It's important for them to rest and recharge just like us."

She lifted her pendant up towards the ceiling and watched the light of the lamps dance on its smooth, colorful surface. *I have to be careful not to overuse it... I have to be careful to not let it shatter as well.* She let her mind wander with the knowledge she had obtained in the past two days.

A descendant of the moon... Only females of my blood are able to use the stone. She recalled her family history being all male heritance for the past seven generations. *I'm the only one that can use the moonstone since...*

She closed her eyes and let her mind drift.

The princess allowed herself to float from her bed and up into the sky from her practice of the levitation spell. She watched the sleepy town fade further into the mountain's crevice until all she could see was the dim glow of their blue lights.

She was well above the mountains with the stars scattered above her. She expected it to be cold up this high, but the air was warm and soothing.

The sky may have been dark, but it was painted with colors of purple, shades of blue and even streaks of pink.

She floated on her back, watching the stars that rained across the sky to a rising melody of harps and flutes that played beneath her.

A festival of the stars, she remembered it being called, *where they played music and danced beneath the star shower.*

All the stars fell in a diagonal across the sky. All,

except one, that seemed to appear out of nowhere and was falling towards her direction, head-on.

Taemi sprang from her back and watched the star continue to flare down and strike the planet beneath her. She felt the impact—even while floating in the sky—as pockets of air bubbles flew past and pushed her through the air.

A large, smoldering shadow appeared from where the star landed and spread across the land—releasing black creatures with glowing, red eyes. They ran across the ground like fleeing centipedes, spewing a poison with no antidote. They caused famine, poverty, and death to all life while consuming the whole planet.

Off in the distance past the Cloymein Plains, she felt a beacon pulling at her. She was able to see the path of a thin thread reflecting in the light of the moon.

It called to her and she ran. The night sky faded out of sight and she was running in the woods. The shadow wolves chased her from behind, slowly gaining more visual of her eyesight as they flanked her. She couldn't outrun them.

Her body slipped on the wet ground and she slid through a dark puddle. The beasts surrounded her, with curled horns, long fangs, and six, red eyes. Three jumped forward, but the double sword-wielder appeared above her and sliced off their heads.

"Princess!" Taemi turned and saw Kio running towards her. She got to her feet to escape, but the shadow wolves began to surround him as well. One by one they jumped and tackled him to the ground.

"Kio!" Taemi ran, but the darkness pulled him away and all she could see was a red river streaming down towards her...

Taemi sprang awake, damp in cool sweat. Her heart raced, wondering if she had a premonition as to what was happening to Kio while she was safe in Laquar. *I have to go to him… before it's too late.* She could only hope she'd be able to save him.

Her heart skipped a beat as a knock came from her door. Layla, the young servant elf, allowed herself in, carrying a tray.

"Oh, so you *are* up. The Oracle said to give you this." The tray held a pot, a single cup, a small cookie, and a tiny pillow that smelled of lavender, rosemary and roses.

"Tea?" Taemi blinked as Layla placed the tray on her lap.

The elf nodded, "The Oracle said you'd been having nightmares, so white peony tea should help you sleep better." Layla explained as she filled the cup with the hot tea. "The dream pillow should help you calm down a little too." Layla put the pillow behind Taemi and bowed respectfully before leaving. "Rest well, Lady Equillis."

The princess' hands still trembled as she held the hot cup and sipped on it with caution. It had a root taste, but she didn't mind it as she normally would. *I suppose I'm getting more acquired to it…*

The memory of Kio was fresh in her head and she felt guilty for forgetting to ask the elders to help him. *They took him because of me… but maybe it is too late now…*

No… Taemi remembered that the woman never said she'd let Kio go if she went with her. *She planned on taking him whether or not I agreed to go. But why* him *if they were after* me?

The unknown answer was the reason she had to get him back. *He stood by my side since the beginning. It's only right I stay with him till the end!* Taemi enjoyed the small snack and drank another cup of the hot tea before lying back down to a dreamless sleep.

CHAPTER 19

The Moon Child

Sunrays beamed through the window as Taemi requested to see Era, the head of the elf council, first thing that morning. After her nightmare, Taemi was determined to save Kio. She knew that if she didn't, it would become her biggest regret, not knowing if he was alive, dead, or worse.

Layla smiled brightly, placing the breakfast tray down. "Actually, the Elders would like to see *you* after breakfast, to learn how your studies are going."

"Oh... *they* want to see *me*?" Taemi picked a berry off the plate and consumed it.

"Yes, they wanted you to rest from your long journey here first."

The girl held back her laugh as she chewed, *Ha, I wouldn't call what I did the past two days much of resting...*

"I'll escort you to the Crystal Hall when you're ready."

The Crystal Hall was located in the Vivacity Tree, which grew in the center of the elven city, surrounded by a large garden. The Vivacity Tree was the largest tree that grew in Laquar, and the only one that bore fruit and tealeaves from its flat, oval leaves.

"It is our mother tree," Layla continued. "It's the

life of the city, as we wouldn't have been as prosperous without it."

The tree itself reminded Taemi of her castle. It housed the council members and their servants, as well as the meeting rooms to negotiate, and large ballrooms for performing and celebrating unions—their term for marriage, as Layla explained on their walk. The tree was certainly sacred to the elven culture.

They walked under the large arch of the main entrance, but instead of going to the front doors, Layla led Taemi to a path in the garden. The maze of twists and turns brought them to the back of the Vivacity Tree where a hole burrowed in the bottom of the trunk. The opening was barely illuminated enough to see the steps.

"Down this way is the Crystal Hall." The young elf stopped and pointed to the staircase. "Only the Elders of the council and the Oracle are permitted to enter. I'll be here to escort you back when finished."

The steps were shallow and two-to-three paces wide as Taemi entered. They led her down into a spiral further into the ground beneath the tree. Small, thin roots hung from the ceiling and cascaded down the dirt walls. The musky, earth scent intensified as Taemi continued into the cool ground.

The stairs opened to a grand dome room, supported with white columns. Clusters of large, blue quarts sprouted from the walls, casting a soft light that illuminated the room, though Taemi wasn't sure what generated the light beneath them.

There were two dark hallways opposite from each other, and a grand silver door before her. She heard patted footsteps from the shadows coming from the hall on her right.

Five figures came into the main chamber as the princess reached the bottom of the stairs. She recognized

Era from the group who led the four others behind. "Lady Equillis, welcome to the Crystal Hall. We are the Council of Elders," Era bowed and introduced her company.

The oldest elder among them was Tarahoot who possessed stark, white hair and a leathery face that drooped. "Tarahoot was a child when the last Moon Child visited us a hundred and ninety years ago."

The older elf gave a shallow bow, "I can see the resemblance in you. You have the same dark hair as she once did..."

The second-oldest was Mezmala. Her hair was dark with strands of silver scattered throughout, giving it a gray tint above all else. "It's an honor to meet you, Moon Child."

The last two were Irene—a female with dark hair that still had its velvety shade—and Vellraniece, a male whose silver-blonde hair began to have stands of white. Neither of the two appeared to be much younger than Era herself, but they expressed their energetic manners with deep bows and bright energy. "It's a pleasure to finally meet you, Moon Child."

The princess returned each of the bows after Era introduced them. "Likewise, it's an honor to be here... In Laquar and the Crystal Hall." She wondered why she was permitted to the hall where only the elders and Oracle could enter.

"Well," Era began, "let's get started." Era led the group across the chamber and down the dark hallway on the left. Irene and Vellraniece summoned small, glowing orbs to light their path. Down the hall, there was a memorial carved into the stoned wall of the hallway. There was an image of a creature with large eyes and curled horns at the side of its head, and beneath it were scriptures written in elven.

Era halted the group to explain, "We created this memorial from the old transcripts of our ancestors who wrote the history of the Moon Child on parchment. But over time, the parchment began to deteriorate, so we carved them into stone to withstand the years of future generations. We Elders will continue to pass down the story to our people, so they, too, can tell the history to the next Moon Child.

"Today, we are going to share with you the origin of Moon Child, so that you can comprehend the source of your power and what it's for.

"More than three thousand years ago, a meteor hit our planet, exposing a dreadful toxin across the surface."

Era paused and they walked to the next memorial a few paces down where the carving of the beast was being attacked by the elves' magic. "Our ancestors attempted to fight off the behemoth and the thousands of other demonic beasts that came with it, but to no avail."

The next memorial showed a young girl with the same pendant as Taemi, "We prayed to the celestial sky for help, and they sent us down a star—a small child with a glowing pendant.

"She performed a spell we call Seal of Pentacles and trapped the beast beneath the terrain." The carving had the same design as the seal in the Forest of the Damned—an intricate weave with the crescent moon and seven stars.

Era continued on, "The seal may contain the beast, but its dark power festered into what is now the Forest of the Damned, populated by the demonic monsters. Over the years, the seal will corrode—awaking the monsters—and then sometimes enough for the behemoth to walk the surface. However, as the seal decays, we are blessed with the reincarnation of the Moon Child who returns to reseal the behemoth once again. If her blood ever spills on the seal, it will completely unravel its prison."

Irene nodded, "There has been no record of decay on the seal for over a thousand years. Usually, the forest is dormant, and creatures don't venture outside, but our scouts have been spotting more fenirs that ventured south over the past ten years."

"Yes," Tarahoot's voice creaked like an old tree, "The last Moon Child came to only recite the Seal of Pentacles as a cleansing ritual. But, for you I'm afraid at its state; it will take more energy to fully restore its crest."

Era smiled towards the others with assurance, "I have no doubt of Lady Equillis' ability." She turned to Taemi, "Madeem has informed me of your progress. It's quite impressive what you can manage with only a few lessons, thus far." She smiled.

The carving of the seal was the last mural and they re-entered the main blue dome of the Crystal Hall at the opposite side from where they began.

"In order to cast the Seal of Pentacles," Era stopped in front of the silver doors, and the elders fanned out around her, "you'll need to harness magic from all the five elements at once—Air, Water, Earth, Electrostatic and Fire—so we'll let you get back to your studies now."

"I have the scriptures for the incantation..." Tarahoot spoke weakly, "I will have someone run it over to Madeem... for you."

Irene and Vellraniece already had the large silver doors open as Era and the two oldest elders turned to leave. "Now that you are acquainted with the history, we hope that you can sleep better with ease."

Sleep with ease...? Her memory replayed the meteor shower where the dark star fell, releasing the damned creatures across the planet. *That's why they were showing me these memorials, but...*

Kio! Distracted by the history lesson, the girl almost forgot to request their assistance, "Oh wait Era—I mean, the council of elders." They paused and looked back at her quizzically, "My friend... he's still held captive by the two sorcerers... I would like to ask for your assistance in helping me save Kio... I don't know where he is, but..." She hesitated under their eyes, but continued, "I have to save him."

The other four whispered among themselves, as Era walked towards Taemi to answer, "We can not."

"What? Why not?"

"With the behemoth's seal weakening," Irene filled in, her voice echoing through the hall, "it is unwise for you to be outside the safety of our walls."

Era's gaze was almost motherly as she looked down at Taemi, "Especially when there's pending threats after you..."

The girl shifted under that gaze and regretfully understood that they were right. Her dreams even showed her path of what once had been and what will still come. "I understand..."

The golden-haired woman smiled and stroked Taemi's head softly. "It is our priority to train you to use your magic ability until the day the seal breaks." She began to walk back to the silver doors with the others.

Their concerns for the princess were completely clear. Taemi knew that she had to learn the Seal of Pentacles spell. She was never aware of the responsibilities of being the Daughter of the Moon until now. *If I'm the only one who can... I shouldn't be putting myself in danger...* But, she couldn't convince her heart to think the same way.

"But, could you send some of your own out to save him?" She could see the slight irritation form on all their faces from her plea, but continued, "Aren't you worried about two strong rogue sorcerers? Shouldn't they be stopped?"

Mezmala looked at Vellraniece and Irene looked to Era, but Tarahoot stood silent and studied the floor tiles without an expression on his face.

Era spoke with caution, "If... this friend of yours means that much to you, we will consider the task."

The other three elders nodded in agreement

and smiled back at Taemi. The oldest elf simply stared down at the ground and entered through the silver doors without a response. There was something about his lack of participation that concerned Taemi.

As soon as the doors closed behind the elders, the girl sighed and started her return up the stairs.

"They won't be sending anyone."

Startled by the soft, young whisper in her head, Taemi paused and looked around the Crystal Hall. She saw the small figure a few paces away shift from behind a pillar, staring at the silver doors. Her dark hair blended with the shadows, while the white of her pale skin and plain dress was nearly the same shade as the marble pillar. Taemi wondered if the others knew the Oracle was standing there this whole time.

"Are you serious about saving him?" She asked. Her voice was still a whisper inside the princess' head.

Taemi clenched her fists, imagining all the times Kio was by her side protecting her. She nodded and returned the answer as a thought, *"I... I have to do something!"*

The Oracle's white eyes flashed in Taemi's direction, *"Then come with me..."* She slipped back into the shadows. *"Quickly, before your escort comes for you!"*

CHAPTER 20

Lady Hero

Stepping lightly through the dark passages within the Crystal Hall beneath Vivacity Tree, Taemi followed the Oracle's guide, *"This way... Now turn right. Keep going straight—now another right—take a left."*

The passage tunneled lower and the marble flooring dissipated to the natural, soft soil of the earth. Her footsteps were soft thuds as she continued. *"Here— through that door."* Taemi brushed the thin, fragile roots from her face and extended her arms out to search for the door in the dark tunnel. She felt only the repulsing touch of the cold, soil that beaded the wall. A small hand gripped her wrist and pulled her through.

"Okay, come sit with me here," Oracle said out loud, but when her hand fell away, Taemi was completely lost in the dark.

"...Where? ...I can't see anything."

"Oh!—I'm sorry!"

A sudden burst of light flashed brightly, forcing Taemi to flinch and shield her eyes. "I can see well in the dark, so I forget that others need light."

As Taemi's eyes adjusted, she saw that the surrounding light came from three, large, erect, white, translucent structures. They were circular, in a way, but their flat edges made it appear so.

The princess couldn't resist touching one of the lamps. They looked like ice formations with frost near the tops, but they were merely cool to the touch. She drifted her hand across the flat edges, touching the thin, vertical ripple of its layers. Her nail caught on the edge, creating a mark, and she immediately pulled her hand away.

"It's okay," the Oracle giggled. "Satin spar is a soft formation. I sometimes scratch them too." She sat on a thick cushion on the floor near a large clear crystal spear that sprouted from the center of the room.

Taemi followed the spear up and gasped at the glass-like ceiling that extended for stories above her.

"It's not really that high; we're beneath a large quartz tower that's above ground." Despite the young girl's words, Taemi still couldn't pull herself away from the fascination.

The Oracle waited patiently, allowing the princess to study the rest of the room that she was led into. The white marble floor was back beneath her feet. The same translucent rock for the lamps lined the walls of the room, reflecting the light with a metallic sheer. Where its walls extended out and stopped made good use to shelf a vast range of assorted colored crystals.

Most were small—between the sizes of a small pebble to a large man's hand. They were arranged around the room by color, accenting the white, slick walls like a rainbow. There were only a few large ones near the bottom. One side was polished smooth—exposing a reflective flat surface of swirling bright color, while the surrounding edge was left to be the natural, rough rock.

The room was fairly small and towards the back, there was a small cot and a white, smooth washbowl that reflected the light just the same as the walls.

"Is this..." Taemi turned back to the young child, "Is

this your room?"

"Yes." The girl's voice was soft, but with a hint of pride. "This satin spar cave is my bedroom and where I like to be until the Elders call for me."

The room was starkly unusual compared to what everyone else in the city had. *This child doesn't even have a window,* Taemi thought, feeling a little sorry for the girl, until she remembered her eyes. *...I guess she wouldn't have a need for a window—but she would at least enjoy the breeze and sense of having one.*

She heard the Oracle breathe deeply from where she sat, with her eyelids closed, "I am at complete comfort here. Please have a seat so we can begin."

"Begin?" The princess obeyed and sat on the other cushion across from the girl.

The child's lids popped open with a small smile. "You want to find your friend, right?" Taemi nodded in response. "Good. What I need you to do is place your hands around this quartz and think of deep emotions. I will place my hands over yours to find the thread to where your energy will pull me towards."

Despite how clearly she explained, the princess didn't fully understand how she would be able to locate Kio. She placed her hands on the smooth quartz anyways and breathed. *Deep emotions?* The first thought that came to her was guilt—guilt of letting him get taken away so easily.

"Try again." The Oracle's voice was soft, but stern.

Taemi dismissed the guilt and thought deeper... *What else?* She imagined the times of when he was close at hand to protect her, *slashing at the Mydrallchob—*

"Something else." The Oracle cut through her thoughts and continued softly, "...think *deep* emotions."

The girl took a deep breath and dug down. *Deep emotions?* She enjoyed their conversations together, and how his stories made her laugh. She liked how he didn't hesitate to tease her and...

No—when he caught me in the ballroom of Sandar and how his brown eyes lit up the dark night when he smiled. She felt anchored holding his hand while his starry eyes stared back at her like she was the only one who mattered in the world. She imagined the way his face reddened when Morlisa teased about...

"I found him."

The words broke through Taemi's thoughts and her face flushed as she opened her eyes to the Oracle, wondering if she felt Taemi's emotions.

"He's south from here in an abandoned fortress at the edge of Narpal." In the large crystal quartz before them, showed an image far to the south of a single-standing ruin of a stone tower attached to a small decrepit fortress overgrown by vegetation. "He's being held somewhere beneath this building... but."

The princess' breath caught, wondering if the Oracle was going to tell her if he was injured *...or even still alive!*

The young girl shook her head and placed her hand on Taemi. "No, that's not it." The vision faded from the crystal. "There are wards in the basement, preventing others from teleshifting in and out."

Teleshifting... "Like a traveling spell?"

The child nodded, "You probably haven't learned that one yet." The light shake of Taemi's head answered her question, "—they probably don't intend to teach you that one anyways." The child got to her feet and started packing crystals in a satin pouch. "To teleshift, you have to be familiar with the destination. I'm not able to see the inside of the fortress, but I can send you there." She handed Taemi the gem-filled bag. "These should aid with the spells you've learned, and this one—" she picked up a stone that matched the structure of the wall, "I can't go with you, but keep this one on you, and I'll be able to bring you back once you're outside the fortress' wards."

Taemi glanced at the bag's contents and then back at the collection of crystals where she saw the black hematite. "Can I have this, too?"

The child's face twisted, repulsed. "Why would you want *that* one?"

The princess was set aback at the question. "Um…" and couldn't find a reason other than a spark of intuition.

But it was enough to convince the child. "You can take it, but be careful using this. You won't be able to cast spells if you're touching it, but…" she cupped her chin, "I suppose if you are fighting powerful sorcerers, it should be useful."

Taemi placed it in the satin pouch while the Oracle pulled out a white box from beneath her cot. "You should put this on, too," and laid the fabric contents on her bed. It was a plain, green, silk tunic with wooden buttons. Its short sleeves were slit to expose skin, and reattached in a pattern of strings. The tunic was accompanied by a pair of white trousers made of a cotton-mix material for sturdiness and comfort. The outfit was completed with a pair of knee-high, soft, leather boots, leather cuffs to protect her forearms, and a leather belt with a pouch to hold the satin bag.

"Change my clothes?"

The Oracle's face bubbled with pride. "You should look like a warrior before your enemies."

A warrior… Taemi ran her hand over the fine silk, generating the image of what she would look like with it on. *Just like the heroes in my stories…*

"It took some time for the seamstress to prepare it for you, but it's exactly what I had envisioned."

The princess looked at the Oracle in bewilderment.

Prepared it for me?! She knew *since I arrived, I was going to leave to save Kio...* "You knew I would go, but why, if the elders said—"

"They neglect matters of the heart."

They did kind of feel distant towards my request...

"But also..." She whispered and touched Taemi's face, "I can see what they can't. You have to go because the moon can't shine without the Sun. If you stay here, you'll only perish mending the seal."

Taemi was distraught by her words, now aware that if she didn't go, she'd die when it was time to perform the Seal of Pentacles. She forced a smile, wondering if she was evading death by going to save Kio. "Thank you..." She realized that she didn't know the child's name. She was always introduced to her as the Oracle. "What is your birth name?"

The child looked away, "I don't have... a name."

"Really?" *She's only a few years over a decade, how could she* not *have a birth name?* "What do your friends call you?"

"I don't have..." The girl's words faded and it was her turn to shift uncomfortably, staring down at the floor. "Everyone just calls me Oracle..." Taemi was about to leave the matter alone until she continued in a soft voice, "But... my parents used to call me Azla when I was alone with them."

"Oh... Can I call you Azla... when we're alone together... Like we are now?"

The child's head nodded, enthused, but her voice was still timid. "I would like that... very much." She stopped suddenly, as if she heard a noise, and gathered the clothes off her bed and pushed them into Taemi's arms. "Quickly, they've started looking for you."

Taemi hurriedly undressed and Azla helped her change into her outfit—tying up the sleeves to her tunic and the leather cuffs to her forearms. Once dressed, the Oracle grabbed the girl's head into her hands and silently began the incantation for the teleshifting spell. Taemi watched the child's lips move, forming the words as her surroundings shifted from the small white room to a damp forest. The pressure of the child's hands vanished from Taemi's head, and the brisk, wet chill of the wind hit her face.

The air was misty, with a low, dense fog close to the ground, but she could make out the stone tower not too far in the distance. Immediately, Taemi tucked her moonstone beneath her tunic, and dug out the hematite stone from her pouch to clench in her palm. She stepped lightly over wet soil, avoiding areas of slick mud and deep puddles as she ventured through the forest.

She stopped twenty paces away and scanned the land ahead. There was nothing outside guarding the two wooden doors of the front entrance, but she wouldn't put past the thought of invisible traps hidden around.

She bit her lower lip; *it would be stupid to just walk through the main door…* Staying at a distance, she continued around the structure for another way in. The tower was completely closed off without windows. She cleared the back and stopped when she reached the overgrown terrain of the fallen rock of the second tower. If there was another way in, it was blocked off by the collapsed debris.

She sniffed in frustration and hesitantly turned back towards the main doors. She hoped the hematite would be enough to resist traps if there were any.

The wooden doors were nearly rotten and covered with moss. Taemi didn't think they'd been opened in years. She grabbed the cold, damp iron ring of the handle and pulled it open as quietly as she could. The door slipped off the top hinge—rusted away to nothing—and sank in the mud, but made it easier to open just far enough for her body to fit through.

Oil lamps were mounted on the dimly lit walls of the main entrance. Her nose filled with a repulsing scent of musky mold. She stepped quietly inside on a decorated cloth that once was lavishing, but now peeled back, exposing rotten floorboards that sank under her weight.

She crouched up the front steps—studier beneath the cloth as the flooring became brick—not knowing what to expect on the level above.

The main room was spacious enough to have hosted elegant balls in its younger days, but now, water stained the wooden beams black, and the walls drifted with unraveled tapestries, flowing in the draft like cobwebs. The flooring of the main hall was brick that used to be covered by the same cloth fabric as the steps, but now, the rigid, unpolished stone was exposed and covered with a layer of sand or dust.

A single throne chair was placed in the middle of the empty hall. Its furnishing stood out of place as the polished wood still gleamed in the light, and padded with vibrant red cushions untouched by the same time that deteriorated the rest of the fortress.

The princess stayed near the walls as she passed through the hall to keep within the shadows. While trying not to be detected, she also wanted to avoid touching the wet, fragile material of the welting tapestries.

"Welcome Princess... you're right on time."

Needles spiked through Taemi's chest and she halted halfway across the hall. She peered around for the source of the voice. A shadow shifted from across the room, directly from where Taemi crouched. The soft clicking of metal on stone echoed, and from the darkness appeared the double sword-wielder in her pink garb.

"Don't mind the mess," her voice chimed as she directed towards the overall space, "we're undergoing renovations." She peered up at the ceiling, and her lips coiled in repulse. "Would you like something to drink?"

A goblet of red wine appeared at Taemi's side, floating in the air. Taemi's eyes widened at the trick itself, but her body refused to move a muscle.

"No?" The sorceress sighed and the wine disappeared. She strolled casually to close the distance between them, "Well then, if you don't mind following me upstairs, I'll take you to see Mr. 'Rashi."

"I'm here to see Kio!" The woman paused at Taemi's demand. The princess held her stance, tightening her fist around the hematite. *"Confidence can move a mountain!"* She recalled from her studies.

The other woman raised her brow, summoned a drink for herself, and took a long sip before responding. "You can see him after your appoint—"

"I want to see Kio first! Where is he?!"

The sorceress answered with poise, "Uncooperative as always, I see..." Her voice was quiet. If this was a battle of queen's mannerisms, the other woman certainly has won.

"You can't use your magic on me!" The words left the girl's lips on an impulse—*stupid!*

"Oh?" There was a silent pause while the woman attempted to do *something*—Taemi was sure—"I see..." But the threat didn't keep her from walking closer and summoning a sword to her hand.

Taemi was defeated. She knew how well the sorceress danced in the Forests of the Damned—*without* her use of magic. Taemi would have to somehow save Kio first in order to stand a chance against this woman *...maybe.*

"Okay, I cave." With a shrug, the other woman raised her sword up towards the princess' chin, and placed her other hand on her hip. "You can see your *darling* soldier boy—but promise—you'll behave after?"

She didn't answer the woman.

"Move. Down the hall," Taemi led with the woman

behind and followed her instructions. They went down a corridor and through another rusty door that swung open on its own. There were stone steps that descended down without a banister guarding the right side of the stairs precipice. Her eyes glanced around as they walked, searching for the Adrienian soldier.

Taemi was guided inside an empty, windowless room at the bottom of the steps. She whipped around in defiance—raged at the woman's deceit—and then she saw Kio down the hall behind her. He was chained to the wall near the steps where she entered the basement. His head hung limp while his arms were fastened to the wall.

"Kio!" Taemi called as soon as she saw him, but he didn't respond.

"Here, allow me..."

The boy suddenly screamed out in pain—at whatever spell the woman cast on him—Taemi immediately pleaded to the woman, "Stop! What are you doing to him?!"

Kio's scream receded to a pant as the woman responded to the question. "I was just waking him up for you."

"...You witch." The harsh whisper softly trailed through the basement while Kio's head hung towards the floor.

"See," she gestured, "alive and well."

"Kio!" Taemi yelled, trying to get his attention, but he refused to acknowledge her.

"...Another one of your tricks?" he whispered.

"You're being quite rude to our guest, Kio-*shoo*" The woman didn't say any incantation, but Taemi watched her finger move in the air—as if she was physically touching someone's chin—and moved Kio's head up to see them.

"Kio..." was all that the princess could say, not sure how to make him believe it was really her.

The boy's eyes widened after adjusting to the light.

"Princess...? Princess—what are you doing here?! How did they get you—?!" He thrashed against his restraints. "You stay away from her—you witch!"

The sorceress glared at him and Kio's words were suddenly silenced, yet Taemi could still *see* him yelling.

The woman rolled her eyes, "See—no wonder he's tired, but that's enough catch-up." She inched Taemi further into the cell, and held out her hand, "Give me the moonstone."

The girl fumbled at the pack on her belt for a crystal, until she felt the coolness of the sword's blade against the bottom of her chin—forcing her to look up at the woman.

"The one around your neck, *Princess*."

Taemi forced a swallow and pulled at the chain to reveal the pendant that was tucked away underneath her tunic. She undid the back clasp and handed it over to the woman.

"Thank you," she smiled. "Well, I guess I'll go get my master and tell him the good news." She stepped backwards keeping the sword up and her smiling gaze on Taemi. When she cleared the room, the heavy, solid door closed and locked—trapping Taemi in the windowless, stone cell.

Taemi pressed her ear up against the door to listen for the woman's departure, but heard nothing. She banged on the door and cried out, "Kio! Kio!" *Does she still have him silenced... or can he not hear me?* "Kio, are you okay? Kio, can you hear me?" But the walls of her prison were too thick to hear an answer back.

With a sigh, she gave up and sat on the cold, hard floor, emptying the contents of her satin pouch. "Don't worry Kio, I'll get you out of here!" She picked up the purple amethyst and concentrated on drawing its power. *If I could just summon a ball of air to break this door...* She focused all her attention—forming a ball in her mind and saying the words—but it was to no avail.

It seemed that Master Madeem's words about me needing the moonstone in order to draw energy from the crystals proved to be correct. She frowned and made a fist. *But I have to keep trying!* She continued to focus and tried her hardest to tap into the crystal's power.

CHAPTER 21

Recollection of Alliances

wo decades ago, Reiji-Arashi peered through his crystal mirror looking for a purpose for his power. He grew bored of Narpal and its small, trivial council. He once was the advisor to a great king, and Arashi brilliantly expanded Narpal's territory, using his wolves as spies on the battlefield. The king worshiped him until his death.

The kingdom's new successor, however, did not share the same views as the former king. He wanted peace instead of war, and to become allies among the surrounding territories. The new king not only ignored Reiji-Arashi's advice, but also removed him from the council completely!

Fools they all were! "They will never expand their territory more than it is," he growled. "...They are weak, too!" His ploy to invoke another nation to attack and take over the sad excuse for a nation was all too humorous for him. He brushed his chin and laughed. "After that, it would be all too easy to show them how pitiful their conservative decisions were... and I can take that same army and continue on, taking over another one at a time."

He scanned his crystal disc, searching for the perfect victim sitting in the high seats that would be easy to manipulate for his scheme.

The crystal surveyed and then spun rapidly out of

his control. Arashi snarled, trying to ease it back to where he wanted to search, but the vision went dark and a shadow spilled out into the room...

Through the crystal came an ominous, low, raspy voice, "Who is this...?"

Arashi growled, "The same question I'd like to know. How dare you interrupt me!"

"Ah... you are an egotistical one... I like that." The lights in the room diminished, amplifying the darkness of the circle pit within the crystal. "You wish to show all those weak fools your power? To have kings bow and worship you, yes...?"

"So, what if I am? I'm great enough."

"Yes... Yes, you are. I can tell... but you can be even more..."

The voice piqued Arashi's interest. Who is this person? A mage of the north? *He was sure he could out-master any of those self-learners. "Are you... an Elf?"*

The voice boomed with uncontrollable laughter, "Hahahaha!!—I am... beyond *their power!"*

"If that's so, then why are you hiding in the dark?"

"I am... resting... But not for long..." The shadow in the crystal swirled. "Do me a small favor, and when I'm fully rested, I will reward you with more power than you can imagine... to do whatever you wish on the surface."

On... the surface? Arashi wondered what creature would want to rule beneath *the surface.*

The voice continued, "What do you know of... the Moon Child?"

Arashi knew nothing of the sort.

"She will be born soon... I can feel her presence close... when she's untied with the moonstone, I'll be able to find her... but I won't be able to reach her. If I show you her... bring her to me. She has a gift that can fully awaken my slumbering body... Do that for me, and all shall be rewarded."

Reiji-Arashi frowned. Bring him a girl with the celestial stone of the stars...? *It seemed to be too simple of a request. He was wary of anything that was too good to be true.*

"One more thing..."

Ah, there *was* a catch.

"There's a strong sorceress to your north. She possesses great power beyond yours."

"Let me guess, you want me to go to her for mentoring?" *The silver-haired man became vexed at the very notion.*

"Find her... kill *her...*" *The crystal spun, and the dark shadow slithered back inside. The flame to the lamps re-lit and the voice was gone, and didn't return.*

Reiji-Arashi lay against the backboard of his bed, holding the bloodstone to ease the pain of his stump. He never found out who the ominous man was that he met nearly two decades ago, but he finally understood those last words, and now regretted the decisions he made since meeting Nars.

He was sure his useless lackey wouldn't be able to summon anything after drinking the wine spiked with valerian root. He was so close to crushing her throat while she clawed desperately at his forearm.

And then...

Where her hands touched him, his bones shattered like an explosion. *She's a monster. That's why she was pent up in the room—she had more power than she led on.* He frowned. *That's why* he *warned me to kill her...* Arashi drifted back to the day he went to see Nars the first time, wondering what it was that changed his intentions. As the voice requested, he went north, interrogating the mages and asking the locals to find out what power she held in those kingdoms.

Most of the mages knew nothing of this sorceress,

but soon he started picking up rumors of a mysterious, young, gorgeous woman who resided in the nation of Eithsa; yet, none of those spreading the rumors witnessed the woman herself.

The rumors went on to say that the woman obtained the luxury hold within the castle at a young age by the stupidity of men and women who were taken aback by her witty charm. As hard as it was for Arashi to believe, the woman could be thought of as innocent at times. She did have a habit of misleading those who didn't know better. *She even fooled me... She was under my skin the whole time!*

While he investigated these rumors, he learned of how she mysteriously took over the kingdom of Eithsa and lived away in the shadows with all the freedom to do whatever and have anything she could ask for. She possessed a special skill she called *contortion*.

This reputation was why Arashi began to thirst for her, despite what he was told. *He* was powerful, yes— but in comparison to her, she was masterful in not only sorcery—*the woman doesn't even have to say incantations or gestures, she merely has to* think *it*—but also in the art of manipulation to get whatever she wants.

All of this power, yet she did nothing with it?! That's what made the silver-haired sorcerer scowl in envy. *Maybe at that point, killing her was out of the question. If she wasn't going to use it, why let her go to waste?* He went to Eithsa to see her, to use her skills so that *he* could own kingdoms, be the king—worshiped and feared.

He remembered meeting her for the first time quite well, entering the castle casually, and a guard led him straight to her chambers up in a quiet inhabited tower.

When he entered the room, a young-mannered woman with the look of early twenties—not that she ever aged a day since, for some reason—*simply sat in a high-back leather chair. It was highly cushioned and slightly reclined as she sat there reading her book. Her hair waved, untamed, around her face. She was dressed in light silk clothing of a vivid sky blue—the color of her piercing eyes—and loosely wrapped in a thick robe with furry white slippers on her feet.* She was living in luxury, indeed— but clearly was uninformed of her meeting with him.

There were three cats in the room sleeping next to her. *Rumors also noted that she took in the strays, cared for them, and in return—they were her eyes and ears of the kingdom. A tabby lay on the back of the chair, a calico nestled in her lap, and a large breed—as big as the two other cats put together—lay on the windowsill with its long tail swaying, curling at the tip and then back again.*

She didn't have tigers until Arashi took her to his fortress in Narpal and introduced her to the large beasts, but the large cat was close to their kind. It had thick, silver fur with stripes down its legs towards its massive paws. Its narrow face resembled a smaller lion with a bushy mane around its collar and large whiskers that extended out from its muzzle and head. Its ears and tail extended out three times longer than a typical stray. Long fur tufts sprouted from the tips of its ears. It was the only cat of its kind that Arashi had seen, and only had seen since.

Spies, they were—all of them. *They roamed the city and told the woman of everyone's weaknesses and schemes, and then she made her plans, accordingly—what a clever tactic! She always had a soft spot for cats, and how she came to use them was unimportant. The woman's method of understanding them was magic of her own. Arashi admired the ability as he had the same with his wolves.*

"Bring us some tea, Lenal—one of the delicate ones infused with jasmine." The servant bowed and left as Narcissus—the name purposely given to herself after her noted conceitedness she openly flaunts. If she had a birth name prior, it was unknown to Arashi, but he couldn't care *less. It was her skill that he marveled for. She marked her spot in her book and set it down. "Arigie Rashi was it?" She stood up, disturbing the calico's comfort, only to sit on the table beside the chair. The cat stretched and curled back up in the chair.*

"Reiji-Arashi." So, she has been informed.

She waved her hand as a gesture to purposely show she didn't care—rude, arrogant, and ...intriguing. Letting such people know the things that she pays no mind to. "And what is it that requires you to come to me... personally?" She arched her eyebrow.

She had complete control over any of the high lords to do as she wishes, but she'd rather let others take over matters while she lounged in the back. She was no queen.

"I would like you to serve me."

She eyed him up and down and barked a laugh. "Ha, Mister Rashi—I'm not some common whore. You think I do what I wish simply because I let a few of the high lords enjoy a night of pleasure?" She asked the question, but didn't pause for an answer. "No, I'm much more than that—and I can prove to you that I will not be taken by whomever wants me."

"My... lady." He hesitated at how to address such a creature as self-centered as himself. "That's not what I meant."

The door opened with Lenal approaching with a cart of a white porcelain teakettle decorated with designs in blue lacquer with matching teacups and saucers. The servant poured the hot tea into the cups and handed one to Nars, and another to Arashi. He wasn't particularly fond of tea, but there was no use in refusing—just in case she was the kind of woman to take offense. Then Lenal slipped away with a nod of Nars' head.

The woman took a sip of the tea and continued, "Elaborate for me."

He began with the quests of gathering powerful crystals he heard stories about—one that resided in the belly of a kraken beneath the ocean, another within a valley of volcanoes near the eastern islands—and his most prized possession of the stones—that laid deep under the earth. Each required Nars' help and magic. The real goal was to somehow persuade her to serve him as a leader to obtain the world. One controls and conquers quickly with the power of others below—just as well as Nars controls Eithsa. He could use her, but he had to bribe her.

After the explanation, the girl looked back towards the large cat that stirred from the sill and raised its head. He stared at her with his large, deep, orange eyes that reminded Arashi of the deathly, autumn moon. The woman briefly glanced at Arashi and then back to the cat, having a silent conversation with it, and then nodded solemnly. "Okay. I guess I can help." The cat yawned and went back to sleep.

Arashi was amused that Nars agreed to help. She left Eithsa with him, and from there on, she continued to be his *loyal* servant—*or at least playing the role.* She achieved gathering every crystal he requested. They feasted off kraken for days, the volcanoes were engulfed in an ice age, and there was now a whirlpool where she pulled up his prized, black crystal. She was quite reckless—distorting the balance of nature, but she always returned with his desire, un-phased by the challenge.

She still kept control on Eithsa—keeping tabs on her position, thinking she'd return—but she kept her place next to Arashi. He soon figured out that the only reason she agreed to help him was because of the sheer boredom of living in luxury alone with the mindless puppets she created.

He saw her personality change over the years—from a dry, bland girl lost in books into a witty, clever woman—*however old she may be*—with a fiery attitude. She began to lust for him and keeping her around only made it easier to get what he desired. He even became fond of her like one would towards a favorite pet—and had forgotten all about the warning from the ominous shadow.

A knock on his door disturbed his thoughts. "Reiji, my Lord." Her voice alone angered him. He could feel the pain of losing his hand all over again. He was smart to set wards up to keep her out of his room. *Monster! I was a fool to trust her!* She knew he mostly used crystals to harness his power. *But I need hands to use them!* He was safe in his room from her and she wouldn't be able to get in without his permission.

She sighed on the other side of the door. "I have the stone you wanted. The girl is locked up in the basement along with the soldier."

A lie. She's tricking me to come out with THAT lie? She wants to take my other hand, is that it? He got up and teleshifted to his storage room filled with crystals. He'll keep an eye on her with his crystal mirror. He shuffled through his shelf, grabbing the stones he thought might be useful if he encountered her.

CHAPTER 22

Dragon's Breath

 "My Lord, Reiji..." Nars waited for an answer, but couldn't hear anything beyond his door. Arashi hadn't left his room since the incident and she wasn't able to enter due to his wards he always had up, and a new one that kept her from kicking in the door.

She sighed, "I finally got the girl for him, and now he doesn't even want her." *It's his fault for losing his temper... If only he had just listened to me and waited a few days...* She left him alone and walked down to the main hall.

"Maybe I should disappear to Sandar..." She formed Mel's handsome face in her mind and smiled, imagining what a new life would be like with *him*. The image flickered with a flash of light and his gorgeous face became charred remains of a broken skull. She leaned against the stone wall for support and shook her head to remove the image. *Though... that* would *be his fate around* me.

The sorceress' head jumbled with the visions that she drank to forget, but they were a harsh reminder of the overwhelming guilt of what she was... *a monster*. It'd been so long since she felt the pain of emptiness twist her insides. There was no escape from it for years until...

That day I met Reiji. He praised her on so many accounts that made her feel proud. It was a relief to finally be around someone just as terrible and vile as she was. The man was immune to both her contortion and manipulating charm, so he always saw who she really was.

Even without contortion, most men typically caved into her beauty and seductive smile. However, she quickly learned her place with Arashi when she returned from completing one of his quests.

She came into his chamber to offer him a drink. He accepted the goblet as she straddled herself up on his lap. He took a long gulp while she brushed her hand across his chest and down to wrap around his inner thigh.

Without taking his eye away from his cup, Arashi shifted to grab her wrist, and harshly applied pressure onto her veins with his thumb. He didn't let up until Nars slipped off the man's lap and pulled away.

She rubbed the sore spot as he spoke coolly, "Don't degrade yourself like that. You're not some common whore who trades a night of pleasure for whatever she wants, remember?" Arashi rose to his feet.

"I..." Nars choked. That's true, I *did* say that... but that was before I... *It certainly wasn't love that she felt towards him, but she was fond of him. He was someone who understood what it's like to be feared by others.*

Except Reiji-Arashi loved *being feared. That was what she admired about him.*

She cleared her throat, "All I want is to serve you, and if you wanted..." She allowed her sentence to trail off as she cast her eyes to the floor.

"If you need to blow off steam, go to a tavern. I'm not running a brothel."

Nars stood dumbfounded. He treats me like some stray cat...

Arashi cupped her chin, forcing her to look up at his stormy eyes. "I know how manipulative you can be, even without that fancy mind spell." He grazed her cheek softly. "A woman's power relies on a man's greatest weakness... and I refuse to lose and fall for your empty tricks."

It was then when Nars was struck by the sudden realization of how much power he held over her. While nothing but his plans for revenge and strong magical crystals drove him, all she wanted was the basic desire of his affection. As long as he would never succumb to the same weakness she had, he would always remain as her master.

As powerless as he constantly made her feel for their decade together, she never anticipated being in this situation. *He was supposed to be a strong sorcerer, but... even that wasn't enough to protect* him *from* me. She felt conflicted.

It was a mistake to ever leave my stupid solitude.
But... we had so much fun together...
If only I knew how to re-attach that arm...
The one where you shattered the bones into splinters? Her eyes began to burn, reminded by the sight. *I'm a curse... Why can't I ever be strong enough to undo these things?*

She reached the main hall and collapsed on her cushion throne in the middle of the room. It was the perfect seat for her to curl up on and drown her feelings with the one thing that never let her down—the one thing that has never failed her—her unlimited and dependable wine.

Kio yelled, enraged, as he watched Taemi hand over her pendant to Nars. The princess didn't even falter to look in his direction since being pushed further into the cell. *Why isn't she listening to me? That stupid girl! Why is she here?! Damn it all! She was supposed to be safe in the Laquar Forest with the elves!*

The door closed shut to the room and Nars walked up the stairs, ignoring his calls. He clenched his teeth, remembering the choice of words she used to provoke his rage last time. *"My master is not a gentle lover..."*

And now she's here... *sitting in the cell for his taking...*
"BLOODY DAMN-IT!"

"Kio? Kio, are you all right?" He heard her muffled voice through the thick door.

"Y-yes, Princess. I'm... I'm... okay." He was far from okay.

"Don't worry, Kio, I'll get you out of here!"

The words stunned him. *Taemi... you* stupid *girl...* She was beyond ridiculous to have ever thought she would be able to rescue him. *You came to get put in the cell and now that man will* use *you!*

He stirred in his iron shackles. *She said it would be easy to break these with* any *spell?* He hadn't bothered thinking about it before, but now it was different. *I have to get free, but how? Water could rust them. Air could break a link, but even if I could do something, the question was— how? Where do I even begin?*

Nars didn't teach me any *spells.* She didn't use words or gestures he could mimic. *She just sat on my lap, laughing and trying to tick me off.*

He breathed in and closed his eyes. *Okay, what if it was all thinking? What if I imagined them breaking?* He visualized it, over and over, but didn't feel anything happening. He didn't feel anything from within that convinced him that he was a sorcerer. *No, The woman had to be wrong... I'm not a monster like them! There's got to be a different way...*

What if there isn't?

"My master isn't a gentle lover..." Her words chimed through his mind again.

Why was she trying so hard to provoke me? Why would she want me to escape so badly? What did she know? Have I really been somehow using it?

He couldn't think of an instant where he had.

"Maybe you killed your own family?"

Impossible, the day he came home—they were all covered in their own blood. *They were already dead when I arrived home.* The image of their mauled bodies, lying lifeless, was still clear in his memory. The shadow wolves already tore through them and then they surrounded *him.*

But then what? He tried to remember how he came to survive, but even in the dream, there was a blank as to what happened.

There was a fire. The fire that engulfed them...

What caused such a fire?

That was because the food was burning...

This isn't working... The pain of losing his parents was now only a hollow ache—a scar long-healed by time.

Rage... emotions... how are they linked? What was it about rage that Nars wanted me to trigger? He always saw Taemi calm and serene when she used her pendant. *How are we different?*

Think—how do I trigger my inner emotions... to save Taemi. She's the only thing that matters. I made a promise to protect her and if I don't—

The cold expression from the platinum sorcerer slipped into his mind, and he growled. *That sick, slimy bastard.* His thoughts went dark and became his own enemy. *If I can't get her out, Arashi will finally have what he's been after—the princess and her power!*

The platinum sorcerer would have her as one of his puppets... A soulless doll responding to his every command like a slave! He'd use her to become king of Adrienan and send the countries into war—spiraling her home into chaos.

Stop, he thought, but he pushed himself to visualize the worst. *If can't get out of here...* it would be a fate worse than death for the both of them.

The lands would be in turmoil of war. Their peaceful home would be bloody battlefields and masses of

Adrienians dead. Kio would still try to reach the princess—fighting to get close to her. He'd call out to the queen as she sat on her throne—allowing the kingdom she loves fade to nothing. Kio would try anything to break her free from Arashi's spell—but she'd only look down on him from her throne with those sad, lifeless eyes. Kio would never be able to reach her....

It'll only get worse yet...

The memories of him would be gone.

Her cheery smile would be gone.

Arashi would laugh, appearing from the shadows behind to cup the chin of Taemi's empty vessel with a slithery smile. *He'd be her master and she would do whatever he commanded...*

Kio began to shake as the metal cuffs burned around his wrists. *The princess...* the woman that he loved would be gone and never to return to his arms again.

No... I won't let it happen. I'll never let him touch her—

He tossed his head back with a yell, "I WILL DESTROY HIM!"

The small flame of energy that circled inside his chest splashed out through his hands. He breathed, storing the white fire—hot enough to melt rock—in the back of his throat. It was hot... like a burning flame and the fiery breath of a monstrous, scaled creature.

Hot like the explosion that fumed out of the woman's mouth with a phantom whisper...

"Dragon's Breath!"

The energy spilled out, and his numb arms fell to the cold stone as the shackles disintegrated. It was gone in an instant. His vision speckled from nausea and his head slid to the cool, stone floor. He took heavy breaths, slipping out of consciousness and restraining the urge to vomit.

"Kio? Kio?" Taemi called out in the distance.

Taemi sprang to her feet, as the door to her cell was set ablaze with a white flame. She watched it with caution from the back of her cell. Without a trace of smoke, the door completely burned away, and the flame dissipated.

That was... fire magic. But it wasn't from her; she couldn't draw out anything from the crystals without the moonstone. She sat in her cell for over an hour, trying. Her breath caught—*Kio!* She peered over the door and saw the boy lying on the ground.

She gathered her crystals to pack them away and ran to Kio's side. She pulled him into her lap with her dark hair spilling over her shoulders. She studied his face while stroking her fingers through his soft, brown hair. *Is he sleeping?* "Kio, what happened? Are you all right?" His breath was heavy, but he didn't answer. Her lips pursed and she wondered if this was another dirty trick of the sorcerers.

The princess glanced around—watching the shadows. At any moment she expected either of the two sorcerers to appear, laughing to make her feel more helpless than she already was without her moonstone.

The boy stirred in her lap, touching the hand she used to stroke his hair. His eyes were only open to a slit as he whispered, "Taemi... I'll protect you." His hand reached for her face, but settled for touching her long, black hair and sliding his fingers down. "That Arashi bastard... he won't lay a hand on you..." He closed his eyes again and drifted to sleep.

The girl let him sleep, but she wondered what could have happened. The wall to which he was chained to was completely smooth. *Why would the sorcerers suddenly set us both free...?*

No, she wasn't free. *I have to get the moonstone*

back! Even if she and Kio could get outside, she couldn't leave without the stone.

Maybe the elves could help... Even if she *could* get help from the elves, she was the one who disobeyed by leaving and then losing her stone. *This is my fight, not theirs.* She also had a feeling they weren't going to be so forgiving towards her even if she did get back to Laquar.

The princess had to think of a plan, but all she had was the hematite, crystals she couldn't use, and Kio's sword, lying against the basement wall. She laughed to herself, *Yea as if I could out-sword* that *woman...*

The boy took a deep breath and his eyes opened. Taemi caressed his hair, quietly, patiently waiting for him to reach full consciousness before bombarding him with her questions. She met his dark, brown eyes with a smile.

It only took the boy a moment before realizing where he was and whose lap he rested on. His eyes widened and he sprang up, pushing himself away with his face flushed with color. "T-taemi! I'm sorry, I... I..." He touched his head where her fingers were and then glanced down at his hands.

He looked up against the wall, then back at his hands—rubbing around his wrists with an expression of awe. "I... I did it..." He whispered. His eyes met hers with a little more excitement to his voice, "Taemi, I did it!"

Her expression was blank. *Did what? What even happened?*

He began to explain, looking down at his hands again. "The chains..." He cast a quick glance to the room across the way. "The door! I did it!"

The door... The door burned away under a white flame. She wasn't sure if she understood him right. "You... you did *that?*" *But only sorcerers could...*

The light from Kio's face diminished and he looked back down at his hands with a look of distaste. "Nars said...

I was one of *them*."

"Nars...?"

"The sorceress. I didn't want to believe her, but—Taemi; I had to get you out! I'm not like them, but..." He sighed. "I just had to..."

The girl didn't say a word as the thoughts trailed in her head. *Kio... a sorcerer...? He can... do magic?* She wondered why it shocked her. *I can do magic,* and yet, his energy was different from hers, like the red garnet. *Something about his power simply felt...*

A plan to get the moonstone back immediately sparked in her head. *That's right!* He *can use crystals!* "Kio!" Taemi's burst of excitement shocked the boy, and she reached into her pouch for the blue lapis lazuli stone. "Here," she grabbed his hand and looked into his eyes, "Say *Hi-reme-ki*—and imagine, like... a sudden burst of light!"

The boy looked down at the stone in his palm, and then pushed it away, shaking his head.

Taemi crossed her arms. "Just do it!"

At her command, Kio held the stone and closed his eyes to visualize, *"Hi-reme-ki!"*

Taemi shunned back as the dark basement flashed white, blinding her eyes for a moment. She counted the seconds it took to see her surroundings clearly again. "That's perfect!"

The soldier's expression only showed that he was lost.

"We're going upstairs to get my stone back! Wait until I'm close to the woman in pink and then—"

"You don't get it, Princess. Even if I could do that same trick again, we don't stand a chance against Nars, and I haven't even seen what Reiji-Arashi is capable of—"

Taemi raised her feet with a sniff, and placed her fists on her hips, "Well, we can't exactly just sit here twiddling our thumbs, now, *can* we?"

Her comrade sighed, giving a hesitated nod, "Yes... your majesty." He pushed to his feet.

Taemi continued as he equipped his sword to his belt. "It's odd that they left us down here for this long... But! They can still show up at any moment. I wonder if that woman, Nars will still have the stone or if she gave it to..."

"Reiji-Arashi is his name. I've only seen him once."

Taemi nodded and opened her palm to expose the hematite. "They can't use magic on me as long as I'm holding this, so once we find out who has the stone, you distract the other one, and I'll get close. When I'm next to them, I'll close my eyes and you create the flash. That should stall them both just long enough for me to get my pendant back. After that..." She looked up at Kio, but didn't have much more to say to him.

The boy smiled and swiftly pulled her into a tight hug, pressing her head onto his chest. "I'm glad you came back for me..." She could feel his heart race and breath shorten, "but you have to get back to the Laquar Forest. No matter what."

CHAPTER 23

Release of the Hound

usic played softly through the fortress as the princess and the Adrienian soldier exited the basement and crept down the corridor to the main hall. They halted near the entrance to stay undetected in the shadows. There was a polished grand piano and a small string quartet that populated the hall with the single throne chair that Nars lounged on, drinking her wine.

The piano played a soothing melody while the strings harmonized in sections. Nars' voice hummed with their composition, letting her voice ring like a well-known ballad. The louder she sang, the more relaxed Taemi felt—knowing that the sorceress was oblivious to their presence.

The woman cast a quick glance to where they crouched in the shadows and smiled over her wine, without skipping a note. When the piece ended, her voice echoed through the hall, "Any request? They're quite skilled."

The pianist and violinist just stared at their instruments, waiting. Their eyes were hollow and didn't move until Nars had allowed them. Kio tensed up and flared his teeth. "She's treating them as her *puppets*..." He growled over the last word.

Nars sighed, "I could sure use the company... It's *boring* drinking by myself..."

Kio drew his sword and walked out of the shadows, "You let them go!"

The woman's expression was quizzical with a hint of shock. "Not a fan of music?" She rose from her chair and glanced at her artists. "Fine." The piano and quartet vanished from the room without a sound. "What kind of host would I be if I didn't accommodate my guest?"

Kio almost choked on his laugh. "Oh, you're accommodating now?" His voice was layered with sarcasm. He kept his sword up with a hand out to guard Taemi.

"Of course." Her answer sounded honest. She was out of the chair, but leaned up on its back, twirling her glass, "You passed my test and became one of—"

"I will *never* be a monster like you!" he shouted the words before she finished.

Her expression stayed composed, despite being rudely cut off. "Well then... Whatever. Stay. Leave. Do as you wish." She turned her gaze towards Taemi. "I'd be happy to play another game of *Spells & Monsters*, with you, *Princess*."

Kio narrowed his expression and looked back at Taemi confused, but the woman continued, "Seems like my lord is still indisposed, so I don't know when he'll have time for you."

Nars' choice of words hit a nerve with the boy and he exploded with rage. "Shut up! Shut up and give us back the pendant!"

She held up the chain and the moonstone swayed. "This?" She took a sip and shook her head. "No... I think I'm keeping it."

She walked towards them. Kio kept his distance, side-stepping near the wall with Taemi following close behind.

"I'm doing you a favor... Without this, you're just a normal princess without a care in the world. Why would you want to have anything to do with magic, anyways?" She laughed and then her voice became soft, staring at the stone. "It only causes trouble..." She paused and her face went solemn, "a *curse*, really..." The chime fell from those words.

She flicked back to her usual self in seconds. "Reiji-Arashi can see you on his own time."

The name of the sorcerer was enough to provoke Kio to charge forward. The woman vanished from sight.

Taemi felt the icy fingers stroke her cheek and called out, closing her eyes, "Kio!"

She heard him say the incantation, and when the light flared, Taemi pushed back on the woman behind her with a sharp jab of her elbow. They both hit the stone floor and Taemi tried to pry the silver chain from the woman's grip.

Nars flailed her arms blindly and a sword materialized in her free hand. The princess quickly threw all her weight on that arm—forcing the sword out of her grip and tossed it a few paces away. Taemi shoved the hematite in the woman's curled hair to keep her from using magic and then she sank her teeth into Nars' hand until she released the pendant.

Immediately, the princess received a blow across her face, and a hard kick to her chest, tossing her across the hall.

The pendant bounced out of her hand and it slid across the stone floor. Taemi heard the sorceress grumble in exasperation as she stretched out her right hand, "What? Why isn't it working?!"

Kio picked up the pendant and handed it to the princess.

Snarling her teeth, Nars picked herself off the floor with the sword back in her hand. "That's a cute trick, *Princess!*" she stated flatly, eying the damage to her pierced hand and back up at them with an icy glare. "Whatever you did, I'm sure it's temporary—but I'll have the two of you severely mutilated before that!"

Kio lifted his sword and stood between Taemi and the sorceress. "You head for the door and get out of here!"

Taemi stepped away, but she didn't intend to leave Kio behind. *Nars may not have her magic, but she was violent with those swords...*

Nars casually stretched and made a stance. She exhaled and lunged forward in the flash of lightning with all her strength.

Kio blocked the hit with his sword—using the palm of his other hand on the flat side of the blade to match her. His feet slid back on the stone floor. She pushed herself away, jabbing her heeled boot into his chest and kicked off.

The boy recovered and charged back.

Taemi watched Kio dance swords with Nars. The sorceress spun around him amusingly with her blade effortlessly playing with him. She blocked his strikes, tripping him to the ground and paraded around, waiting for his next move. Kio's face was red with sweat, panting for breath, but she never advanced to making the first move.

He's like a toddler compared to her... He needs more speed to keep up! Taemi took a breath and held the moonstone in her palms. *"Tah-meo!" Cast Haste!* She focused the energy from her moonstone onto him and watched his pace grow as she supplied him with more and more speed.

Nars staggered from hearing the incantations and retreated a few paces to avoid Kio's unpredicted alacrity. "What's *that* gibberish?" She shot Taemi a glare, but she recuperated and adjusted her velocity to match Kio's—blocking his attack and sending him back with a counter.

Nars is marvelous... Taemi gasped as she watched the two dance blades. Kio was able to keep up, but couldn't get an opening on the sorceress. *She isn't even utilizing her magic!* The hematite would prevent her from using it. *But... neither of us can use magic on* her.

"Stop, Moon Child!"

She heard the voice yell in her head, but it didn't sound like Azla's.

"She's not your enemy—"

"Remind her!"'

"Please remind her!"

The voices talked over themselves, pleading for her to stop the two from fighting.

"Agh! What's that noise?!" Nars flinched back and struck forward, clashing hard against Kio's sword and driving him into the ground. "Quit making that sound!"

"Her memories—"

"She can't focus."

"Remind her!"

"Tr'u me Ah tare-os ess..."

"Say it."

"Say the words." The voices echoed through her head.

"Tru-me-ah-tare-ossess?" Taemi repeated softly, trying to understand the pronunciation. She didn't know the spell, but she knew that those were the same words Nars recited back in the Forest of the Damned.

Nars cried out in agony, and stumbled down to one knee, holding her head as if it pounded pain.

A large gust of wind sent Taemi to the floor, and the ground trembled. *Oh no, what's happening? Did she remove the shard?*

"Shut up! Shut up!" Nars screamed. She grinded her teeth and placed more force behind her counter-attacks, pushing Kio back, and then clutching at her head again.

Taemi couldn't see what spell she activated, but she also knew that she didn't do *anything*—the moonstone was cool in her hands. Nars retreated back, holding her head and screaming in pain—*just as she had in the forest when she stepped on the strange pattern. And again... when they encountered the poisonous six-headed beast.*

Oh no! It's that *headache...* The image of the beast melting replayed in her mind. *Nars was able to use the magic in that forest through her pendant and... and...* Taemi saw the path of energy generate within the ground, about to erupt. Her heart panicked, "Kio, wait!" But he didn't pause.

Kio danced—dodging the areas of concentrated magic. He jumped as spikes spiraled up from the ground where he once stood and he threw his attack at Nars. The woman blocked it with her sword while cradling her head and flinching from the pain.

Suddenly, Kio's sword shifted into his other hand and he swiftly impaled the sorceress through her stomach. Taemi's insides cringed at the sight. She turned around to avoid the image, but she could still hear the woman's cry echo as he pulled his blade out, and her body thumped to the stone floor.

"Are you okay?" Kio was by her side now, wiping the blood from his blade. The princess answered him with a hesitant nod while swallowing the distaste that pooled in her mouth.

"We shouldn't have to worry about her now," Kio glanced back. "She's mumbling something like, 'Why isn't it working?'"

"I put the shard in her hair." She said it so fast. Something made her feel uneasy. *Why do I feel so guilty? She was attacking us!* But for some reason, she didn't hate the woman enough for this.

"Shard...?" Kio questioned.

"The hematite—she can't cast magic because it's in her hair."

"I don't think she'll find it before..." He paused and turned to Taemi.

"Ironically, who would have thought you'd ever be as weak as a kitten?" A man's voice filled the hall.

Taemi glanced over to see a tall man, dressed in black with shoulder-length platinum hair, lure over Nars' body lying in a red pool.

Where did he *come from?!*

Nars was curled on the ground holding her wound as she reached out with a bloodied hand towards him "... Reiji ...Please ...I can't."

He tsk'd and kicked her harshly in her in the gut. Taemi covered her mouth. Nars moaned and spat blood to the floor. "Pitiful. You said she'd walk right in and practically hand you the stone? Ha! You useless witch." He kicked her again and she stopped moving. "You didn't bother taking *their* hands..." His last words were strained.

"Stop it!" Taemi yelled.

"Stay back, Taemi..." Kio grabbed her arm and shoved her behind him. "That's Reiji-Arashi, the sorcerer who's been after your stone."

"What... What do you want with it?"

Arashi tossed his hair out of his eyes and laughed. His ominous tone filled the hall. "My dear, it's not the stone I was after," he played with a black crystal in his hand as he approached closer, "but you to be my queen."

His words felt like a wet snake on her skin and her fear consumed her. *That's why he sent that woman after me?* She glanced down at the lifeless body. *If he would do something like this to his own comrade...* Taemi didn't want to imagine what he'd do to her. *He would make a terrible king...*

Kio growled and charged at the man. "She'll never be yours to have!"

"You look worn out." The man merely waved his hand and flung Kio aside with air magic. "Have a rest." The man's laugh echoed.

Taemi clutched her cloak, her fist turning white. She was glad that they didn't have to take on both of the sorcerers at the same time, but she didn't know anything about this man. His aura was as dark as the shadow wolves he cast.

"Taemi-*che*, come to me."

Her heart stopped. The vision of the dream rippled through her head as the beast called for her... *the behemoth called me Taemi-che...*

She was frozen in her stance as the man approached her slowly. He held a large, black crystal in his hand while his other arm was tucked away in his cloak.

The sorcerer staggered suddenly as if he was hit with an invisible rock. He shot a glare at Kio who stood panting over his blade. Arashi's lips coiled in distaste. "You are an insufferable brat."

The mild distraction broke Taemi away from her trance and she backed away.

"Looks like that monster was right about you..." Arashi lightly hinted towards the woman lying in her own blood with a small shift of his eyes. "No matter." He flashed out the hand that held the crystal and raised it above his head. "I'll finish the task I gave go her, myself! Cerberus— come forth!"

The room spun with a strong pull of gravity as the black crystal absorbed the energy from its surroundings. A single stream of dark, black smoke circled around the stone and then spilled out into a cloud, covering the space of the room. It condensed, forming a large shadow wolf. The smoke continued, sprouting two more heads with fiery pockets for its eyes. Its mane blazed with orange flames. Its body was a whirl of hell fire, contained by the black smoke.

"*Mirra-Mirra!*" On instinct, Taemi cast the reflective spell, and the thin shield formed in front of her and Kio. *If Cerberus is anything like the three-headed chicklet...* She hoped that it wouldn't amplify Arashi's spells any more than they were.

"Look out, Taemi!" Kio darted to Taemi's side and sliced at the head that was about to engulf her whole, but the smoke dissipated before Kio's blade could strike. The head reformed behind him and shot out a ball of burning fire from its mouth.

The fireball reflected off their spell and was directed back towards the wolf, but the beast merely sniffed the flame away with a flash of its teeth.

"Mirra!" The princess didn't skip a beat to re-cast the spell. *If I missed one moment, we would both be charred.* She dodged the third head, running away from the creature to give her time to pull out the opal from her bag. *If it's a fire element, I'll have to douse it with water!* She began the spell that Master Madeem had her perfect on the second day, forming a ball of water in her hands and shooting it at the creature.

The water hit the wolf like a giant, hot iron—steaming away with a hiss—and it did nothing to deter the hellhound.

Kio continued to slash at the heads, but never landed a single hit as the smoke vanished and reappeared.

The third head dropped to the ground and opened its mouth, exposing its flaming breath. Fire danced out slowly and began to spin in a cyclone. The wolf whipped its head, and the spinning flame moved across the floor.

The boy ran, teleshifting Nars' blade into his second hand and then pivoting back with the blades crossed in front of him and sending out a slash—the air spell drifted up and sliced the twister in half—dissipating the flames.

Arashi's laughter echoed off the wall at every failed attempt.

Taemi panted. *Defeating the giant three-headed wolf is futile... We can't... it's too strong.* She glanced towards the sorcerer who merely watched his pet feast on them. *If we took* him *out... The magic would disperse.*

The princess clenched her teeth as she glared at the man. His very presence repulsed her. *He attacked my kingdom on* my *day. He hurt my people, tearing the innocent into shreds when* I *was the only one he was after. He made me run into the night—abandoning my home and family. He made me sleep in the cold, damp woods. He trapped Leviathan and made him sink the* Zazen. There was no end to this man's persistence of vile corruption.

Even the creatures residing in the Forest of the Damned were better-mannered—only killing what they needed to feast on!

White energy gravitated around the girl's hands and solidified. The Bow of Light flared effortlessly into her grip. She centered herself within the fiery chaos that surrounded her as she breathed in—allowing the transcending flow of energy to encase her. She slid the blazing arrow of light back across her cheek. She exhaled and released.

With a trail of blinding light, the arrow flared across the hall towards the silver-haired man.

The arrow hit the man's counter-spell and skewed it into the nearest wall.

Taemi cursed—forming another arrow—but her target flickered and re-appeared over her. Air grabbed her by the hair and lifted her up to her toes. Arashi smiled while watching her wince from the tearing pain at her scalp, and slid his cold, leather, gloved hand beneath her chin. "You think you can match my strength with only a few days of using the moonstone?" The girl tried to pull away, but he clutched her jaw sternly—his face only inches from hers, and he whispered, "I will teach you to submit and worship me."

The words slithered down the girl's spine, wrapping her in his dark, slimy aura.

The fortress suddenly filled with a deep vibration, bursting with power so strong, it stopped time. She heard his words close to her in a deep growl of hatred, "Don't you *touch* her!"

The girl watched Kio float in the air before her—leaving a gaping hole swirling through the center of Cerberus who stood between him and Arashi only a few seconds earlier. Time drifted slowly for her and the wolf, but Kio's movements appeared at natural speed, as he pulled back his arm and struck the sorcerer in the face with an electrostatic punch.

Taemi fell to the floor.

The force threw Arashi back, and the boy followed with another jump, moving through the air towards him.

The sorcerer stumbled back again by an invisible attack seconds after Kio's reflection spell shattered away. Arashi revealed his stubbed arm from beneath his coat to help keep his balance. His mutilated arm was wrapped in cloth and leather straps, holding crystals against his stump. The sorcerer cast ice around Kio's feet, but it only staggered the boy slightly before shattering beneath his fury.

Kio's moves were lightening—his energy ricocheted off the ground and walls, filling the fortress with the booming sound of thunder. The girl sensed the power pulsing in him. He didn't know how to control his magic into spells, but it coursed through his muscles, enforcing his strength and speed, fluently.

While Kio distracted the man, and Cerberus slowly regained its form, the girl got to her feet and created the Bow of Light again. Once the arrow was pulled across her cheek, she yelled out, "Kio!"

In a blink, the arrow shot off and the boy dashed out of the way before the sorcerer saw what was coming. He screamed as it pierced him up against the stone wall and burned at his skin. The man vanished out of sight.

"Taemi, look out." Before the girl could focus on her surroundings, Kio took her in his arms and they tumbled to the ground to avoid Cerberus' last bite. They watched the creature's body break into a smoldering, dark cloud as it evaporated away.

Kio panted on top of Taemi. His body was hot and wet, and his skin was coated in dirt from the stone floor. Sweat dripped from his damp wet hair onto the girl's face. He glanced down, "Are you okay?"

She stared up at his gorgeous, brown eyes, unable to move.

He brushed the dark hair from her face.

She was exhausted from the amount of energy she used to create the Bow of Light.

The boy's mouth curved into a half smile. "Let's get out of this place, Princess." Kio pushed himself off the girl and hoisted himself to his feet. "You said the elves can teleshift us to Laquar once we're outside?" He held out his hand to help her up.

Teleshift... "Morlisa!" Taemi disregarded Kio's help and stumbled to her feet, pushing herself towards the sorceress.

"What are you doing?!—Get away from her!"

Taemi knelt down near the woman and hesitated. She didn't know anything about healing magic, it just happened on its own every time. *She's already lost too much blood... it might be too late...*

"Taemi! Just let her die here!"

Ignoring Kio's warnings, the princess checked the woman's arm for a pulse and gasped. *Her body is still warm and the wound stopped bleeding awhile ago.* It only appeared to be a deep cut now. As soon as she touched the woman, her pendant glowed and she watched the rest of the wound fasten together; not even a scar was left behind.

The Adrienian soldier exhaled a deep sigh and

mumbled quietly behind her, "You're such a softy..."

Taemi couldn't explain her impulse to save the woman. She enjoyed her time she spent with Morlisa—*Nars I suppose her actual name is*—even if she was only trying to capture her.

There was something else about this woman that had Taemi captivated. Nars had the same familiar presence as Leviathan after Taemi released him from his trap. *The voices said she's not my enemy...* She knew they were the same as the floating lights from when she fell into the mysterious hole.

"I want to take her with us. She could maybe help us find Arashi..." *Or maybe use her* against *Arashi.* She doubted the woman would still favor him after he abandoned her.

"Fine," Her soldier didn't hide his anger. "Let her live. Death is a mercy anyway. But, she'll be punished!" Kio responded harshly.

EPILOGUE

Return of the Blazing Sun

The kingdom of Adrienan rejoiced at the return of their missing princess. Lady Equillis paid her respects to those who perished in the shadow wolf attack—including her father who passed away from his wounds while she was traveling to the Laquar Forest. The princess grieved, regretting that she wasn't able to be by her father's side in his final moments, but she wouldn't let it deter her from remembering his lectures to be the queen that her people so desperately needed in their time of sorrow.

The Council of Elders was greatly offended by her leaving and she was refused to see Azla, the Oracle, as a rebuke. The elders would relay any news the Oracle foreseen if they involved the Moon Child.

But they also agreed to allow Taemi to return to her kingdom and rule while practicing the Seal of Pentacle spell during her free time. She was accompanied by Master Madeem to oversee her magic lessons with the moonstone.

Kio was also included in these teachings as he was able to summon energy from the crystals, as well as the natural pool that radiated within him. Master Madeem was astounded at his ability and how quickly he was to learn. But the boy vowed that he would only use the skill to protect his queen and kingdom.

For his valiant efforts, Kio was appointed to be the queen's first commander. As he patrolled the corridor of the castle, ensuring it met with her safety, he stayed alert for Arashi's shadow wolves. The elves placed protection wards to keep the sorcerer from attacking without a warning, but Kio hoped that the man perished from his burns after fleeing.

He reached the courtyard and paused.

Queen Equillis, in an elegant, green satin dress—with a gold rope belt and long, bellowing sleeves of the elven fashion—laundered in the garden, practicing the spells to grow flowers. The boy could feel his heart pound in his chest, adoring how the color of her dress only enhanced her vibrant green eyes. Her black, silk hair was tied back into a loose braid. She matured quickly over the few months, but she still enjoyed her sweet tea and cakes in the garden.

The day was particularly warm as the sky only showed the vast brilliant blue. The hot sun was high, making it about mid-noon. A light wind blew past, carrying the fragrance of magnolias. The queen stopped in her practice and glanced up at the sun's position. *Right on time,* Kio thought as she grabbed a small basket next to her and ran out of the garden towards him.

"Oh, Kio! How are you today?" He knew where she was going at this time and he always tried to intervene, if only for a moment, to see her. Since her being queen and him the first commander, their duties kept them further apart than he anticipated.

Kio bowed at her acknowledgment. "My Queen, everything is at—"

She gripped his arm and smiled, "Look what came in today!" Her informal closeness was well out of place, but he welcomed her touch regardless. *The queen can break any rules as she wishes.*

Queen Equillis pulled out a round, orange fruit from her basket, "This came in from the south of Nishe! Here—have one."

The boy couldn't stop smiling at her excitement over a few oranges. "I hope they're just as sweet, my Queen."

She nodded. "Nars will be excited too! She'll be happy for something..."

The boy sighed as he escorted the queen out of the courtyard, *right on queue.* Taemi treated the prisoner as if she was her long-lost friend or fur companion—catering to the woman's wishes and bringing her treats. In return, Nars secretly taught Taemi spells that even the elves didn't know. Kio hated when she talked about her. *That woman is bound to get Taemi hurt!* Since then, Kio tried to make a point to accompany her on her visits, or find a way to distract his queen entirely, and hastily deliver the monster's lunch himself.

"Did you know that the correct healing spell is actually reversing time instead of hastening it?" The queen continued as they walked down the castle halls, "She says that it completely eliminates scarring and permanent damage that could come from a broken bone or..."

Up ahead, Kio saw Mr. Tanner shuffling through the halls frantically. "Oh! There you are, my Queen!" He exclaimed when he saw the two of them. "The High Lord Wallace and Lady Neena are here to see you about a request of their border."

The queen sniffed and rolled her eyes, "Of course they are!" Kio was well-informed that the two have been constantly requesting her attendance to bellow about their petty quarrels with their neighbor lord. When alone with her, Queen Equillis constantly mimicked their request in a high-pitched voice, *"Their tree is too close to my land. What am I to do if lightning stuck it and it fell into the dirt path?"*

Mr. Tanner bowed, "They expressed that the matter is urgent and they are waiting in the main hall."

Taemi's eyes widened with audacity. *"Urgent?!* Ha! I will not be summoned like a servant! I will see them when I have the *time* for them!" She stiffened upright and recomposed her queen-like serenity. "Now, if you would excuse—"

The first commander halted her with a slight tug of her sleeve, "My Queen... they have the south border, it could be something with the forest." He didn't have to finish its name; its curse bordered every kingdom.

The queen turned to him with flames in her eyes. "For *their* sake—it *better* be!"

Kio smiled, hoping it would ease her temper. "Look, I'm sure it will only take a moment, and I can take care of..."

They never really thought of a code name for the prisoner they hid below the castle. He pulled up the basket, "—take care of this for you."

The young woman pulled the basket out of Kio's hand and then smacked it into him with force. "Fine." She pointed her finger up at him and stated sternly, "You be nice today!" With a bow of his head, his queen twirled on her heels and briskly paced down the hall with Mr. Tanner following after.

Kio sighed and slipped through the tapestries, walking the narrow alley until he entered the dungeon quarters located beneath the castle and even further below the cellars. He nodded to the men at guard and entered the dimly lit corridor. The cells reminded him of the stables with wooden doors, barred walls, and a space just big enough for a horse. Straw was brought down to help cover the smell and the queen provided clean water for baths once a month, yet Kio felt she was too generous at that.

The prisoners talked among themselves when they're first brought in, but they silent down as the days carry on in their dark cells. Now, they merely mutter whispers when one enters, wondering if it was mealtime, or if someone was up for an execution.

The queen didn't allow many of those, either...

As he approached the end of the hall, he stopped and grabbed one of the torches from the wall. He located the only key that was made for this particular cell, unlocked the door and entered.

The cell was empty at first glance, but after three steps forward, the illusion faded away to a woman huddled up in the corner with her head resting on the wall and gazing down at the ground. Wooden chopsticks pinned up her dark, greasy, hair as it had been days since it has been washed. Stray strands found their way to frame her face. She wore shackles around her wrists and neck, chained to the wall that only allowed her a few paces of freedom.

The queen was proud of the illusion spell that kept this particular woman a secret from the rest of the guards and prisoners. She even put up a sound barrier to keep her from calling out, and others from overhearing when the queen did come down to speak to her. The shackles were forged using the special iron ore of the mountains that surrounded the Laquar Forest. As long as the mineral touched her skin, she couldn't use any of her magic. They had additional wards scripted on them as well for extra measures.

"Is that my knight in shining armor?" She asked as Kio entered with the light, but she didn't stir.

"I'm no more *your* knight than you are a free woman."

"You're words sting me..." Her voice chimed sarcastically, "yet, I have a chance, as there's no ring on you yet." She commented without glancing up, but she always said something of the sort every time he visited. "She's made you her hand, but she hasn't given you hers? How sad."

"That's enough. I only came to feed you." Kio's voice was flat as he threw the bag on the floor. Her eyes watched the orange roll out across the floor.

"...But I'm so starved for conversation," she laughed. "How come you haven't asked for it?"

Kio's lips formed into a snarl, "You mean that trick of yours? Forget it. I refuse to lower myself to a monster like you."

The woman burst out laughing so hard, she held herself up against the wall for support. "*You?* You couldn't possibly be *anything* like *me.*" She gained her breath and stared up at him through the strands of her hair. "You can't without my help."

"That's reassuring... because I don't want to be *anything* like you." Kio kicked the bag of food closer to the woman and she gazed down disappointedly at the contents that spilled out.

"...You know, it's ironic how the tables have turned between us."

"Yes, but this time I have no intention of touching you." He replied coolly.

The woman's eyes narrowed, "*...and* at least I was kind enough to feed you *quality* meals."

The boy almost felt sick to his stomach just thinking back at the raw meat she fed him. *She's lucky to even get meat scraps and she complains that they're overcooked!* He couldn't keep himself from glaring down at her. "If it weren't for the Queen's kindness, you'd be long dead."

The sorceress scoffed and rolled her eyes. "As if *living* is all such a blessing..."

"Spare me your pathetic melancholy; you're barely middle-aged." By the woman's appearance, she was likely only a few years older than Kio.

Nars smiled softly with the dim candlelight dancing in the reflection of those crystal blue eyes that searched the shadows. "...Middle-aged? That barely scratches the surface of me."

Kio knelt down before her and lowered his voice. "Well, if that's the case, I'll at least make the *rest* of your life a living hell." Kio glanced around the cell thinking of the improvements he should make. "This cell is much too nice for the likes of you."

But those eyes were infatuated with the shadows, and the woman became nothing more than a vacant shell— lost within her own thoughts.

The boy sighed and left the cell.

Reiji-Arashi sat in the dark with the black, spinning void seeping through the crystal disc. The room was uncomfortably cold when the ominous man spoke to him.

"You failed me Arashi-che..."

The sorcerer sipped his wine, ignoring the presence's voice.

"I told you to kill that sorceress from the north, but you were greedy with her power. Now, she sits in the protection of the Moon Child."

Arashi had no words for the man. He retreated quickly to relieve the burning pain of the princess' attack. But when he returned to confirm the monster's death—she was gone. He never anticipated the girl would take Nars captive, much less heal her to stay alive, but... that's because Arashi only expected her to be a child.

She was much more than that, he realized now. He underestimated her since the beginning. *She was a reincarnation of a celestial deity!* It was the shadow's fault for not informing him properly.

"Very well." The voice responded to Arashi's silence. "I will inform you of the last forbidden crystal hidden on your planet. It is by far the most difficult to obtain, but the reward is well-worth its spoils."

Arashi listened with half of his attention. He'd have to obtain a small army of mages to equal the power he had at his command to achieve this crystal. He hated the self-taught—they were weak and reckless. None of them would even know Nars' magnificent contortion spell. But with the loss of his arm, he too, was now handicapped. He threw his drink at the floor. The ominous voice had long departed while the man was lost in thought.

About The Author

Born in Wisconsin, Simon L. Swink spent her summers swimming beneath the willows, kayaking down rivers, running through prairie-grown fields, and exploring the dark, pine forests. Her birthday was always celebrated on snow-covered stands where she and her family deer hunted.

As a girl, her favorite sports were archery and horseback riding. She enrolled in summer camps to perfect her skills. Later she worked at a local horse ranch where she aided young, horse-loving campers like herself, how to groom, lead, and tackle up their saddles. She also became a certified archery instructor and volunteered her time to teach young girls, the how to and safety of archery.

Like many Midwesterners, she traveled across the country with her family to hike the Smokey Mountains, cartwheel down the sand dunes and learn to lobster trap on the Atlantic. She collected interesting rocks, gorgeous gemstones and colorful quartz on her family vacations.

Simon L. Swink currently resides an hour north from her hometown with her loving husband, and three adorable cats.